PRAISE FOR *AR(*

"I was absolutely en
character. Such a rich
thriller."

...ere is nothing cookie-cutter about this

—*Michelle Rene, award-winning author of **I Once Knew Vincent***

"Janet Shawgo weaves an intricate tale of espionage and suspense that draws you in and puts you in the driver's seat! Hang on, this romance writer is about to rock your world with her new thriller!"
—*Michael Byars Lewis, award-winning author of **Surly Bonds** and **Veil of Deception***

"Janet Shawgo is a talented writer who possesses a vivid imagination and the ability to create complex characters and interesting story lines that draw readers in and leave them longing for more."
—*Kaylin McFarren, RWA Golden Heart® Finalist for **Flaherty's Crossing**, and author of the multi-award-winning Threads series*

PRAISE FOR THE *LOOK FOR ME* SERIES
Look for Me

"Janet's story line was captivating, and it beautifully illustrated the wonderful profession of nursing, which has no boundaries. After reading this book, anyone thinking of joining the nursing profession will have a solid conviction to pursue that career path."
—**Christopher Walker, MD, FACOG, FICS**

"Shawgo captures the true essence of what nursing is all about. Her first attempt at novel writing is an inspiration to the writer in all of us."
—**Patricia Hensley, BSN, RNC**

"A wonderfully written, heroic saga of a woman's determination, strength, and resourcefulness in giving unselfishly on the battlefield while putting herself in danger."
—**Rosemarie Masetta, BSN, RN**

"I found the book engaging and difficult to put down. I felt like I was actually there."
—*Melanie Reis, CNM, ARNP*

Wait for Me

"As a lover of historical and medical fiction, I found it a special treat to find the combination done with such skill. The characters in Shawgo's first novel helped me to remember the true reason why I chose a vocation of healing. These characters also made me proud to be a woman. This second novel does not disappoint, and it more than reinforces these sentiments. I challenge you to try to put it down!"
—*Elizabeth Hutcheson, MD, FACOG*

"I find Janet's writing style very compelling, leaving the reader to wonder what will be found just around the corner. This is a tribute to all females who sacrifice their lives in the service of others."
—*Christine Leblond, Colonel, United States Army, (Ret.)*

"*Wait for Me* catches your attention from the very beginning. Janet has shown the courage of women during a time of war. They answered the call to serve their country, and went where the need was greatest."
—*Pamela L. Little, Captain, United States Air Force, NC*

Find Me Again

"I have read and enjoyed all of Janet's books, and after reading the first few pages of *Find Me Again*, I know I'm in for another great ride. Janet writes strong and wonderfully self-sufficient women, and she captivates her readers with powerful story lines that flow without friction. I am a huge fan and will continue to be for years to come. Bravo, Janet!"
—*Neeley Bratcher, author of The Victoria Childs series*

"Janet does it again with the final book in the *Look for Me* trilogy. Set aside plenty of time to read, as you will not want to put this one down. There is a larger sense of the paranormal element in *Find Me Again* than in the others. The love story was brought to a wonderful ending with a great lead into a spin-off series. I can't wait to see what else is in store

for us from this wonderful indie author!"
—*Stephanie Shaw, Steph's Book Club*

"Janet has done it again—a wonderful story from the first to last paragraph."
—*Michael Cacciatore, MD OB/GYN*

AWARDS AND HONORS FOR THE LOOK FOR ME SERIES

Look for Me

Winner, Romance Division, 2012 International Book Awards
Winner, Historical Fiction Division, 2012 Chanticleer Book Awards
Four-Star Review, 2012 Chanticleer Book Reviews
Finalist, Historical Fiction Division, 2012 International Book Awards
Finalist, Romance Division, 2012 Next Generation Indie Book Awards
Finalist, Mainstream Division, 2012 Chanticleer Book Awards
Finalist, Laramie Awards, Historical Fiction Division, 2013 Chanticleer Book Awards
Finalist, Romance Division, 2013 USA Best Book Awards
Historical Novel Society acknowledgment, 2015

Wait for Me

Winner, Chaucer Awards for Historical Fiction, Women's Fiction/WWII Division, 2013 Chanticleer Book Awards
Finalist, Chatelaine Awards for Romance Novels, 2013 Chanticleer Book Awards
Finalist, Romance Division, 2013 Next Generation Indie Book Awards
Finalist, Best Design Fiction, 2013 Next Generation Indie Book Awards
Finalist, Romance Division, 2013 International Book Awards
Five-Star Review, 2014 Readers' Favorite
Finalist, Military Fiction Division, 2015 Readers' Favorite International Book Award Contest
Winner, Military Fiction Division, 2015 Beverly Hills Book Awards
Finalist, Historical Fiction Division, 2015 Beverly Hills Book Awards

Find Me Again

Grand Prize Winner, Chatelaine Awards for Women's Fiction and Romance Novels, 2014 Chanticleer Book Awards

Finalist, Romance Division, 2014 Next Generation Indie Book Awards

Finalist, Action/Adventure Division, 2014 Next Generation Indie Book Awards

Finalist, Romance Division, 2014 International Book Awards

Five-Star Review, 2014 Chanticleer Book Reviews

Winner, Mystery & Mayhem Awards, Romance Division, 2014 Chanticleer Book Awards

Finalist, Clue Awards for Suspense and Thriller Novels, 2014 Chanticleer Book Awards

Finalist, Paranormal Awards for Supernatural Fiction, 2014 Chanticleer Book Awards

Finalist, Somerset Awards for Literary and Contemporary Fiction, 2014 Chanticleer Book Awards

Winner, Chatelaine Awards for Women's Fiction and Romance Novels, Blended Genre Division, 2014 Chanticleer Book Awards

Five-Star Review, Adventure Division, 2015 Readers' Favorite

Honorable Mention Fiction Intrigue 2016 Readers Favorite

BOOKS BY JANET K. SHAWGO

Look for Me series

Look for Me
Wait for Me
Find Me Again
You Just Can't (e-book only)

ARCHIDAMUS

2018

Jacki

Meet Caydon!

Here is something different!

Sincerely,

[signature]

ARCHIDAMUS

HE NEVER FORGIVES, HE NEVER FORGETS

JANET K. SHAWGO

NORTHLOOP
BOOKS

NORTH LOOP BOOKS
2301 Lucien Way #415
Maitland, FL 32751
407.339.4217
www.NorthLoopBooks.com

ISBN-13: 978-1-63505-214-5
LCCN: 2016914785

Distributed by Itasca Books

Cover Design by Jim Arneson, JaadBookDesign.com

Printed in the United States of America

If you are a patient man, all things will come to you . . .

—Aaron Reece Caydon

Caydon

ACKNOWLEDGMENTS

As an author, I have discovered that the people around you are filled with information and support. A simple phone call, text, or email can make all the difference in minutes or hours of research. *Archidamus* has been one of those books that, without the help of family and friends, could not have been completed. A super "Thank you!" to the following:

Joan Acklin . . . My twin sister, who always tells me the truth about my work, whether I like it or not.

Beta Readers...Thank you for your time and input.

Brittany Masetta, LMFT... Your direction to the correct psychology of my character made him interesting and deadly.

Luke Graves . . . The detailed military information you provided assisted in the story.

Tracy Comerford, Aoife Comerford, and Maggie Comerford . . . My Ireland ladies. I appreciated the pictures, information, and invitation to come visit. (I'm working on that trip!)

Eric Acklin . . . Thank you for agreeing to be a part of this project.

Sarah Monroe . . . You were able capture what I needed for *Archidamus*, and you brought Aaron Caydon to life.

Jackie Belair . . . Thank you my, friend for the French translations.

Sèan Barrett . . . My appreciation for your time clarifying the Gaelic translations.

My gratitude and appreciation to the staff of Hillcrest Media Group, my publisher, for your constant encouragement of my work. And huge hugs to my readers. You keep me going and going and going . . .

Janet

PROLOGUE

Aaron Reece Caydon sat in the home of his onetime friend, Bevan Benjamin. They had been fellow agents at the NSA, partners, but that had been a lifetime ago. Bevan had progressed quickly up the ladder, had swum past the political sharks, and he now advised the president and chief of staff on possible threats to national security. Aaron's name was included with those who were possibly a threat to the red, white, and blue. Bevan was no longer his friend; now, he was Aaron's enemy. Their recent conflicts and the interference of the NSA in his private business had pressed this private meeting, a final warning of what he was capable of, what he would do to those closest to Bevan.

Aaron patiently waited, drinking a beer and listening for any signs that Bevan's dog or the young agent sent to detain him might be waking from the sedatives he had administered. The young agent had thought he was up to the battle, but Aaron had proved to be the better man. He would always be the better man. The military and his father had seen to that.

Laura Edwards, Bevan's fiancée, shifted in the chair in front of him. She had been securely but gently restrained. Footsteps coming up the walk brought a smile to Aaron's face. He finished the beer, and crushed the can in his hand. Aaron watched as Bevan entered the front door and sat down in front of him.

It pained Bevan to see the woman he loved tied to a chair. "Laura, are you hurt?"

Laura shook her head.

"Bevan, what a question for you to ask," Aaron chided.

"Caydon, why all the theatrics?" Bevan asked as he motioned to Laura.

"I'm making my point that none of you are safe. You can see that it is easy for me to get to anyone, anywhere, anytime and make them disappear if I wish. Tonight is the last time I will leave without taking from you. No more checks. Back your people off. You now have more to lose."

"I want you to go. I'll do what I can to leave you alone—for now," Bevan replied.

"She's pretty Bevan; let's keep her that way. Oh, and congratulations . . . Daddy," Aaron said and smiled. "I'd appreciate it if you two would sit tight for about twenty minutes before calling for help."

Aaron headed to the back door. As he stepped outside, he hoped his warning had been taken seriously. He began to holster his weapon when he was knocked to the ground, and the gun fired, grazing the side of his left foot. The next thing he felt was a sharp and burning sensation down the left side of his face and shoulder: someone was cutting him. He turned to see someone small backing away, preparing to strike again.

"I don't think so!" he said.

Aaron had had enough of this tick. He was bleeding, and his injured foot was making it difficult to keep his balance. He threw the small man to the ground, and he realized his attacker was light. Was that perfume he smelled? It didn't seem possible that a woman could have inflicted all this injury upon him. He leaned down and backhanded her to unconsciousness. Aaron could hear sirens, and knew he had to leave. The boning knife covered in his blood was lying in the woman's hand. He relieved her of the weapon and placed it in his belt.

"Impressive, but I'll be walking away tonight," he said, and disappeared into the darkness.

CHAPTER ONE

Jackson Hole, Wyoming
Sunday, November 3, 2002
7:00 a.m.

Aaron stood among the trees, breathing clean, fresh mountain air, and listened to the sounds of the morning. He had replayed that scene in Bevan's home in his head every day since it had happened almost a year ago. He stood motionless, and watched a large black bear sow and her cubs leave the area before he began his trip back to the house that had been his refuge for the last year. As he approached the house, he stood for a moment and checked his surroundings, looking and listening for even the slightest change from the day before. He had to be cautious these days; even though Bevan had said he would stand down, it didn't mean the promise had been kept.

Aaron entered a door that led downstairs to a lap pool and gym, removed his running clothes, rinsed his body, and dove into the pool. He thought about his life, businessman, ex-military, and for a time, mercenary. After being injured he had come to Wyoming looking for a place to heal. Aaron's sanctuary had been secured by Gordon Morres, a retired physician. Gordon owed Aaron his life, and he was now fulfilling a promise to Aaron made many years previously. Stroke after stroke, lap after lap, Aaron kept his rhythm. Strength. Endurance. Stay focused. Don't waver. He remembered the first days of his arrival on the mountain, and Gordon's concern for his injuries.

Gordon had been visibly upset. "Jesus Christ, Aaron! This is a mess!"

"Just fucking fix me."

"These aren't going to heal well. You'll have permanent damage; there will probably be numbness in your foot and a permanent scar on your face. Some nerves have been severed, and the muscles on your back will take months to heal properly. Christ, you've been sliced to the bone back here! The person who did this knew what he was doing," Gordon had told him.

"She."

"What did you say?" Gordon had asked.

"I said it was a fucking woman who did all this to me."

"Well, she filleted you like a fish. Who is she?"

Aaron had shrugged. "Not sure, but she belongs to Bevan. One of his special agents."

"Damn it! I told you, warned you. You've become arrogant, lost your focus. Next time, you could die," Gordon had spat.

"I should have killed her. Next time, I *will* kill her!"

Gordon had seen to the injuries, allowed him to rest and prepare for his next plan of action as he focused on healing his body. Gordon had been correct about the time it would take to heal; it had taken longer than even he had expected. This woman was an admirable foe, one Aaron could not misjudge. One he must find. Aaron stopped mid-lap and pictured her face. *I will kill you.*

Twenty minutes later, he sat naked in the sauna, looking at his body. The muscles were defined again on his arms, legs, and abdomen, all as they should be. He had refined his diet to cut all red meats and to add fresh fruits and vegetables. Gordon had planted a garden, which had kept them stocked over the summer while he recovered. His daily meditation helped him to center and focus on the plan ahead. Aaron and his men now spent hour after hour in the gym. Gordon had hired a physical therapist, and had paid him highly to keep quiet about his patient. Aaron dreaded each session with the bastard, as the injuries to his back were painful. The therapist didn't seem to care about his pain, and pushed each week with more difficult exercises.

Aaron looked at his foot and rubbed the spot where he had been shot. The injury had caused him issues with running, his foot giving way at times, but he had overcome it. Thousands of rounds had been fired on a private range; this would only sharpen his skill. He had procured a shipment of new weapons that would be waiting for him and his men in their new location. His contact hadn't specified what was being shipped, but the items were new military acquisitions for the next year. He was once again a step ahead. Physically and mentally, Aaron felt he was ready.

His search for information on his attacker remained just that: a search. No information could be found. This was probably due to his old friend, Bevan, one of the NSA's best. The lack of information meant she was something very special, but he would find her. Something special . . . for a time, *he* had been something special. You were always special until there was no longer a need for you. But Aaron had discovered a better way to live, a financially healthier way, a way that was on *his* terms.

Aaron left the sauna and dove back into the pool for one last cooldown lap. The steam from the shower invited him to complete his morning ritual. He stood under the hot spray as the thought of a morning in Glenfinnan entered his thoughts.

"Kyliegh." The word slipped from his lips. Tall and slender with long, red, shining hair, a woman who understood him accepted him. There had only been one other woman in his life who had meant more than a one-night affair. His first love had been violently taken away from him many years ago. This had caused him to guard every emotion. Until Kyliegh.

Aaron reached for the shower wall remembering the last time he had seen Kyliegh, and the fresh scent of flowers in her hair. His body ached knowing how she felt lying beneath him as they made love. *Too long, too long.* He moaned with an unsatisfying release, and then watched as the hot, steaming water rinsed away his need. There would be a day when he would return to Kyliegh and never leave.

Aaron wrapped a towel around his waist and stood, staring at the reflection in the mirror. He touched the scar on his face and thought about all his time in the military. Until that moment, the only mark on his body had been the Special Forces tattoo on his lower-right arm. Even when he was in the private sector, he'd never been wounded—not even a scratch. But now he had a constant reminder that he had lost his focus.

"Time for a change," he said. Aaron cut his hair, and then shaved off what was left with a straight razor. As he finished dressing, he looked at the boning knife in the place of honor he had made for it. He picked it up and wondered who else this blade had been used on, who it had killed. He would do some research on the blade once he found information on its owner. Yes, he knew this blade had been used to kill. He ran his thumb down the blade, causing blood to seep out of the cut. Aaron licked away the blood. He had used a number of knives in his military career, but this knife was one of the sharpest he had ever possessed. It was his; he had paid a heavy price for it. But he would return it one day and leave it in her heart. He replaced the knife and went downstairs to meet his associate for a late breakfast.

Gordon could hear footsteps, and he looked up from his book as Aaron entered the dining room. "Well, that's a new look for you," Gordon commented.

"It's time. I've been too soft. But never again."

"Things have progressed. Your prey is in the air. He should be here by dark," Gordon said, walking to the buffet for coffee.

"I knew the offer would be too much for him to refuse."

"And his brother?"

"Out of the country on his honeymoon. It'll give me the time I need before contacting him. Is everything prepared?" Aaron asked.

"I'll prep his glass with a sedative. I've made arrangements at the airport. You should be able to leave Tuesday, if the weather holds," Gordon said.

Aaron had finalized arrangements several weeks previously with associates outside of the country. Money had been transferred, and now he waited. He was a patient man. If you are a patient man, all things will come to you. His father had forced him to repeat that phrase almost every day of his life.

Aaron sat down with Gordon, and ate in silence. When the clock on the wall began to chime, he broke his silence to address Gordon. "Gordon, I'll be upstairs the rest of the afternoon, until your meeting."

"I left some new meditation CDs in your room."

Aaron nodded in acknowledgment, left the table, and headed to his room for meditation, yoga, and mental focus.

His room had a large window that held a view of the mountains. That day, clouds were beginning to grow, and each day the chances for snowfall increased. Everything had to go as planned or he could be spending another winter here. He placed the new CD in the player and took his position in the middle of the floor. As Aaron relaxed, his mind regressed to a time that felt like a century ago, but it was as fresh now as it had been the day it had happened.

"Du bist spezielle." He was special, his parents had told him. He had been capable of memorizing everything that he saw, read, or was taught since the age of four. Aaron had been labeled first with a photographic memory; now, the proper title was eidetic memory. This curse, as he had first called it, later became his biggest asset. There was a long list of individuals that were indebted to him, some honor-bound to come at his beck and call, others financially obligated to him. Those who failed to fulfill their debt to him, or disappoint him in any way all died.

He remembered the day his biological parents had died, and the story he had been told by the military about an accident. He thought of the lies he had been told about his daughter, Caren, by foreign men who'd sought to use him. It had taken years to find her and the men who had murdered his first love, Vanora. They had died as all his enemies did: slowly and mercilessly. Caren was protected and hidden from everyone, including the government that would harm her or use her against him.

Aaron could feel his pulse beginning to race over these memories and lies. He listened to the bells from the CD deeply chiming. The demon had attempted to rise, but the anger to kill slowly disappeared, replaced with calm and control. There was no need for physical actions when simple words were enough to convey his intentions. The completion of the music indicated that his meditation was over. Aaron now indulged in one simple pleasure: reading. Several hours later, the arrival of the Land Rover forced Aaron to stop and mark his place in James Patterson's newest novel. He had become quite the fan of the Alex Cross series after having met Patterson through a mutual friend. Aaron had read all of Patterson's works to date.

He walked to the window and smiled as the tall young man, who had been so easily manipulated, exited the vehicle. Aaron dressed in professional attire and began his trip downstairs. He stood in the shadows, watching from the adjoining room as rum and Coke was served to his prey. His cue to enter the room quickly approached.

GORDON MORRES FOLLOWED the instructions and the script Aaron had given him. The fireplace in the main room of the cabin presented a warm and inviting sanctuary to all who entered. Eric Shaw, twenty-four, was a photographer and the younger brother to billionaire Taylor Shaw. He had so quickly succumbed to the ruse. Eric had been born into money. His family owned the *White Daily Journal*, one of the oldest newspapers in New York. Eric received a small allowance, but he was not dependent on Shaw wealth, hence the ease in luring him to Wyoming. A pity, as Gordon knew this young man's future.

"Welcome to my home, Mr. Shaw. Whiskey, scotch?" Gordon asked.

"Thank you; rum and Coke, please. I'm excited to be here. Your offer was nice—a bit extravagant for the work you want done," Eric said, and he took the drink offered to him.

"Not at all. Your work is well known, and I always get what I want. Cheers." Gordon raised his glass.

"Cheers. When do you want to start?" Eric asked, and downed his drink.

"Now will be fine."

Eric looked perplexed. "I don't understand."

Gordon walked over to him. "I would like to introduce you to the man who arranged all of this."

Eric turned and dropped his glass on the floor. The man before him was a wanted criminal, a possible terrorist, and a kidnapper.

"I believe it's time we were properly introduced. My name is Caydon, Aaron Reece Caydon, and we have unfinished business." Aaron smiled as Eric Shaw fell, unconscious, to the floor.

CHAPTER TWO

Aaron watched his associates remove the casket, which held the drugged body of Eric Shaw, from the hearse and place it on his jet at the Jackson Hole airport. The sun was beginning to peek over the mountains, and the skies were clear. A year's worth of planning had gone without issue. He now had what he needed to complete his plan to retire from this life and disappear forever with Kyliegh.

He walked over to Gordon. "I will not return; your debt has been paid in full," Aaron said and shook hands with him.

Gordon smiled and handed a large envelope to Aaron. "I will always be in your debt. If you should need anything, you have my number."

"How long are you staying?" Aaron asked.

"I'm leaving in the morning. The cleaning crew will arrive shortly after I'm gone. All transactions were in cash; no paper trail can be traced," Gordon answered.

Aaron nodded, and he turned to enter the plane.

"Wait," Gordon called suddenly. "What do you want me to do with this?" Gordon held up Eric Shaw's cell phone.

"Destroy it. Since 9/11, they all have tracking systems in them, and that's the last thing either of us needs. I know how to contact his brother," Aaron responded.

"Consider it done."

Aaron stopped at the cockpit. "Are we cleared?"

The pilot acknowledged the question with a nod and continued with his final checks. Aaron looked toward the back of the plane, where the casket containing Eric Shaw had been stored. He saw his right-hand man, Dan, in position. Aaron's military upbringing continued even into his private life. He was the general, and Dan was his lieutenant.

"Everything's working properly?" he asked Dan.

Dan replied, "Fine, for now. But I may have to make some adjustments as the trip continues, and he could be quite sick once the medication begins to wear off."

"As long as you don't kill him, he'll get over it," Aaron said.

It would be a long flight. He had about six weeks before he would send the official ransom letter to Eric's older brother, Taylor. This would give him time to prepare, to think, focus, and finally to find the woman. Aaron looked at the envelope lying on the table in front of him. He knew he should open it, but his thoughts drifted again to a New Year's morning on the loch at Glenfinnan with Kyliegh. Once he closed his eyes, rest and actual peace came quickly.

THE PILOT COMPLETED the final check and plotted the fuel stops along their route. This was going to be a long one, but having relief would help lift the burden. He looked back at all the men on the plane. Each and every one of them owed Aaron either his life or a debt. This would be his last flight. His age and his time served meant that his service had come to an end. He was financially secure, and his debt was paid in full. He would miss the others, but it was time for him to disappear.

"You ready?" the copilot asked.

"Yes. Course set for Innsbruck, Austria," the pilot answered.

"It'll be about fourteen hours, maybe more with fuel stops and customs," the copilot confirmed.

"Sounds about right. Maybe I can talk Aaron into stopping overnight so we can all rest."

"Good luck with that. I think he has other plans or we wouldn't have the extra pilots on board."

"I think you're right. Time to go; we've been cleared," the pilot said and announced to the others to prepare for takeoff.

Six hours later, the pilot cautiously approached his sleeping boss. He leaned forward and shook Aaron's shoulder.

"Aaron, we're landing for fuel. I need everyone's passports and the papers on our 'deceased.'" He smiled. "Did you have a nice nap?"

"I guess I did. How long was I out?" Aaron asked, handing his friend a large envelope, which contained all he had asked for and a substantial amount of currency.

"About six hours, give or take. We'll be landing in about twenty minutes," the pilot said before heading back to the cockpit.

Aaron looked out the window at the blue water, which turned into land, buildings, and a small runway, where men waited. Plans had been made before they'd departed to make this stop—and all stops to come—proceed without incident. He watched as the fuel truck pulled up and connected to the plane. All was as it should be: flowing fuel, smiling officials, and no problems.

Aaron opened the envelope and pulled out two files. The first was unmarked and held multiple photographs of Bevan, his wife, Laura, and their infant daughter, Sarah. There was updated information on Bevan's activities since last December. Laura's new job was close to home, and baby Sarah went to work with Mom every day. Bevan had a family, a life. Bevan needed to remember his warning; there was more to lose now. Aaron remembered the family that had been taken from him: mother, father, lover, and almost his daughter. He believed that there were more memories that hid in the shadows of his mind, but anything before his fourth birthday had not been retrievable.

"Aaron, we're all finished and ready to go. If the weather holds, we should be there in eight hours," the pilot said, interrupting his thoughts.

"Good," Aaron replied, and he turned to Dan. He handed a phone and piece of paper to him. "I need you to call this number and tell the man that answers what time we should be arriving. Tell him to have everything I requested at the airport. One more thing, I expect him to be there; no substitutes."

"Are you expecting problems?" Dan asked.

"No, and I intend to keep it that way."

Aaron put Bevan's file away. As the plane leveled, he began to relax, and he reached for the next file, which was marked "Private." Aaron opened it, and shock appeared on his face as he looked at the face of the woman who had attacked him.

Innsbruck, Austria
5:30 a.m.

AS AARON WALKED off the plane, he was impressed by the fleet of black Mercedes that was waiting for them. His men quickly moved the casket and equipment to the vans that had been provided. His pilots had been instructed to make arrangements for the jet to have a new paint job, which would include numbers indicating Innsbruck as it origin. Aaron shook hands with his senior pilot. "Good luck, and thank you for your service to me over the years."

"My pleasure," the pilot said, and walked toward the other men to say his goodbyes.

Aaron then looked toward a rotund man shifting from foot to foot. He motioned for him to come forward.

"Mr. Caydon," Tomas's voice quivered.

"Tomas."

"I hope the arrangements I have made for you will be acceptable. The castle is isolated, just outside of Innsbruck. It's fully stocked, and no one will bother you. The guards at the gate are being paid to not ask questions."

"How long is this open to me?" Aaron asked.

"For as long as you need. The guards will notify me when you leave."

Aaron continued to question Tomas. "The shipment I asked for?"

"Arrived, and it has been taken to the castle," Tomas answered, wiping his forehead.

"The local authorities?" Aaron asked.

"Paid."

Aaron turned away. "I'll be in touch."

"Whatever you need, sir you have my number." Tomas wiped the sweat off his face once more, despite the cold wind that blew. He turned to leave, but stopped when he heard his name.

"Tomas . . . if you have failed me in any way, your debt will be extended to your grandchildren," Aaron said.

"It has been done! I swear it on the lives of my children. No one will bother you. I am the mayor of this city, and my word is not to be questioned by those below me," Tomas assured, his voice quivering.

"We will see."

Aaron entered his designated Mercedes, handing Dan the address to enter into the GPS.

"It's about an hour maybe two, depending on the mountain roads," Dan said. "What about our guest?"

"I would like for him to be stable and upright," Aaron responded, settling into the front seat.

"He'll have a headache, and he'll possibly be nauseated and disoriented for a few days," Dan answered.

"He is an unwilling participant, my pawn. He will be treated well and kept comfortable. In the meantime, I have a job for you."

"Back to the States?" Dan replied.

Aaron handed him a file. "Possibly. It depends on what you find over the next few days."

Dan opened the file and looked at the picture of the woman. He recognized her instantly. "I've seen her before. I was almost caught by her and Blain Benjamin last year while I was following Bevan."

"What's her name?" Aaron questioned.

"Don't know. I tried to find out, but she's a ghost," Dan replied, putting the car into drive and slowly making his way out of the airport grounds.

Aaron mused on this, staring out the tinted windows. Then he commanded, "Find her and all the information about her that you can get your hands on."

Dan nodded and headed onto A12. "I'll need to go back."

"How long to get everyone settled?" Aaron leaned back in his seat as the car picked up speed quickly on the autobahn.

"A week, maybe two, and I'll have everything in running order here," Dan replied, keeping his eyes on the road. "Then I'll be on my way back. If I need to leave sooner, I'll leave Miguel in charge."

"Do it." Aaron closed his eyes, thinking over his plans for the days to come.

CHAPTER THREE

Fort Meade, Maryland
Sunday, November 10, 2002
8:00 a.m.

Zaveen "Zack" Keens, twenty-four, and her new partner, Lane Brigham, thirty-one, sat in the conference room, waiting for their boss, Bevan Benjamin. Lane had been with the NSA for five years, and he had been on assignment when he'd been compromised. He had been sent back to the states and reassigned in the last year to a temporary job in DC. Lane had a military background, and he was six feet one with a stocky build—all muscle—and red hair. The most unusual thing about him was that he had different-colored eyes. Zack tried not to stare, but one eye was hazel and the other was a deep blue.

He had been handpicked for this assignment by Bevan. Zack had read his file, and she already knew that he had some questions about being partnered with a "little girl." She knew that only having a couple of years with the company still made her a rookie, but her special abilities helped to offset the lack of experience. Zack smiled, but she knew it would not be easy to gain Lane's confidence. She was more concerned about how he would accept her gift. Not just anyone would accept a partner who could read their thoughts and know things that others didn't.

"Do you know why we're here on a Sunday?" Lane asked.

"I have an idea. Do you know of a man named Aaron Caydon?" Zack replied.

"No. Should I?" he retorted.

"You will," Bevan said as he entered the room. "Zack is already familiar with him on a personal basis; you have a lot of catching up to do. But it shouldn't take long."

Zack remembered the boxes of classified information the CIA had gathered on Caydon. It had taken weeks for her and her former partner to trudge through. It would take Lane at least two weeks to go through them, maybe longer, depending on his reading abilities.

"Paper or computer?" Lane asked.

"Paper," Bevan answered.

He nodded and began making plans for his cram session. "I'll need this room, twenty-four hours, coffee, two boxes of those little chocolate-covered cake donuts, a gallon of cold milk, two bags of chips, four ham sandwiches, six PayDays, and two gallons of sweet tea."

Bevan smiled. "I can do that."

"Oh, and I need to get some CDs out of my car to play while I work, and an hour in the gym before I get started," Lane added.

Bevan nodded. "Whatever you need to get this done, Lane. Zack, I need to see you in my office. Lane, once you're done with the other material, there will be one more file you'll need to read, too. An hour will be all *you'll* need to get through it."

Bevan made a call to his secretary, Darlene, and left Lane's food order with her. Then he directed to Lane, "You have an hour to get ready; I'll have all the records here."

"Be back in an hour," Lane said and headed out the door.

Bevan turned his attention to Zack. "I know you've read Lane's file, but there were a few things left out, just as there are things left out of yours. It's always best to not give away everything you know. Let's go, and I'll fill you in on your new partner."

"Speaking of partners how is Blain? I know Caydon did quite the number on him," Zack said.

"Doing well. He was finally released medically, and he's been retraining. I don't think he's happy with his progress, but the injuries he sustained were meant to delay recovery—something else Aaron

Caydon is good at. You were both lucky," Bevan answered as they entered his office.

As they walked in, Darlene said, "Lane's food request has been ordered and will be here soon. I'm heading to the archives now since there is so much to bring over. I also ordered lunch for you two."

"Thanks just let us know when it arrives. We're going to be busy for the rest of the day, or rather, Lane will be busy. I'm leaving after lunch—wife, daughter, family thing, you know." Bevan smiled and closed the door.

Zack looked at Bevan and knew there was something else, more information that could not be shared inside the walls of the office. "I assume this has to do with the box in your car," Zack offered.

"Yes. After lunch, after Darlene has gone, I'll meet you at my house. Sorry you have to make the drive."

"Why the charade?" Zack asked.

Bevan paused before answering, choosing his words carefully. "The files I have are not the government's, they're mine. They're from before his time with the NSA, before the military, before he was Aaron Caydon. There's one in particular, a binder full of my own notes, which you need to pay attention to."

"I thought that Caydon was a product of the military. At least, that's what is indicated in his government files," Zack probed.

"As I said, there are always things that are left out of files. The military only enhanced what he already had naturally," Bevan replied.

"There's something else you're worried about," Zack said as she walked toward the door.

"Yes. Since the incident last year and your report on Caydon's connections here, I've found myself doubting everyone in this building. Where are you going?"

There was a knock on the door, and Darlene entered with drinks and food. "I'm going to leave now," she said and handed the sacks to Zack.

Bevan shook his head. Zack was amazing, and her abilities seemed to be growing stronger.

"That was fast," Zack commented.

"Not a lot of backed-up orders on Sunday," Darlene said and smiled. "Lane will be quite content when he returns."

"See you in the morning," Bevan said, then waited until Darlene left the office before continuing. "I have some things you need to know about your new partner. First, why don't you tell me what you know, what you personally have discovered."

"Well, I didn't know about his memory capabilities until this morning. He has a military background, black ops, and he's a weapons specialist. I don't think I need to go into the two operations that keep him awake at night. He's single now—just broke up with a nurse named Paige. He hates his red hair, loves dark beer, has terrible eating habits, has an iguana named Fred, and he thinks I'm a little girl who he'll have to watch after," Zack summarized.

Bevan smiled. "Lane was recruited, like you. I handpicked him for the company years ago, and most of his work was covert until he was compromised. His ability to recall will strengthen both of you. He comes from a large family—four brothers and two sisters—and he speaks five languages."

"Five? His file says two," Zack said.

"As I said, never show all your cards. Blain was not the partner you needed, he's too much of a cowboy. He was predictable and it got him hurt. I need agents that work smart, think before they act, and anticipate Caydon's next move. I believe the two of you will be able to accomplish that, once he realizes you don't need him to protect you. I'll cover that with him next week. Lane was born in Ireland to an American father and an Irish mother. He is intelligent and can move silently and quickly, despite his size. The only thing that may be a problem is his diet." Bevan laughed as he unwrapped a PayDay and began to eat it.

"I would've thought he was more the healthy type. Go figure," Zack laughed.

Bevan continued more seriously. "When I recruited him, I was already aware of his metabolism. Physical or mental exertion causes a tremendous use of calories for him. I would suggest you keep extra candy bars with you. I understand his favorite is PayDays." Bevan motioned with the candy bar in his hand, then looked at his watch. "Time to go. Laura will want you to stay for dinner."

Zack smiled. "Love to; it's been a while since Aunt Zaveen has seen Sarah."

"Oh, really? Laura said you two had lunch last week."

"A technicality. We only had an hour. Now I can have the day," Zack said.

"I want to check on Lane as we leave," Bevan said.

"He just got back to the conference room, and he's opened the first box. He's quite intrigued by Caydon."

"Intrigued is not what I want to hear. I need Lane to understand how dangerous Caydon is, and he needs to be more concerned about how to catch him without getting you both killed in the process." Bevan was perturbed.

Zack reached into her bag and dropped her car keys as she pulled them out.

Bevan picked them up and looked at the picture of Zack and Eric hanging off the key chain. "I meant to ask you earlier if you've heard from that tall fiancé of yours."

"No, it's only been a week, and I don't expect to hear from him until probably the first of the year. Eric said this job would take him out where cell coverage isn't really possible, but that he would email if he got a chance. I did get a message from Jace. She and Taylor are going to extend their honeymoon and go to Munich for Christmas. They'll be home New Year's Day."

Bevan thought about everything Zack, Eric, Jace, and Taylor had been through. Brothers Taylor and Eric Shaw were heirs to the White-Shaw family fortune, and they were tied to one of the largest newspapers in New York, the *White Daily Journal*. Their recent inheritance had made both of them targets. Aaron Caydon had previously attempted to tap that inheritance by abducting Jace Bowen, Taylor's then-fiancée who was now his wife, and who was also related to Zack. The abduction attempt had failed, but it had left questions that Bevan had not been able to answer. Bevan was concerned about Zack not hearing from Eric. Aaron Caydon was still out there, and Bevan felt he wasn't finished with Taylor Shaw.

Bevan watched as Zack got into her car. He sat for a moment before starting his. Eric Shaw had shown little restraint in his feelings for Zack before leaving for his business trip; how was it possible that he hadn't sent word, even if it had only been a week? As Zack drove out the gate in front of him, he just couldn't shake the feeling that something wasn't right. Bevan opened his phone and hit number three. His brother-in-law, Ron, who worked for the FBI in Hawaii, was always good for running down information he needed on a more personal basis.

"Ron, can you contact the Shaws' lawyer, Bentwood Milton, and see if you can get any information on the job Eric Shaw is working on? Then I need a check on his bank account, withdrawals or deposits, and finally . . ."

Ron finished for him. "All activity on his cell phone for what, the last month or so?"

"Yes," Bevan confirmed.

"Problem?" Ron asked.

"Possibly."

"Call you in a few days," Ron said.

Reston, Virginia
7:00 p.m.

ZACK HAD ENJOYED the afternoon and evening with her boss and his family. She wanted to stay longer, but had work to do and a box of files to be studied. Zack picked up Sarah and headed to the child's bedroom to put her down for the night.

"Zack, you don't have to do that," Laura said.

"It's not a problem. I need one more hug before I go," Zack replied.

"You're spoiling her," Bevan teased.

"Like that's a problem? She's growing way too fast."

"I'll walk you out. Laura, I'll be back in a minute," Bevan said.

Zack and Bevan walked out to his car, where he opened the trunk and took out a medium-sized box, handing it to Zack. "Don't lose this. Besides Lane, it's for your eyes only," Bevan cautioned.

Zack put the box in her car and looked in the rearview mirror as she left the Benjamins'. She loved spending time with Bevan, Laura, and the baby. Zack had spent a lot of time lately at work, reviewing files on Caydon, improving her skills, conducting harder workouts at the gym, and pushing herself at the range. In her downtime, she had been flying to keep her hours and log up to date. What she really wanted was time back home in Louisiana, to go out on the land and to be with her family. Home would have to wait this year, and Zack knew Mama would be sad she could not come home for Christmas.

Zack looked at the ring on her hand. She missed Eric, and she hadn't thought about there being a problem until she'd read Bevan's concerned thoughts. Eric had told her it might be a while before he called, but now she was worried. She would call when she got home; at least, she could leave a message. She thought about the box in the back seat, and wondered what more there could be to the story of Aaron Caydon than she already knew.

When she arrived at home, Zack sat for a moment and looked around before getting out of the car, smiling suddenly. She took the box out of the back, locked the car, and headed toward her apartment. Just before she got to the front door, she stopped and turned around. "I thought you said it would take twenty-four hours," she called out.

"I still have a couple of boxes left to go through, but I needed a break," Lane said as he walked out of the shadows.

"I think you might have driven a little far for a break," Zack remarked, and she handed Lane the box she was carrying.

"You got any beer?" Lane asked.

"No dark beer, but I do have light beer," she answered.

"Guess that'll have to do," Lane allowed.

Zack opened the door to her apartment and looked up at Lane. "I know you didn't drive all the way over here for a beer. So come in, and I'll see what I can do to alleviate your fears about whether or not I can truly handle myself against Aaron Caydon and cover your six."

"Is it that obvious?" he asked.

"Not really; you see, I have this ability," she began.

Lane nodded vaguely, not fully understanding. He walked into Zack's apartment, taking time to look at his new partner's life. There was a large collage of family pictures. At the center of these was a picture of Zack and a tall young man. Lane had seen the engagement ring she wore, so he assumed that this was her fiancé. In front of the picture sat a fetish, the image of a raven. Zack's apartment wasn't large, but she had what she needed and didn't live beyond that. As he looked around the apartment he thought about his new partner. He knew she was competent with weapons, but he was still concerned he would have to be her protector in the field. She was petite, which could be an issue in hand-to-hand combat.

"His name is Eric Shaw, and you really need to stop worrying about me," Zack told him as she handed him a beer.

"Thanks, but how did you . . ."

"How did I know what you were thinking? I'm capable of reading minds, possibly controlling thoughts. It's a gift from my family, something I'm continuing to learn how to better control," Zack replied neatly.

Oh, shit! This could be a huge problem for me, he thought.

Zack smiled. "In the past, I wasn't able to control my abilities. Even with the training I'm receiving at work, the flood of information is overwhelming at times. As much as I want to tell you that I won't invade your thoughts, I can't promise that."

"Well, I guess that will have to do," Lane said. "I know you have access to my files, and you obviously have done some research on me, so I feel it's only fair to ask you some questions."

"Ask away. I have nothing to hide," Zack countered.

Over the next three hours and a six-pack of beer, Lane asked every question he could think of about her family, education, fiancé, and the run-in with Aaron Caydon. He discovered Zack had been injured in the altercation, and a Keens family heirloom, a boning knife, was taken by Caydon.

"Just a couple more things, then I'm heading back to the office and finishing up. How long will it take you to go through that box from Bevan?" Lane asked.

"About a week, maybe more. I don't read quite as fast as you," Zack admitted.

"Do me a favor, if you find something I might need to know before you're finished, will you call me?" Lane asked.

"Definitely," Zack assured.

"Next time, I'll bring the beer; I hate light beer." He grimaced. "By the way, something else you need to know is that I speak eight languages, not five. I haven't had a chance to tell Bevan."

"Tell me which ones," Zack prompted.

"Irish and Scottish Gaelic—there's a difference—Greek, Latin, German, French, Spanish, and Russian. And I just bought Rosetta Stone discs on Mandarin. I love linguistics."

"I'm impressed. I speak French, Spanish, Arabic, Kurdish, and Farsi. At least we can converse if necessary in French and Spanish," Zack said.

"I have a gift; I'm able to memorize and retain. It's not eidetic memory because I do have to study and sometimes I have to read it several times, but once I have it, things stick. The only exception is language. That comes easily to me," Lane said proudly.

"I think that Bevan feels we're well paired to find Caydon," Zack said.

"He has quite the web of connections, and it seems to be everywhere. You said you have some ability to control thoughts. Do you think you'll be able to do that with Caydon?"

"I'm not sure. He's different, and I'm hoping that the new information from Bevan will help me understand just *how* different he is from everyone," Zack said.

"Well, I need to go. I have something to run by Bevan in the morning, and if he approves, you'll need your passport," Lane said cryptically.

"See you tomorrow then. We'll all be in the office, even though it's a holiday, as usual," Zack said, following Lane out.

Lane walked away and felt better about his partner, even though she didn't have the best taste when it came to beer. He had confidence in his boss, and he knew Bevan wouldn't put him with someone who couldn't hold their own in a fight. Lane wasn't sure he believed the mind reading or controlling abilities Zack claimed to possess. Over the years, he had developed an ability to read a person, which was probably what Zack was doing. Maybe she was just better at it than most. It just wasn't possible to have the type of gift that she claimed. As he drove back to the office, he stopped by an all-night diner and bought a few things he would need to get him through until the morning.

"That'll be fifty-two dollars even," the waitress said.

Lane paid and took his order.

"You must be having a late-night party," she said.

"Nope, just a snack for me," Lane said before he left.

ZACK LOOKED AT the box sitting on her small kitchen table. She knew there was information within it that she needed to know, but it would still be there tomorrow. Right now, she needed to at least leave Eric a message, and hopefully he would get back to her in a week or so. She had to trust him and let him work. The last thing she wanted to ever be was a suspicious or nagging fiancée.

She dialed Eric's number. It went straight to his voicemail.

"You know the drill: leave your message, and maybe I'll call you back." Beep!

"Miss you, call when you can," she said simply, and then hung up. She looked down at her cell phone again, a chill ran across her back.

CHAPTER FOUR

Austria
Monday, November 11, 2002
3:00 p.m.

Eric Shaw attempted to open his eyes, but the nausea came again; it was relentless, wave after wave. How long had it been? Was it day or night? He tried to sit up, and it came again. He searched for the bucket that had become his friend since awakening from what he could only assume had been a drug-induced slumber. He retched and retched, but nothing came up. His throat burned. Eric looked at his left arm. There was a tube attached to it with some type of fluid running into a vein; it seemed to be the only thing that was keeping him alive. He turned his head when he heard the door open. A blurry figure came to the side of the bed and put something in the tube. It burned when it reached his arm, but it seemed to calm the raging hammer in his head and ease the burning, twisting knot in his stomach.

"Now you should start feeling better tomorrow," the man said.

As Eric fell back into darkness, he spoke one word: "Zaveen."

DAN WALKED TOWARD the curtains as Eric Shaw spoke. As the light of the Austrian morning shone down on his patient, he made a quick assessment. Dan had been a medic while in the military, and he knew the medication that had kept Eric Shaw asleep would be out of his system soon. The intravenous solution would keep him hydrated until he could start taking food and drink.

"How's our guest?" Aaron asked as he entered the room.

"Improving. The medication and gas I used had a little longer effect than I expected. I'm hoping he'll be able to at least sit up tomorrow and drink something," Dan told him.

"Good. How are things progressing here in general?" Aaron asked.

"I had everyone up at five this morning to finish unloading and unpacking everything we brought with us. Four crates containing our new weaponry have been opened, and the weapons have been distributed to each man. I have two men out on the property, checking for any possible problem areas not covered by the so-called guards Tomas hired," Dan reported.

Aaron walked over to the window and looked out on the sunny day. "They are being paid to be stupid, so I didn't expect much intelligence or military background from them. Who is assessing my new acquisition?"

"Miguel, and boss, I have to tell you the Beretta M9A1 and the ARES Shrike are very impressive," Dan said with satisfaction.

"Then why don't we take a walk and you can show me. We need to be ahead of everyone. The Beretta came with the seventeen-round clips, correct?" Aaron inquired.

"Yes sir, and the ARES with hundred-round belts. Sorry for asking, but the ARES is not available for the military at this time, right?" Dan questioned as they headed downstairs and into the library.

"You're correct, and let's just say it was a gift. Miguel has found the privacy we need for practice?"

"Yes. Actually, there's an old building, partially destroyed at the back of the property. We won't be heard." Dan walked over to a crate and handed Aaron one of the ARES Shrikes.

"Perfect. Do you feel comfortable leaving a week early?" Aaron asked as he looked over the weapon and began to familiarize himself with it.

Dan nodded. "I can leave Miguel in charge to finish what I didn't accomplish."

"Since I feel that Bevan is watching for us, your trip back will take you to Texas first. I have something I need for you to pick up and ship here for me," Aaron instructed him.

"Winery stop?" Dan asked and handed him a Beretta.

"I've acquired a taste for the wine there. See if there's anything new, perhaps a nice dry red." Aaron loaded the clip into the weapon.

Dan smiled. "I'll enjoy that stop. Where are you sending me? Dallas?"

"No, Amarillo. I don't think there will be prying eyes at that airport. Rent a car and continue, as in the past. Don't stay in one area for long, and change transportation frequently. I need you in New York to check on return dates for the newlyweds, then on to DC. Oh, and one more stop in Boston to drop off a letter and package," Aaron said. He walked over to the window and opened it.

"With all that, I'll be gone at least a month, maybe two. By the way, our guest called out."

"To who?" Aaron asked.

"Couldn't make out more than a whisper. Maybe Irene, Maureen, Eileen. Sorry."

"Well, it's a start," Aaron replied; a moment later, he fired the Beretta. He handed the weapon back to Dan and walked out of the library.

Dan looked out the window to see a dead cat hanging over a tree branch. "Damn."

Aaron walked back upstairs and into Eric Shaw's room. He looked down at his captive and smiled. "If you are a patient man, all things will come to you."

archidamus

Fort Meade, Maryland
7:00 a.m.

BEVAN ENTERED THE front door of the NSA building and headed straight for the conference room. He wanted to see if Lane had finished. As he opened the door, the smell of fried chicken and tacos was overwhelming. There were food wrappers, empty milk containers, and drink cups lying on the table and floor. The only thing left was a half-eaten PayDay. Lane was asleep in the corner of the room, covered with a throw that sported the Irish flag. Bevan shook his head, backed out of the room, turning the light off and locking the door. The cleaning crew would hate him later for the mess. Bevan headed to his office; as he turned the corner Ethaniel "E." Long was standing at his door.

"Morning, boss. You're running late, aren't you?" E. said jovially.

"That's what happens when you get married and have a family," Bevan retorted.

Ethaniel Long was head computer geek for Bevan. He was related to the Keens and Bowen families, and had grown up at the family Long-Bowe Bed and Breakfast in Waynesboro, Georgia. The B&B was not far from where Bevan's parents resided. Once a large tobacco plantation belonging to the Bowen family, the modest Long-Bowe was currently run by E.'s parents, Daniel and Denise. E. hadn't followed his parents into the hospitality business. His advanced computer skills had made him highly sought after, and E. had been hired right out of high school by the NSA. He was responsible for many of the highly successful programs for the company. E. was more than valuable: he was a necessity.

"Speaking of marriage, you need to get fitted for your tux," E. reminded Bevan.

"I already have an appointment. You know, if you two hadn't picked the biggest day of the year to get married, things might not be so frantic. Was it your idea to get married on Valentine's Day?"

"Definitely not my idea—Deanna's. I'm leaving all this in her hands."

Bevan laughed. "And I'm sure it will be one for the social page."

"Yeah, that's what worries me," E. said, rolling his eyes.

"She must be out of town or you wouldn't be here."

"She's in Italy, looking at material. Don't ask. Something about summer designs she needs to get done before the wedding; I don't pay attention. I'm updating programs, running new systems, and looking for hackers."

"You're still checking for movement on our friend?"

"Every day, and for now, we've picked up on nothing, not even his private jet," E. answered.

"He's out there. Just keep watching, and do me a favor: put some tags out for anyone checking on Eric, Taylor, Jace, or Zack."

"Problem?"

"Not sure; I'm having Ron do some checking in Hawaii," Bevan said.

"Oh. By the way, I've put in for time off for the wedding and honeymoon. I'm going to suggest that we get the same replacement person for me that helped last year," E. said.

"That's fine; just make sure she keeps a little tighter watch this time. I can't have Caydon slipping in and not know about it for a week," Bevan said.

"On it. Let me know if you need anything. I'll be here all day and into the night."

Bevan waved him out. "Go do whatever it is you do."

Lane walked in just as E. was departing. "Hey, Lane. Whoa, you smell like a bad taco." E. pinched his nose jokingly.

"What's up, nerd?" Lane grabbed E. and rubbed his head. "Tell that fiancée of yours I'm available and better looking than you."

"Yeah, whatever, dude—brains over brawn." E. pointed to his head, then left Bevan's office.

"How that nerd ever got that gorgeous woman of his is beyond me," Lane said, shaking his head and laughing.

"I take it from the destruction in the conference room that you're done."

"Except for the box at Zack's apartment, yes." Lane yawned. "Bevan, I need a shower and a change of clothes. When will Zack be in?"

"She's probably coming through the door, so make it quick."

"I have an idea that we need to discuss. It'll mean us leaving the country for a while," Lane said.

Just then, Zack strode into Bevan's office. "Oh, man you look bad," she commented to Lane.

"Well, I can tell that I'm not going to get any work done today," Bevan sighed. "Zack, conference room; Lane, shower. We'll all meet in the conference room in fifteen. Now, get out of my office."

He looked up as Darlene stuck her head in the door later. "Is it safe?" she asked.

He smiled. "Come in."

"I've contacted the cleaning crew, and they're headed to the conference room. All the files have been taken back. Your appointments for the week are in your computer calendar. And Ron Edwards called and said he would contact you later today," Darlene reported.

"Thank you. I'll be in the conference room for the next hour. I'll need to contact some overseas agents for reports. Can you block off time for the next six hours for me? And will you make sure my appointment with the tux rental place is still set for this week? I'll also need you to have my reports ready for my meeting in the morning with the president," Bevan rattled off.

"Got it—now, your fifteen minutes are up," Darlene said.

"Thanks, I don't know what I'd do without you."

As he walked to the conference room, he passed the cleaning crew, who were voicing low obscenities as he passed. When he arrived, Bevan was pleased to see Zack and Lane working together. His last memory of Zack and her former partner, Blain, in this room were two agents standing in opposing stances, arguing from opposite sides of the table. This present scene was refreshing, and Bevan knew he had made the right decision. He could see Lane laser-pointing to an area in Scotland. "What's this?"

"We need to make a trip," Lane stated.

"It's not exactly a good time to be sightseeing," Bevan replied dryly.

Lane ignored the gibe. "I don't plan on sightseeing. I have family and contacts that can help us. The information that the NSA and FBI gathered last year indicates that Caydon has someplace in Europe that he goes to for downtime."

"Bevan, is there any way E. can go back over the phone calls and the airport videos from last year, just before Caydon slipped back into the States?" Zack asked.

"I'll see what he can do, but disposable phones aren't traceable. The best I can do is find out where he boarded the ship in Oban," Bevan said.

"Then that's where we'll go first. If the nerd can come up with anything, we can work back from Oban," Lane decided.

Bevan sat for a moment, getting accustomed to the idea. He knew that Lane had a good plan and that they should go. "Zack, have you started on the box I gave you?"

"No. I was going to start tonight," she said, shifting guiltily in her seat.

"Then you need to work from home the rest of the week until you've gotten through it. Focus on the file marked 'Archidamus.' The rest will have to wait. Lane, set up what you need, and I'll have Darlene make arrangements for both of you. I want you to read that file, and my notes within it, before you both leave, no excuses. If the file isn't read, you don't leave," Bevan said in a tone that settled the matter.

"I'll touch base with the nerd, then make some calls," Lane said.

"Any chance we can leave after Thanksgiving?" Zack questioned.

"You going home?" Bevan asked.

"Well, if Lane will come with me, we can leave from New Orleans," Zack offered.

"New Orleans? Home cooked meal? Hell yeah! I'll come," Lane said. Zack smiled brightly at him.

"Any word from Eric?" Bevan followed up.

Zack wrinkled her brow. "No. Any word from Ron?"

Bevan shook his head, running his fingers through his hair. He couldn't seem to hide his thoughts from her. "I'm waiting on a call. I'll let you know."

"I wasn't worried at first, but I think something may have happened to him," she began, with concern coming through in her voice.

Bevan cut in, reassuring her. "It's probably nothing, out in the wild chasing rabbits, but I'll feel better once I talk to Ron."

"I'd appreciate a call once you talk with Ron. Lane, can you stop by tomorrow evening? I have dark beer, and I'll order pizza," Zack wheedled, brightening.

"See you around eight," Lane replied before he headed out the door.

Zack turned back to Bevan. "So, what's in the file?"

"It's something you have to read for yourself," Bevan said vaguely.

Zack tried to read his thoughts, but this time there simply wasn't anything there that made sense. She shrugged and left the conference room, heading toward the elevator. Bevan watched as she left, then headed back to his office. He sat down, and immediately his top phone line lit up.

"Ron, tell me you have something," he said wearily after answering.

"Nothing from Milton, and nothing out of the ordinary on his accounts. There was a large deposit made to his account before he left. I'm checking, but it appears to be from the job he's working on now. The only thing strange is that the deposit was in cash, made here in Honolulu," Ron told him.

"Something's not right."

"No, I didn't think so either, so I had his cell phone checked for the last two weeks. Calls to Zack, calls from her to him, and then nothing."

"He's out of range, possibly," Bevan offered.

"No, the phone has either been turned off or destroyed, so there's no way to trace it."

"Damn it. Something is wrong," Bevan said.

"Agreed. Where was he going?" Ron asked.

"Wyoming. Jackson Hole, I believe. See if your people can locate an address where the phone was before it went dead. If you can't, I'll put E. on it."

"OK. If there's a kidnapping possibly involved, I can work on it from here. I'll have some agents make inquiries and get back to you in a week. What are you going to tell Zack?" Ron asked.

"Nothing for now. I need her focused."

"Yeah, well, good luck with that—and with trying to keep her out of your head," Ron said before he hung up.

CHAPTER FIVE

Alexandria, Virginia
Monday, November 11, 2002
6:00 p.m.

Zack spent more time than she'd planned shopping after she left work. The last stop was at the market; if she was going to work from home, she might as well be stocked up. On her way into her building, she stopped at her box, it had been a few days since she'd checked her mail. Zack smiled at the letter from her mother and a postcard from Jace and Taylor.

Once she got into her apartment, she saw that there was nothing on her home phone from Eric, and no email from him either. She tried not to worry, and reminded herself that he had said it could be a month before she would hear from him. But Zack just couldn't shake the feeling that something wasn't right. She pushed it aside for the moment and put away her groceries, then read the letter from her mother. There was news about home, church, and family, and her mother's reminder to say her rosary and come home soon to visit. Zack smiled and made a mental note to let her mom know that she and a friend would be there for Thanksgiving.

She looked at the box on the kitchen table. Zack took the lid off and began to thumb through the files. She ran across files dating back to 1890 and 1900. The file "Archidamus" was large, containing operational reports, medical reports, psychological testing logs, arrest records, and training paperwork.

Zack picked up a binder, and several black-and-white photographs fell out. One was dated 1935, and it showed a small boy of about four or five in a martial arts uniform with a dark belt. There were military officers and people who appeared to be monks standing with the child. On the back of the photo was written "Archidamus." The next black-and-white photo was dated 1945, and it showed the same boy. But it *couldn't* have been him—by that year, he would have been about fifteen, but he barely looked eight years old.

She put the pictures aside and began to look at the file marked "Medical." The information on the first page made her hands shake. Zack sat down and read the page again. "This can't be true," she whispered, then pulled out her cell phone. "Lane, I need you to come over to my apartment—*now*." Zack's voice was trembling.

"What's wrong?"

"It's the box of files Bevan gave me—us—to look over. If what I'm reading is correct, Aaron Caydon is a product of genetic experimentation, and he's in his seventies," Zack said.

There was silence on the other end for a few moments. "Meat lovers' supreme OK with you?"

"Fine."

"Good. And I'm bringing Fred; he's been lonely," Lane said before hanging up.

Lane stood still for a moment. Surely he hadn't heard her correctly. Maybe she'd just misread something or there was a misprint on the file. The pictures he had seen of Caydon showed a man in his midthirties.

He speed-dialed his favorite pizza place. "Three meat lovers' supreme with extra cheese, please."

"Pickup or delivery?" the female voice asked.

"Pickup."

Lane went to his fridge and grabbed two six-packs of Guinness, then stuffed four PayDays into a bag with a change of clothes and his Irish throw. "I hope her couch is comfortable," he said as he picked up his iguana. "And you need to behave."

◉

ZACK SAT AND waited for Lane. She needed to make sure that the medical information in the file was correct. How could this kind of scientific experiment even be possible in the early 1900s? What she read sounded like a story from her brothers' Marvel comic books. She began to look online for information on reversing the effects of aging. She found information on human growth hormone, discovered in the 1920s, but not isolated until the mid-1950s. She needed Lane there to read over the files dated 1890 and 1900. All of this was too much to absorb, and she really needed to concentrate on the binder that Bevan had insisted she read. Zack's phone rang.

"I could use a hand downstairs," Lane said.

"Be right down," Zack said, and she headed out to help. She raised an eyebrow when she saw the bag throw, and Fred.

"I hope you don't mind; Fred's been lonely I just couldn't leave him again. I figured that with all that you told me, I might be here for a couple of days," Lane said, handing Zack his Irish throw and the beer. "I also called Bevan and told him I would be here helping you with the special files, so not to expect me in for a few days until we get through everything."

"What did he say?"

"Not much, really; he actually didn't sound too surprised," Lane said.

"Thanks for coming. There's more here than I can read in a month and make any sense of. I'm hoping that with both of us working on this, we can throw ideas and suggestions out there and get through this faster. My main focus is on Bevan's notes on Archidamus. I need you to read over everything else, and then we can decide what's most important," Zack said. She put the beer in the fridge, grabbed some paper plates and napkins, and they sat down on the floor to eat.

"First, I have to tell you that all this sounds like a bad horror movie. But I've read some books and medical journals on age reversal," Lane started.

"Well, aren't you a surprise," Zack replied cheekily.

Lane continued on, ignoring the interruption. "Things change so quickly now you have to keep up. I can find anything on the Internet, and I find medical journals very interesting. But I'll have to contact someone I know to see how this could be possible in the early 1900s."

Zack sat down at the table with a pen and pad to make notes. "I'm going to get started."

"Which files did you want me to go over first?" Lane asked.

Zack reached in and handed him four files. "This should keep you busy for a couple of hours."

Lane grabbed another piece of pizza and opened the files from 1890 and 1900. He began to methodically place paper after paper in chronological order, side by side. Lane looked up to find that Zack was staring at him. "Don't worry. There is a method to my madness."

"Whatever works to get us through all of this—and quickly," she said.

She turned her attention to her own pile of files, and the pages handwritten by Bevan that had been collected in a binder. She was soon deeply engrossed with the notes.

Summer, 1985

The following pages are my private notes, thoughts, and personal story on Archidamus Karsten Werner, born the first day of April, 1930, to Karsten Wilhelm Werner and Liesel Ivonne Graf-Werner. Both parents were German-born. Karsten was a biologist, a geneticist, and a man ahead of his time in reversing the aging process. Karsten's history is in a file dated 1890. Liesel's file is dated 1900. Liesel taught Shakespearean literature at the university in Berlin. A favorite story of hers was The Winter's Tale, *and she loved the name "Archidamus."*

Karsten and Liesel's marriage was arranged by the German government, but what the government didn't count on was the love that grew between them. The two had talked many times of leaving Germany so that they could be free to raise their children one day away from the prying eyes of the government.

Years came and went, and the children that they had hoped for never came. Then, when they both had given up, Liesel became pregnant, and Archidamus was born. Karsten's genetic work brought offers first by the British government and then from the American military. The promise of freedom to work for Karsten and a job for Liesel brought them to America. But, of course, the military was constantly involved in Karsten's work.

The first four years of Archidamus's life was a rapid progression. He walked at eight months and was able to speak full sentences by ten months, and he had the ability to replace items in the exact order he had found them in by twelve months. He was labeled at the age of three with a photographic memory; today, we call it eidetic memory.

Archidamus was becoming more and more an interest to the American government. He was exposed to numerous tests for months and months, much to the displeasure of his mother, who finally said, "No more!" Liesel believed that a child of four should be playing with other four-year-olds, not being tested by the military. It was only two months later that Karsten and Liesel were suddenly dead. A terrible accident on an icy road ended any interference from Liesel in the government's plans.

The military stepped in after their deaths, and Archidamus was placed in the home of an outstanding man, Colonel Howard Frances Caydon. Colonel Caydon was a career-military hero and leader. The colonel had followed *the Werners' lives since their arrival in America. He had received daily reports on each family member, especially Archidamus. The colonel was sent to tell Archidamus that his parents would not be coming back. Colonel Caydon's plan was to make the child his—and the government's.*

Archidamus was allowed to pack a few things to take with him, but Colonel Caydon refused to allow the boy to have any pictures of his parents. How could he groom him to be a weapon if he had ties to the past? As the final insult to his parents, Colonel Caydon changed the young boy's name. Archidamus was not the name of an American hero; instead, Aaron Reece Caydon was born. Aaron's first lesson on that day was, "If you are a patient man, all things will come to you."

Zack looked up; Lane had already finished both dated files. "What has it been, fifteen, twenty minutes? Are you done?" she asked.

"For now, but it's been a little longer than that. I finished the last pizza."

"Tell me what you found out," Zack prompted.

"Pretty much just general information on their lives: where they were born, their education, their arranged marriage," Lane replied.

"What about his work?"

"Genetic studies on reversing the aging process. Pretty much what you thought. He made his son a science experiment, but it took a while due to constant failures in the lab," Lane told her.

"Instead of a family, one perfect child," Zack mused. "What about the medical file?"

Lane shook his head. "Way above my pay grade, I'm afraid. I'm going to need permission from Bevan to show Karsten's work to my contact."

"Did you get a chance to look at the military folder?"

"I did a quick scan; it's quite impressive. It usually takes a career veteran twenty to thirty years to achieve all that Caydon accomplished. The government started training him at five, and he was used on some covert missions during World War II at the age of twelve. He had to have looked maybe eight years old then," Lane continued.

"What? How is that possible?" Zack asked.

"Not sure. I need to take a quick break and run for some supplies. It's going to be a long night. I need to go through the medical and military files again; we need to know what he's capable of and see if we can level the playing field," Lane said as he headed toward the door. "What can I get you?"

"Nothing. I have some things here," Zack said and watched Lane leave. "Back to work."

Aaron was recruited at the age of five into the United States military. The scientists put him through test after test, physical and psychological, to assess his abilities. The continued statement day after day from his father, Colonel Caydon, made him focus on each task before him. The young boy was fearless, and he adapted to every situation he was placed in. Even for his young age, he accepted all physical training in martial arts and weaponry.

This all seems like a bad dream to me as a human. They took a small, intelligent boy and turned him into a machine. Aaron was sent on several assignments as a child, even into war. He was able to complete the missions and return with positive results. It seemed to the government's enemies that a small child was no threat. As Aaron aged, his growth was delayed due to the genetic changes his father had made. This was just an added gift, allowing a child, a preteen, to come and go without challenge, mission after mission.

He accomplished mission after mission, but what was not known was that Aaron had begun to garner favors during those missions. Lives were owed to him, and money was promised then and for generations to come. During one of Aaron's debriefings, a psychologist reported the beginnings of what he believed were antisocial traits. Since the military owned him, or so they thought, they encouraged and built on those traits. What could be better than an individual with little remorse and complete loyalty?

These traits led to issues with local authorities and several arrests for petty crimes. Colonel Caydon's punishments to Aaron for those arrests were more missions, more training, and constant isolation. The colonel watched as his son excelled, mission after mission. Plans were in progress for Aaron's continued military service, with possible missions for the NSA. It seemed that they had the perfect weapon. As Aaron continued to be a good soldier, he began to make plans for his own future: if you were a patient man, all things would come to you.

After the end of Colonel Caydon's life, which all assumed was due to the colonel's love of cigarettes, Aaron volunteered to give his father's eulogy. The church was packed with honored guests; even the president at that time came to honor this man, who had given so much to his country. The following is the short and direct eulogy Aaron made that day. It left many wondering if the colonel had actually succumbed to his illness or if there had been a human hand involved. I will leave it to the reader to ponder.

"My life has been full and structured thanks to the man we honor today. I will now lay all future atrocities at his feet, and as a final statement to his legacy, I simply say, 'I was very patient.'"

Aaron had planned wisely; he'd had the colonel cremated. After the odd eulogy, the military was sent to obtain the ashes for testing. Once the urn was opened, all that was found inside was sand and a note stating, "You're too late." The ashes of Colonel Caydon are still missing, and the only remembrance of him is a headstone in Arlington over an empty grave.

Aaron disappeared for a while after the death of the colonel. This is where my association with him begins.

Zack stopped reading when the door opened and Lane entered with another pizza, a six-pack of Guinness, and a box of PayDays. She smiled and stretched.

"That looks good. I need a break, and we need to talk," she told him.

"Let me fix a plate and open a brew, and I'll be ready," Lane told her.

"It seems that Caydon has been building his financial empire since a very early age. He has individuals that owed and still owe him for some favor he did for them or their family. That's why he's able to move around the globe with ease. Last year, I also found out that he has a web of information coming out of the NSA. It's never direct; information passes from one person to another, and finally to him," Zack shared.

Lane nodded. "Good to know. There's also a psychological folder I need to go through really carefully."

"Caydon has some sociopathic traits. It seems they were built upon and encouraged by the government."

"He's the type of man who doesn't take any type of defeat well. It appears you're the first person ever in his life to hand him that, no matter how small it was. Caydon walked away injured, and that hurt his pride, but most of all, it hurt his ego. You do realize this makes you a target. I don't believe he'll come after you himself, but Bevan gave me a list of names of men loyal to Caydon who are probably working with him," Lane cautioned.

A shiver ran over Zack's arms. "What about my family?"

"We'll talk to Bevan and see what we can do to keep them safe," Lane said.

"They don't know what I do for a living. Well, my mother and brothers don't, but I'm pretty sure my papa knows. I never thought that what I do for work could bring danger to them," she said softly.

"I don't believe he knows who you are or there would have already been some issues for you and your family. When I go home with you for Thanksgiving, we can recon your property. We'll check for weak spots, problem areas. Between the two of us, we should be able to make a plan," Lane said, attempting to reassure her.

Zack nodded, but she didn't look convinced. "I'm tired. If you don't mind, I'm going to hit the sack for a few hours. There's an extra toothbrush under the sink in the bathroom."

"Go ahead. I'll be going over the medical and military files again. By the way, I found this with your name on it." Lane handed the file to Zack.

"Vanora?" Zack asked.

"Don't ask me." Lane shrugged his shoulders and headed to the kitchen for more pizza.

Zack took the folder and Bevan's notes, then headed to her bedroom. She shut the door, crawled into bed, and found the section where Bevan had first come into contact with Caydon.

My first encounter with Aaron Reece Caydon came while I was a police officer in Atlanta. He'd had multiple arrests: petty theft, panhandling, all misdemeanors with minimal time in county jail. I thought at the time that Caydon was a runaway living on the street. I built a relationship with him, and I used him as a confidential informant. The information he gave me was always spot-on, and it allowed me to make several arrests that helped me advance my career and earn promotions. But Caydon had an uncontrollable temper. I spent a lot of time with him and learned to talk him down, slowly helping him control his anger.

I was called one night to come into the station the last time Caydon was arrested. He told me he was tired of all the lies, and he began to tell me the story of his life and age. He was not eighteen, but was actually fifty-five. He had escaped from his military prison (as he called it), and had been on the streets for about two years. Unfortunately for him, others were listening, and he was transferred to a mental institution. Two days later, he was taken away in an unmarked black vehicle by two men in suits.

It was three years later when I met him again, after I was hired by the NSA. Caydon appeared to be a young man in his early twenties then: stoic, hardened, and one of the best and fiercest field agents I have ever known. In the time he had disappeared from Atlanta, Caydon had been taken back and reintegrated into military operations and, finally, into the NSA. Assignment after assignment was given and accomplished. I have never met anyone like him, and I'm still amazed at his ability to memorize and recall every specific detail of every mission.

Unbeknownst to the government, Caydon had garnered favors again on his assignments, and money passed into his hands. He was sent on many missions alone, and he would be gone for weeks. I believe he was renewing old contacts and making sure debts to him were continuing as promised. Can you imagine this man appearing over forty years later, still young, demanding that loyalty to him be continued by your grandchildren? He had built his own empire. I will never know the total worth of Aaron Caydon.

In the time I spent with Caydon at the NSA, I continued to encourage him to better his skills, including his antisocial traits. I now regret that. Shortly before my first promotion, Aaron Caydon left the NSA, with not even a letter of resignation: he just disappeared. What I found out in the weeks to come was that he had "officially retired." When agents went to his town house, it had been emptied of everything, and there was no forwarding address. His compensation was sent to an account in New York, and it is still untouched to this day.

He vanished for two years. Then, ARC Investigations appeared. He had made quite the name with the elite of New York, Los Angeles, Paris, and London. You see, money makes the dirt harder to find. Caydon had built a respectable name for his company, and for years, he stayed off of the FBI, CIA, and NSA's radar. Unfortunately, his name became associated with arms sales to the wrong people, murders, and sales of government information, but neither he nor his men could ever be directly connected to any of the accusations. No charges were ever filed, and he continued to be the upstanding owner of ARC Investigations. I've collected copies of reports from Interpol, Scotland Yard, and a few others, on what I believe are Aaron's involvement.

Zack closed the binder. She was tired, but she wanted to take a quick look at the other file before she went to bed. It contained just two pieces of paper and a picture. The eight-by-ten photograph was of a beautiful dark-haired woman with violet eyes. The first piece of paper was a death certificate for Vanora Sibi Blacach, murdered. The police had had no leads; it was now listed as a cold case in Dublin. The second paper was a badly copied birth certificate for a female, Caer Etain Blacach. Her mother: Vanora Sibi Blacach. Her father: *Aaron Reece Caydon.*

Zack jumped out of bed and yelled "Lane! Lane!" as she burst into the living room.

Lane rolled off the couch dumping Fred to the floor. He then jumped up, holding a huge knife. "What, what . . ."

"Whoa, it's me, Zack," she said, backing away.

"Shit—don't ever do that!" Lane said and sat down tiredly.

Zack's eyes gleamed. "You won't believe it! Aaron Caydon has a daughter."

CHAPTER SIX

Austria
Wednesday, November 20, 2002
12 p.m.

Eric Shaw stood on the balcony of his very expensive prison. The weather was brisk, and he could see clouds building. *Snow*, he thought. Today was the first day he had been able to eat a full meal without vomiting. Slowly, over the last week, he had begun to walk in his room from corner to corner, window to window, trying to get some idea of his location. The one thing he knew was that he wasn't anywhere near Jackson Hole, Wyoming. If he had to guess, it was either Switzerland or Austria. At least they had brought his clothes.

He knew now that Aaron Caydon had kidnapped him, and it would be for money—probably a lot of money. Eric had lost all sense time: there was no calendar, no watch, and his cell phone was probably sitting in the bottom of some lake. His room and balcony overlooked the mountain that the castle was built on, wherever he happened to be. *Not much of an escape chance*, he thought.

Eric held a cup of hot tea and honey, and he thought of Zaveen. He took a drink and was thankful that his throat no longer burned. "God, this is really good."

"I'm glad to see you enjoying the day, and I'm very pleased you seem to have made a full recovery. I must apologize for the side effects of the medication," Caydon said smoothly as he entered Eric's room.

"I guess I should be happy you didn't kill me," Eric responded grudgingly.

"Kill you? Eric, you are my guest until your brother and I come to an agreement on how much your trip back home is worth."

"I don't guess you'd just let me write you a check and head on back, would you? No harm, no foul, so to speak," Eric offered.

"You're quite the humorist, but no. But I will be happy to provide you with books, videos, and, if the weather is amenable, limited time outside," Caydon told him.

"I don't guess there's a gym anywhere."

"Why, yes, there is, and when you're a little stronger, you will have access to it," Caydon said. He turned to leave.

"One more question."

"Yes?" Caydon replied.

"What's the date?" Eric asked.

"Wednesday, November 20," Caydon said, and he left the room.

Eric heard a key lock the door and the top bar being latched. It had been only seventeen days. He couldn't believe it; it seemed like months, but that had to be the drugs. Zaveen: she wouldn't even suspect that anything was wrong for at least two, maybe three, more weeks. Taylor and Jace were still out of the country for at least two more weeks. His only hope was that Zaveen would somehow be clued in by her special ability.

AARON WALKED DOWNSTAIRS and into the main dining area for lunch. Tomas had provided a small staff of cooks and servants to see to their needs. His lunch was served as he enjoyed the last bottle of his Texas wine. Miguel entered the room and sat down.

"Dan left this morning. He said he'll contact you as he makes progress," Miguel reported.

"Was he able to find anything on the woman before he left?" Aaron asked.

"No."

"And the castle?" Aaron asked.

"Everything is set up; we have reconned the perimeter and placed our monitors and alarm systems. The men are in the gym now, and we will be at the range by five," Miguel reported.

"I'll be joining you on the range, and I expect to see perfection today. I'll be leaving Saturday, for two to three weeks. I expect Mr. Shaw to be treated well, and when you feel he is ready, schedule gym time for him. If the weather is decent, allow him one to two hours outside. I'm not truly worried about him trying to escape, but I do not wish to hear of any attempts. Do not underestimate him," Aaron said.

"Understood."

Aaron waited until he was alone, and then used one of two phones he'd bought in town a week ago. One had been sent to Scotland. He closed his eyes and smiled, then dialed the number to the second phone.

"Aaron?" Kyliegh answered.

"I'll see you in three days," Aaron said, then hung up the phone. He took his wine and walked to the fireplace, which was warm and inviting. He kissed the phone, then burned it.

Fort Meade, Maryland
6:30 a.m.

ZACK AND LANE had spent over a week rereading Bevan's private files, searching the Internet, and spending time in the archives at the NSA. They had met early at the office to set up maps so that they could go over their plans for the next six to eight weeks. Their plan would put them out of the country during the holidays and into the New Year.

"What time did you tell Bevan to be here?" Zack asked.

"Seven—and the geek, too," Lane said.

"You give E. too much grief. The guy needs a break; he's getting married soon, and his mind is all over the place right now."

"The only place his thoughts should be is on that beautiful woman of his. He's one lucky man."

"I think he knows that," Zack said, rolling her eyes.

"Well, he better treat her right, or I'll be standing there to take his place," Lane teased.

She changed subjects. "Did you talk to the geneticist?"

"Yes, and then I had to threaten him with what I'd do if he ever told anyone about my visit," Lane said, taking his weapon out and checking it.

"Why?" Zack questioned.

"He almost fell out of his chair when I explained what I needed to know and showed him a part of the formula that Karsten had used. I've never seen a man so excited over numbers and letters. He did say that if what I'd shown him could be proven, it would be possible to slow the aging process."

"To what extent?" Zack asked.

"The patient could live to be up to two hundred years old."

"Did you tell him he was from the planet Vulcan?"

"He begged me for more information; that's when the threat came. He tried to reason with me about all the good that this could do, but I shut him down."

"Do you trust him?" Zack asked.

"I have to—he's my older brother." Lane smiled. "What about you? Any information on the daughter?"

"I was excited about that information, but I've found nothing," Zack admitted.

"That can mean only one of two things: the woman is dead or Caydon's found her and has safely tucked her away from anyone who might use her against him."

"The name on the birth certificate—that person no longer exists. That means her name has been changed, and we have nothing," Zack said and held out her empty hands.

"Pretty much, but maybe the geek can find something. He seems to have a few more resources than we do. I suggest that we pass this off to him," Lane said, and he made a forward pass motion.

"If anyone can find her, it'll be E."

"I do want you to spend a few days with me on bomb ordinances, and we need as much time as possible on the range and in the gym. And I have a question," Lane said.

"Go ahead."

"What's with the raven fetish? I saw it at your house, and I've seen you holding it a couple of times," Lane asked.

"It's a gift from Jace from when I graduated. It's magic, a messenger of great mystery, a change in consciousness. It represents anything we have the courage to face, anything we have the power to transform. Since my run-in with Caydon, I've kept it with me pretty much all the time. I'm spending more time focusing and attempting to control my gift. It's funny—since I've been carrying this, I've gained more insight into my gift. Even my trainer, Mr. Joe, can't believe the improvement," Zack explained.

"What kind of trainer is he?" Lane asked, wondering why she needed a trainer.

"There's a special department here that deals with psychics and empaths. It's been in effect since the 1950s. Mr. Joe was involved in the program during the seventies. He's now the head of the department."

"And you think your gift will help us against Caydon?" Lane asked.

"I hope it will, but after finding out about his genetic makeup, it may have no effect at all. But Caydon's arrogance, the injuries he suffered, and the chance that he has a woman in his life who he truly cares for might give me an edge," she answered.

Lane nodded, then changed the subject. "Did you contact of your family about Thanksgiving?"

Zack grinned. "I called my mom, and she's very excited that we're coming home. She's going to love you since you speak Spanish, and you can talk to my papa in French."

"I'll enjoy going back and forth from one language to another; it's always good to keep up the practice."

"We'll take the four-wheelers and go out to check the property. But it may take a few days; the grounds are pretty extensive. How do you feel about a few nights out in the open?" Zack asked.

"It's not a problem for me, as long as I have a few PayDays."

Zack laughed. Just then, the door opened, and Bevan and E. entered. "I thought you might like a little breakfast snack before we get started this morning," Bevan said, handing Lane five large sacks from his favorite breakfast haunt.

"Snack? Looks more like banquet," E. said.

"You're the man, Bevan. I was getting a little weak with all this mental strain," Lane said.

Bevan walked over and looked at the maps that were pinned on the walls: Ireland, England, Scotland, Austria, Germany, and Switzerland, along with aerial photos of Zack's home and the surrounding land. "I assume that you two believe Caydon is in one of these areas."

"I've plotted all that was possible from the cell phones that were traceable. It isn't much, but it all coincides, except Switzerland and Zack's home," E. said, handing the information to Zack and Lane.

"That makes me feel better about you, Zack," Bevan said.

"Me too," she said, smiling.

"This means that he has no idea who you are yet, and that gives us time," Bevan said.

E. nodded and added, "I'm working on surveillance of your parents' house and land, starting today."

"While we're home, Lane and I will be out to check on possible weak areas. We'll set up cameras and alarms. I'll talk to Papa and tell him what I can. It will help that Lane is going with me," Zack said.

"I'll do what I can, but the less the company is involved right now, the better. The leak here might make it possible for him to go directly to your house if we start sending agents out there," Bevan cautioned.

"Understood. In any case, I know that land better than anyone, along with all the hunting blinds there, which are hard to find unless you're familiar with them," Zack said.

While they were talking, E. had moved to look at a map of Scotland. "I've plotted a course from Oban back through Scotland. The rest are questionable."

"My family's ready for us in Ireland. We'll be staying in Dublin for a week or so before we head out to Scotland. I have contacts that may be able to help us go directly where we need to be, instead of wasting time guessing," Lane said.

"I don't suppose the fact that the Guinness Storehouse is about a block from where you're going to be staying had any influence on your decision, did it?" E. asked tartly.

"You need to worry more about keeping that gorgeous woman of yours happy, and less about my drinking habits," Lane returned.

Bevan ignored them. "It seems the two of you have this pretty well situated, and I approve. I need you to keep in touch with E., and he will directly update me. Darlene has made arrangements for your trip to Louisiana. Lane, I want you to make the arrangements to Ireland from Zack's home. Try to keep the expense to a minimum, would you?"

"Is there a problem?" Zack asked.

"I'm trying not to draw attention to the two of you right now. Since you're going to need time to check your home, I'm sending you both out on Friday. Zack, be sure to see your mental trainer today."

"I will. He says I'm progressing well, with more control and focus," Zack shared.

"Good. E., your turn," Bevan said before leaving the conference room.

"I'm working on cell phones for you two with direct lines to me, plus some disposables for use overseas. I also have a few things for you to take that may come in handy," E. said.

Zack looked at Lane. "We're going to be gone for a while. Who's gonna watch Fred?"

"I have a standing room for him at my vet. They love him," Lane said and laughed as E. grimaced and walked out of the room.

◉

BEVAN ENTERED HIS office and was given a quick update on his schedule for the day by Darlene. "Thank you," he replied. "I'm going to be making phone calls for a while, so unless it's an emergency, take a message."

"Yes, sir," Darlene said, and she shut his door.

Bevan sat down and waited. The top line lit up. "Ron, what'd you find?"

"It's not good."

"Tell me," Bevan said.

"I contacted the office in Cheyenne and talked with the agent there. I didn't give too much information, but enough to get him off his butt and out of the office. He spent a couple of days checking the airport and the house where Eric Shaw supposedly went. The house is huge: lap pool, sauna, gym. It's up in the mountains, very secluded and very much empty. A representative from the rental office walked the agent through the house. It had been cleaned and stripped of all furniture, linens, dishes, etcetera. It's just a shell now, and for sale. It had been rented for a year, paid in cash up front," Ron said.

"Let me guess: false name and no picture identification for whoever rented the house?" Bevan ventured.

"You should have been a detective. There was a photo ID used, and an application was filled out, but they can't find it. The file just disappeared."

"Any chance someone there could sit with a sketch artist and give any type of description?" Bevan asked.

"The main manager is not the one who made the original contract. It was done by a temporary worker, who has since gone back to college. I was able to get a name, and I'll have an agent in Oregon find her, but I'm not hopeful," Ron continued.

"What about the plane?"

"Another great ghost chase. The numbers on the plane were out of Gettysburg, and since the airport in Jackson Hole is small, the flight plan filed was false as it leads to a private landing strip in Tulia, Texas. I'm not even going to waste my time on that. These guys are pros, and they covered all their bases. This is not something that happened overnight. All of this took some time, at least a year."

"Eric's phone?"

"Well, from the last GPS location, it was at the house, but after that we've got nothing. I would bet that it's been destroyed," Ron said.

"It's Caydon, I know it, but until the official ransom letter or call comes in, all we can do is speculate as to where they took him."

"I assume you have Zack and Lane working on things?"

"Laura told me that you and Liz are coming in tomorrow night for Thanksgiving," Bevan said, suddenly switching subjects.

Ron recognized this as his signal to stop talking and to call him later at home. "Sure thing, plane lands around seven. I want some time with that cutie niece of mine before you put her to bed," Ron replied smoothly.

"We'll see you guys tomorrow, and don't forget the beer," Bevan said, then hung up.

Damn it! he thought. *Always three steps ahead. What was it Caydon used to always say? "If you are a patient man, all things will come to you."*

CHAPTER SEVEN

Zack and Lane were breaking down their campsite after spending the last two days and nights out on the Keenses' land outside of Morgan City. Bevan had been correct about Lane's ability to move quickly and silently despite his size. She had purposely taken him through the toughest terrain on the property, just to see how he'd manage. He had even managed to sneak up behind her a couple of times.

Lane had made numerous drawings of what he felt were weak areas that would be the easiest to access if Caydon sent men to her home. They then compared the drawings to the land map her papa had obtained from the county before they had arrived. After making comparisons and new additions of fences and tree lines that weren't on the county map, they had made their plans. E. had sent them enough equipment to set up alarms and cameras from the points that they had marked.

After arriving late on Friday, Zack had asked her papa to follow them out with extra supplies, and to help set up their base camp the next evening. Her mama was displeased and chastised Zack for going out over night with a stranger. Lane had stepped up and made her believe that this was a training mission for him. Of course, telling her in perfect Spanish hadn't hurt, and promising to help cook when they got back.

They had driven for about an hour out on the Keenses' land, and Zack had known just where they needed to go. There was a small clearing that would be perfect for their base camp. Zack's papa had helped unload their equipment and set up their tents. When they were finished he faced both of them.

"Zaveen, what is going on?" he'd asked. "And, please, don't lie to your papa."

Zack had looked at Lane before starting to reply. "Papa . . ."

Lane interrupted and explained in French the reason and necessity of the trip out on their land. Zack watched the concern grow on her father's face as Lane explained the possibility of one or more of Caydon's men coming to the farm.

"Mr. Keens, at this time, we believe that Caydon doesn't even know Zack's name or anything about her. So, for now, we have the advantage," Lane had told him.

"They will not like what they find if they come," Mr. Keens had replied proudly.

"Papa, these men are professionals. They have military training, and they are ruthless," Zack had said.

"My college graduate, you forget while they may be professionals, this is our land—our home—and no one can beat us at home."

Lane had told him they would be out there for at least two days.

"Do not stay longer or your mama will begin to worry and come to find you. Now, let me show you what I've done while you've been gone. Unless you know where these are, no one will find them," Mr. Keens had told them.

Now, Zack smiled; her papa had been correct. The new hunting blinds he and her brothers had set up were all but invisible. This made her feel better. If Caydon's men came, her family could hide for days without being found. She looked at Lane. "We need to hurry; Mama will have lunch waiting."

"Your mama is a wonderful lady," Lane said.

"They're both very impressed with the way you can switch so quickly from one language to the other. Mama told me the first night we were home that it was like you grew up with us. That's a huge compliment," Zack told him.

"So, what are we having for Thanksgiving?" Lane asked.

"The usual: turkey, dressing, tamales, and the coldest beer in the parish. Oh, and I had Papa get you some dark beer."

He smiled. "You are turning out to be the best partner ever."

"Don't thank me yet. You still have to help Mama in the kitchen, and she is tough." Then she asked, "Do you think the system we set up will give them time to get out of the house if Caydon's men come?"

"They'll have about ten to fifteen minutes as a head start, as long as your parents aren't heavy sleepers. The cameras will allow them to check daily on your papa's computer. I'll set it up and password-protect it just for him," Lane said.

She nodded in approval, then changed the subject. "For the next four to five days, we're going to be busy cooking, cleaning, and being with family. Mass is on Sunday morning at seven, I expect you to go, Catholic or not."

"Sounds like any other holiday at my home. But you might want to stand back when we enter the church, as the doors may fall in on me—it's been a while," Lane said. He tied down his tent onto the four-wheeler.

Zack had finished loading. "Have you made our flight arrangements?"

"Yeah, that was something else I meant to tell you. The earliest flight I could get us out of New Orleans was for next Wednesday, so you get a couple more days with your family."

"Good. I'll have Papa set up the targets. How are you with a bow?" Zack asked, smirking. With that, she drove off, leaving Lane in a cloud of dust.

"Damn, is there anything she can't do?" he wondered, then took off in pursuit.

CHAPTER EIGHT

Dan walked from his hotel to the IHOP across the street and ordered the Thanksgiving special. He sat cursing Aaron for his sudden obsession with Brushy Creek wine. *Some of the best wine in the world is not far from the castle, but Aaron has to have Texas wine*, Dan thought.

He had ended up spending extra time in Amarillo due to bad weather and issues with the car rental. The representatives at the car rental office had not been easy to bribe, and he had been forced to use one of his aliases. The trip to the winery had also taken extra time due to weather and road conditions. However, the people at the winery had been friendly, and he had happened to arrive when they were having a special gathering. The music, food, and wine sampling had made for a nice day, even though the weather had been overcast and dreary.

The four cases of Texas wine he'd ordered had been repackaged for shipment overseas, and an extra hundred bucks had kept the clerk at the twenty-four-hour FedEx in Irving quiet about the contents. He had put a rush on the delivery, sending them to Tomas. Dan smiled, knowing that Tomas would hate having to deliver the boxes himself, as he was terrified of Aaron.

When anyone asked for a favor from Aaron, it was like making a deal with the devil. Dan knew that the favor Tomas had requested of Aaron had been for power and money. Once the agreement and terms of payment had been settled, Tomas had received what he had so greatly coveted. But as time passed, Tomas had forgotten his promise, until the demand for payment and political favors had been made. At first, Tomas had ignored Aaron's requests. He had tried to circumvent their arrangements, until the deaths of close associates had forced a meeting between the two men. Aaron had strongly voiced his displeasure at Tomas's failure to fulfill his agreement. To ensure that there would be no further issues, Aaron increased the monetary debt and extended it to Tomas's son. As a final warning Tomas would deliver in the future as agreed upon or pay in blood.

"More coffee?" the waitress asked, jolting him out of his recollection.

"Yes, and can I have cherry pie, not pumpkin?" Dan asked.

"Absolutely. Ice cream or whipped cream?"

"Neither. Just warm it up in the oven," Dan directed.

"I'd be happy to do that for you," she said with a smile.

Dan had received information from several contacts who thought they might possibly know the woman he was searching for and where she could be found. He had cut the list of fifty locations down to what he felt were the ten most promising places. Dan had struck out in the Dallas area on his first contact. Nine to go. He would be driving to New Orleans next to meet with two contacts, who each swore that they had the information he needed.

His flight to New York wasn't until Wednesday, so he would have a few days in Louisiana. He always enjoyed Jackson Square, and he could almost taste the beignets at the Café Du Monde, where he intended to spend several hours drinking coffee and listening to some jazz. There were perks to his job. Aaron didn't care what he did, as long as there were results. He pulled a piece of paper out of his pocket and looked at the reservations for his hotel. The Inn on Bourbon Street was a place he had never stayed, but it was close to those things he enjoyed in New Orleans.

The waitress set the pie down in front of him. "Here you go: warm cherry pie."

"Thank you; do you know what the weather is going to be like tomorrow?" Dan asked.

"Where're you headed?" she asked.

"New Orleans."

"You should be OK, maybe just a little rain and cold. I don't think we're expecting any ice or snow. Drive safe, and Happy Thanksgiving," she said before leaving his bill.

Dan was glad to hear that he might have decent weather for a change. From where he was, it was only about a six-hour drive to New Orleans, and the last thing he wanted was for it to turn into more. He finished his pie, stretched, and left a fifty-dollar bill for the waitress on an eighteen-dollar bill.

Morgan City, Louisiana
2:00 p.m.

ZACK WAS STANDING in the kitchen, loading the dishwasher and listening to Lane tease her mother in the family room. His language skills were amazing: he would speak Spanish to her mama, then answer in French to her papa, then go back to English for everyone else. It was obvious that Lane had come from a large family, as he didn't need to be asked to help. He cooked and he cleaned; wherever he was needed, he lent a hand. Lane had set up the program on her father's computer, and instructed him how to access and move the cameras with the small joystick attachment.

Zack smiled, thinking about how wonderful dinner had been: with family and friends, it had been a decent day. All that was missing was having Eric, Jace, and Taylor there. She would be glad when Jace returned. She missed their talks. Zack began to think of Eric, and she closed her eyes, focusing on where he was at that moment.

"Zack . . . Zack . . . *Zack*!" Lane grabbed her arm.

Zack opened her eyes and stepped back. "Something is terribly wrong," she whispered to him.

"What?"

"It's Eric. I've always been able to find him, to connect to him," she told Lane.

He furrowed his brow. "How? Didn't you tell me he's in Wyoming, out somewhere in the mountains?"

"Did Bevan go into any details about my abilities, besides what I have told you?" Zack asked.

"Not a lot. He felt you and I would talk things out, being partners," Lane answered.

"Well, I can usually tell when Eric is thinking about me," she began.

"How is that possible?" Lane asked.

Mr. Keens walked into the kitchen, holding a cloth bag and shaking it. "Come, Lane, Zaveen—time to play dominoes."

"In a minute, Papa," she said, and then turned back to Lane. "My gift has always been special, but now it's growing—my abilities are growing. I'm gaining control, and that is something I haven't had until now. I'm having one issue, though. It seems I have lost my ability to connect over distance. I'm not sure why . . ."

"I don't understand. I thought you could just read people well," Lane admitted.

"Oh, I read people, alright, but not in the way you think. I thought you understood about my abilities," she said.

"Honestly, I don't really believe you can read people's minds or make them do things. That's just not possible," Lane replied.

"Pay attention when we play dominoes. I'll be able to control the game, to make them—and you—see things that aren't there, to make them play dominoes they shouldn't."

"Bring it then, Zack. I play a mean game, so don't get too upset when I dominate and win," Lane said, laughing, and he headed to the family room.

Zack stood for a moment, trying to digest what Lane had said to her, and then his thoughts betrayed him. He honestly didn't believe her, but he would after that day. She wished Bevan had spent more time talking to Lane about her gift, but there was nothing like experiencing it firsthand. She filled a couple of buckets with beer and ice, getting ready for an afternoon of dominoes. She stopped and closed her eyes. *Eric, where are you?*

Austria
10:00 p.m.

ERIC WALKED OUT of the shower and stood looking out the prison window, toweling his hair. The last five days of gym time had made him start to feel human again. Being drugged and shipped across the world like a piece of furniture was not on his top-ten list of things to ever do again. The two days he'd been allowed outside had been even better: fresh air and sunshine. It was too bad that he had to wear a shock collar like a dog to keep him from crossing the invisible fence.

The men who watched him were obvious ex-military. He was surprised they didn't have any weapons on them when they took him outside, but he was sure that they didn't feel the least bit threatened by him. "If they only knew my stealth and ninja moves, they would fear me," he said aloud, then dropped his towel and struck a pose.

There was a muffled laugh behind him. Miguel had walked in with the snack Eric had asked for, and he couldn't help but laugh when he saw the tall, lanky Shaw waving his long arms like a windmill. "Your snack," he said between chuckles.

"You caught me; now I must kill you and all your friends," Eric said, continuing to chop at the air with one arm while reaching out and taking the plate with the other.

"For a rich kid, you're funny," Miguel told him grudgingly.

"Well, just so you know, I only get an allowance, and up until a year ago, I was pretty much broke. Then I started taking jobs doing what I really love: photography. I was hoping my trip to Wyoming would catapult my career. I didn't know that I would be drugged, boxed up like furniture, and shipped across the world. And, as if that wasn't bad enough, I then spent the better part of two weeks puking into a plastic bucket, hooked up to an IV, and wishing Thor would take his hammer and go somewhere else. And I'd guess all my equipment is gone."

"Actually, no, but Aaron *is* planning to use it," Miguel told him.

"Ah, the old 'here's the proof that we have your brother' tactic. Good move. Will there be a picture of me holding the Innsbruck or Vienna newspaper to prove the date? I'd love to catch up on local news, too."

Miguel frowned. "Nice try, but no, that's not happening."

"Damn, you guys are smart," Eric said, tapping his head.

"Good night, Mr. Shaw."

"Eric—you can call me Eric. Is there any chance me and the guys can hit the slopes tomorrow? I love fresh powder," he said with a grin.

Miguel just waved his hand and left, locking Eric's door.

"Damn, I thought we were making progress," Eric said, picking up his sandwich and walking back to the window.

Things could be worse, he thought. *I guess if I had to be kidnapped by some lunatic, at least this one has good taste. But it's Thanksgiving; surely Zack is wondering why I haven't called.* He pictured his fiery fiancée, her sweet smile and loving arms.

He then thought of his brother and all the tragedy they had been through over the last two years: Their time together overseas, reporting on the war, which had cost Taylor a thumb and a broken arm, and almost his life. The loss of their older brother in the north tower on 9/11. Caydon kidnapping Jace and playing mind games with Zack's boss. Now Taylor would have to deal with the stress of another kidnapping, which would involve the FBI and money.

Eric couldn't understand why Caydon needed more money. Everything that surrounded him was expensive: the castle, the men, and their equipment. He was sure that Caydon had a private jet—that was the only way they could've gotten him out of the country. It appeared Caydon already *had* a lot of money. The only thing that made any sense was that Caydon was planning to disappear forever, to retire from being the kidnapping, murdering psychopath he was. But to do what—Be a regular person? Garden? Sip tea with the Queen? He would have to pay off all his men and then just fade into the sunset. That would take a lot of money—the kind of money Taylor now had.

"Wow, good plan," Eric said out loud and reached for the phone. "Miguel, can I have another turkey sandwich, and do you play chess? No? Well, how about we round up some guys and play poker. Of course, you'll have to take an IOU from me, but I'm good for it."

Morgan City, Louisiana
9:00 p.m.

LANE STOOD OUTSIDE, trying to hold his bottle of beer in his shaking hands. Bevan should have told him, should have prepared him better before throwing him into the fire. He had seen some strange shit in his career, but Zack topped it all. She had done exactly what she had said she would do. He'd pulled a good hand, but the next time he'd looked, all the spots on the dominoes had changed. When he'd looked up at Zack, all she had done was smile. If she could do that, what else had she been training to control? What was it she had said the first night they'd talked?

"That it wouldn't always be possible for me not to invade your thoughts," Zack said, walking up behind him.

Lane jumped and dropped his beer, spilling the rest of the contents all over the porch. "Damn it—that was my last one!"

"Well, if your hands weren't shaking so badly, you wouldn't have dropped it. And there's more; Papa bought extra," Zack told him meekly.

"I'm trying to wrap my mind around all this new information about you. I blame myself for not asking more questions and for not believing you. I'm sorry for that," he confessed.

They sat down on the steps of the front porch. He looked up at the stars and took a breath as a cool breeze blew across them.

"It's fine," she said. "Some days I have an issue with this gift. For a long time, I didn't accept it: I hated it. Then, one summer my grandma on my papa's side took me out on the land and showed me what our gifts could do to help. There was a child who had gotten lost that day; we sat together, focused, and located the child. We passed the information to the authorities, and a life was saved. After that day, I accepted what I had, but no one could help me control it."

"What about your grandma? Surely she had some way to help you?" Lane asked, still trying to accept all he'd been told.

"My grandma told me that my gift was strong, even more than hers. I remember her taking my face in her hands and saying, 'Child, you will have to be strong in the years to come. Don't give in to the vanities of life. You must work to control what is inside you for the good that you can do.'"

"I have to ask about the authorities. Why didn't they question you?" Lane wondered.

"Things are different here. They know that there are people like me. When Papa called, no questions were asked; they simply went where we told them to look."

"That's some weird shit," Lane responded, shaking his head.

"I figured you would be packing to run back to DC to ask for another partner," Zack said.

"Well, that thought did occur to me," he admitted, "but then I thought about all the possibilities and the good this could do for us when we get to Ireland."

"Does that mean you don't quite trust your family there?" Zack said.

"Well, some of them do have questionable histories and even more questionable friends," Lane said delicately.

"And you were going to tell me this when?" she said, flaring her nostrils.

"When we got on the plane," he confessed. "But now I have my very own living lie detector. It will definitely make things easier."

"As long as they don't have abilities to hide their thoughts from me."

"Is that possible?"

"Yes, that is, if you're aware of your own abilities," Zack answered.

"Have you run into anyone who could hide their thoughts?" Lane asked.

"Only one."

"Who?"

"Darlene, Bevan's secretary," Zack said, raising her eyebrow.

"You don't think she's doing something wrong, do you?" Lane asked, concerned.

"No, she's been working with the company for years. Darlene is Bevan's right arm."

"Good to know, especially since she's privy to my eating habits," Lane said, and they both laughed.

CHAPTER NINE

New Orleans, Louisiana
Tuesday, December 3, 2002
3:30 p.m.

Dan sat drinking coffee and eating his second order of beignets at Café Du Monde, listening to the wonderful sounds of New Orleans. He should have watched the news instead of listening to the waitress at the IHOP. His trip from Texas to Louisiana had not been pleasant. It had cost him an additional two hours due to the obnoxious people around him who had no idea how to drive in bad weather. The hotel had been a welcome sight upon his arrival, and he had enjoyed many of its amenities. Dan was not looking forward to calling Aaron before he left on Wednesday, but he would have to update him, good news or bad. Right now, it was all still a dead end; his contacts had been useless.

"Coffee?" the waitress asked.

"Yes, and one more order of beignets, please," Dan said, indulging.

"Be right back."

Dan leaned back in his chair and opened the file, looking at the picture once more. He remembered the night in the restaurant when he had almost been cornered by her and her partner, Blain Benjamin. He couldn't understand how she had known that he was there watching Bevan. He was adept at blending into a crowd; that's what had drawn him into Aaron's crew. Dan was nonthreatening and good at obtaining information.

"Coffee and beignets," the waitress announced, setting the plate of warm confections in front of him.

"Thank you. Could I ask you a question?" Dan asked.

"What can I help you with?" she replied.

"Does this woman look familiar to you?" he probed, handing her the photo of the mystery woman.

The waitress squinted at the photo, then shook her head. "No, I'm sorry."

"Thank you," Dan sighed and handed her a fifty-dollar bill. "Keep the change."

"*Merci.*"

Dan drank his coffee and decided to enjoy his last evening in New Orleans.

ZACK SAT IN the passenger seat of the car, looking out the window as they drove into New Orleans in the early evening, heading toward the Inn on Bourbon Street. That night, she would take Lane to her favorite place to eat in the city. Zack thought about the extra days with her family and the much-needed target practice with her bow. She had spent a couple of hours attempting to teach him how to shoot, but he had never once hit the target. He was, however, an expert with knives, and he'd hit the center of the target every time. It was nice to know they both had abilities with weapons other than guns.

Zack thought about the blade that Caydon had taken from her. It had belonged to Deelyn, her kin, who had carried it throughout World War II. Deelyn had been a Jedburgh; she had parachuted into enemy territory, joined the Marquis, and killed a Nazi spy. Zack vowed to have the knife back one day. It would come back to where it belonged: with her family.

Tomorrow, she and Lane would leave on a midmorning flight into LaGuardia, then change planes and settle in for the seven-hour flight to Dublin around six thirty that evening. Zack looked up as they drove up to the front of the hotel. They parked the car and got their bags out of the back.

"The parking costs aren't cheap here, are they?" Lane asked, grimacing.

"It's New Orleans; like New York, you pay to stay," Zack said simply.

"Who is it that you know here?"

"My uncle Ernest; he manages the hotel. I hope he's here."

"Well, it's impressive on the outside, so far," Lane said, looking around.

They entered the hotel. Zack stopped immediately, practically bowled over by a feeling of deception, a sense of someone's need to find her. It was someone she knew; he was trying to find information on her and her family. It was one of Caydon's men. She reached out and grabbed Lane's arm.

"What's wrong?" he asked, instantly sensing her urgency.

"Someone's looking for me. He's been here," she began, then winced in concentration. "No, wait. He's staying here."

Lane looked at Zack in shock and couldn't speak for a moment. "Are you sure? Maybe it's your uncle; your mama may have called and told him we were coming."

"No, I told her not to call, that I wanted to surprise him. It's someone else. He met someone, showed them my picture. I know him. It's one of Caydon's men. The flag—he's the man who was wearing an American-flag necktie last year," Zack spouted as the information came in bursts.

Lane's hands were shaking again. "Damn, Zack. You're fucking spooky, woman."

"We can't stay here. We need to find another place to sleep. If we don't go, I could put everyone in danger," Zack said, and they turned to leave.

At that exact moment, they saw her uncle Ernest coming their way with delight on his face. "Zaveen! My niece, how good to see you! Why didn't you call me and let me know that you were coming?" Ernest asked loudly as he walked toward them with outstretched arms.

"Damn it; we're screwed," Zack told Lane under her breath.

"How long are you staying?" Ernest asked.

"Just tonight, Uncle. We're leaving tomorrow, going back to DC," Zack said, shooting a look at Lane.

Lane shook hands with Ernest. "Hello, my name is Lane Brigham. I'm Zack's new partner. She was kind enough to invite me to her home for Thanksgiving."

Zack hugged Ernest, resigning herself to the situation. "We missed you at the house for Thanksgiving, Uncle."

"I know, but someone had to work the hotel, and it was my turn. I'll be off for Christmas. Will you be back then?" Ernest asked.

"Possibly, if I can get the time off. Can we check in?" she said, desperate to retreat from the busy lobby as soon as possible.

"Of course; let me check," he replied, leading them to the front desk. "Ah, yes, I have two nice rooms on the top floor. And you two must join me in the kitchen for dinner and wine," Ernest insisted.

"That sounds great," Lane said.

Lane checked them in while Zack walked back to the front door, trying to sense more information. She jumped when Lane touched her arm.

"It's just me. We need to get settled and talk this through before we start drinking wine," he told her.

"Right now, I'd rather have the wine than talk," she said as they headed for the elevator.

They got off on the top floor and saw that their rooms were across from each other. "Drop your bag off and come over when you're ready. I took the rest of the dark beer when we left. We can have a couple and talk before we go to dinner," Lane said.

"Hang on," Zack said. She opened her door, threw her bag in, then shut it. "OK."

"Damn, you're something else. Most women would spend the next two hours unpacking and primping."

"Where's the beer? I need to sit for a moment and have something to drink. Things are running too fast in my mind." Zack took the beer Lane handed her.

"What can I do to help? I mean, what does your mental coach do to help you focus?" he asked.

"Before, when I didn't have any control, I would see things and hear things all at once. Everything came fast, like a dam breaking. Over the last year, meditation and yoga have helped me to focus, to slow the rush and pick out what is most important," she explained.

"Well, I meditate," Lane offered.

Zack look at him and smirked.

"What! Men can meditate, too," he said defensively.

"I know, but you don't seem the type," Zack told him.

"You're not the only one with mental issues," he said, then backpedaled, blushing. "Wait, that didn't come out right. I meant you're not the only one who has problems with focusing. My mental metabolism is like being in a race car that never runs out of gas. Before I learned to control it, I wouldn't sleep for days. Finally, I had to find something to slow the car down and get out of it. Meditation helped," Lane said. He turned on the television, flipping to the channel that hotels were beginning to include to help people sleep. "Sit on the floor, and I'll see if I can help you."

Over the next hour, he talked them through breathing, mental focus, and relaxation techniques. Zack began to calm, to center her thoughts, and then she heard his name. *Dan.* She opened her eyes. "Lane, I know his name: Dan. But . . ."

"But what?" Lane asked.

"Uncle Ernest is coming down the hallway to take us to dinner."

"Is Dan here now?" Lane asked.

Zack closed her eyes. "Yes. He's at the front door of the hotel. His room is on the second floor."

"We need to have your uncle take us down the back elevator to the kitchen. The last thing we need right now is for this Dan to see you or me. Does Ernest know about your gift?" Lane asked, looking up when there was a knock on the door.

"Sort of. It's not something that we discuss on a regular basis, but he knows I have a gift. That's not the only problem we have. Many of the employees here know me. If Dan shows my picture to anyone here, he could get the information that Caydon wants and needs," Zack said, then opened the door.

"Well, you two seem cozy," Ernest said with raised eyebrows.

"Oh, Uncle, Lane has never been here, and I just stopped over to see if he wanted to change rooms so he could see the street."

"You should have said something! I can change your room, Lane," Ernest said apologetically.

"No, that's fine. I'll change with Zack after dinner," Lane told him.

"Uncle, why don't you take us down the back elevator and give Lane the tour of the hotel—and don't leave out any of the history."

"My pleasure. Come, Lane, let me tell you about this hotel and its secrets, and then we'll go on to the kitchen for the best meal you'll have in New Orleans," Ernest said proudly.

DAN WAS RELAXED and full of beignets. He would miss New Orleans, but it was time to go back to work, and that meant a call to Aaron that night with unpleasant news. He would pay his bill, go upstairs, and watch TV before calling and leaving a message. Dan didn't expect to hear back from him, as Aaron was busy in Scotland. He hoped Aaron's time there would make the news that he had not found the woman easier to accept. His flight to New York was midmorning, so he would have time for a nice breakfast and maybe one more stop for beignets.

"Good evening, sir," the clerk greeted him at the front desk.

"I'd like to settle my bill now," Dan said.

"We haven't added tonight's charge yet, sir."

"I'll go ahead and leave enough cash to cover any expenses or added charges, then," Dan said, and handed the clerk $2,000. "If there's any change left over, please keep it."

"Thank you, sir," the clerk said.

Dan knew there would be at least $100 left, enough to keep the clerk happy. As he turned to leave, the clerk called to him. "Sir, you forgot your folder."

As the clerk handed it to Dan, a picture fell out. The clerk leaned to pick it up and recognition passing across his face. Dan could see that he knew something. "Have you seen her?" he asked, trying not to betray his excitement.

"Why, yes. She and another gentleman checked in earlier," he replied.

Dan froze for a second, and then recovered, "She and her partner were to meet me here today. We're working on a case." He then produced a wallet with a fake badge for the clerk to see.

The clerk acknowledged his credentials. "Zaveen is the niece of our manager, Ernest Keens."

"Thank you," Dan said, and he walked away with contained excitement. He wanted to ask for more information, but he would find out what he needed later that night. Dan stopped suddenly, remembering the name Eric Shaw had repeated. *It was hers.* His phone call to Aaron had turned from one of dread into the possibility of an added bonus.

ZACK AND LANE were enjoying their meal in the kitchen and listening to her uncle's stories, but her mind was not there. She worried for her family, for Eric. She was about to take another sip of her wine when she heard her name.

"Zaveen is the niece of our manager, Ernest Keens."

Zack watched in slow motion as her glass shattered on the concrete floor. She looked at Lane and her uncle. "He knows! He knows who I am."

"How?" Lane asked.

"The clerk at the front desk," Zack said, and then grabbed a napkin and pen, scribbling a note on it.

"Zaveen, what is going on?" Ernest asked with alarm.

"Uncle, you must to go to the farm. Give this note to Papa—he'll explain. And don't come back here tonight. You're in danger," Zack told him urgently.

"I don't understand," Ernest said in distress.

Lane stepped in to explain. "This involves a case we're working on. Until now, the people we're looking for didn't know who Zack was, but now that's changed. It would be wise for you and your family to leave for a while."

"Is that really necessary? Can't you have this man arrested?" Ernest asked as Zack grabbed his arm, urging him to get up.

"We could have him detained, but at this time there isn't enough probable cause to arrest him." Lane answered.

"And once released the consequences to our case would be devastating." Zack said.

"How much time should I take?" Ernest asked.

"At least a week." Lane then walked to the kitchen door and looked out into the dining room.

"Uncle, please. Papa will explain in more detail, but you must go *now*."

"I'll have to make some calls. I might be able to take a few days off," Ernest conceded.

"Uncle, do you know another place we can go? We can't stay here," Zack asked and motioned for Lane to follow them.

"Yes, I'll make arrangements," Ernest said.

"We'll meet you outside in ten minutes," Lane said.

"Uncle, don't go back to the front," Zack warned and grabbed his hands.

"Ten minutes," was all he said.

Zack and Lane ran back to their rooms and grabbed their bags. They took the stairs down to their car and waited for Ernest.

He met them there a few minutes later. "I called your papa. He said he'd meet me at our favorite hunting blind. I'll take a few days off."

"I'm so sorry about all this," Zack said.

"Don't worry—family comes first. Let's go."

"What did you tell your staff?" Lane asked.

"Nothing; I'm the manager. I was supposed to have left at seven. The only reason I stayed was to have dinner with you two. As far as most of the staff knows, I left at seven."

Zack and Lane got in their car and followed Ernest to a safer place for the night.

DAN SAT IN his room and hacked into the hotel computer system. His computer skills were compliments of the US government. He was able to obtain information on Zaveen Keens: her address was that of the NSA, and he could find no car information, which meant it was a rental and probably on her partner's information. He searched for another NSA address and found Lane Brigham's name. He would look up Brigham's information later. Aaron would want to know the character of this man.

Dan called their rooms on the third floor; no answer. "Time for a little walk," he said to himself. Dan took the stairs up one level. The keyless locks were a pain, but were not impossible to open. He knocked on Zaveen's door first. When there was no answer, he went in: there were no bags, the water glasses had not been touched, and even the bathroom had not been used. No one had been in this room; it appeared she was gone. He shut the door and went into her partner's room. Someone had definitely been there. There were empty beer bottles—Guinness—and someone had sat on the bed, but as in Zaveen's room, there was no luggage. They were gone, but why?

He went back to his room and opened a prepaid cell phone. "Important information obtained; can't wait until return to update," Dan said, then hung up. He looked at his watch. It was now eleven thirty; in Scotland, it was between five and six in the morning. Aaron would be awake.

The cell rang. "Good news?" Aaron asked on the other line.

"Very," Dan responded.

"Send what you have for delivery on Monday the ninth. Tell Tomas I'll expect him for a late dinner around nine."

Dan spent the next two hours obtaining what he could on Zaveen Keens's family and compiling it into a report. He gathered information on her parents, her brothers, and the family land. He was able to find where she had graduated from college, but after she was hired by the NSA, information became less accessible. He was sure that was due to Bevan Benjamin. Lane Brigham's information was interesting, especially his military service, but again, once he became property of the NSA, less and less was known. A red flag went up for Dan when he discovered Lane had family in Ireland; that was too close to Aaron and his goal. The last thing he included in his report was the possibility that Zaveen and Eric were connected in some way.

He took his computer downstairs to the business office, shut the door, and began to connect the wires. The hotel had given him a password to use the computers in the business office, but he couldn't leave any trace of his presence for the authorities. He scanned all the information he'd obtained, then forwarded it with a message to Tomas: "You personally are expected for a late dinner at the castle on Monday the ninth at 9:00 p.m. Do not be late." Dan smiled as he sent the message and file.

He disconnected his computer and went back to his room. He showered, packed his bag for the trip to New York, and went to bed. His next assignment would be easier; even the common man on the street knew information about the very rich of New York.

CHAPTER TEN

Zack had been awake since five. She'd tried to go back to sleep but couldn't, so she'd gone downstairs and worked out in the small gym at the La Quinta Inn & Suites where they were staying, just outside of the New Orleans airport. An hour and a half later, she'd returned to her room, showered, and dressed, then found the washer and dryers for a fast load of laundry. Zack had hoped that the workout would distract from the worry for her family, but the plan failed.

She finished packing and opened the door just as Lane was about to knock on it. She knew he was ready to go for breakfast. "Damn it, you have to stop that!" he said, sensing her intrusion into his mind. "Did you sleep?"

"Not much."

"I didn't think so; I heard you leave this morning. Did you hit the gym?"

"Yes, I'm worried about my family," Zack said as they headed to the elevator.

"Did you call them?" Lane asked.

"Just my uncle. He and my aunt left this morning."

"Your family is better off on the farm. The warning system we set up will allow them the time they need to get to safety. At least now they know; no more guessing that someone may come. Your papa will be more diligent. Remember what he said: it's his land, and no one knows it better or can beat them on it. This time, you have to trust him," Lane told her.

Zack knew Lane was right. "Well, at least the breakfast buffet looks good."

"I'm starved," Lane said.

Zack watched Lane fill not one but *three* plates. "Did you call Bevan?"

"Yes, and I gave him a full report, including the information about Dan. He said most of the men that work with Caydon were in the military at some point, but that someone has emptied their files, both hard copies and computer. Even their photographs are gone, so there's no way to find out who this guy is. Bevan said for you to focus on the job ahead."

"He's right; I can't stay here and wait for an attack that may never come," Zack said.

"Good. Now, I'm going to get one more waffle before we check out."

"I'm going back to the room. I'll meet you at the car in twenty minutes," Zack said.

"Our flight is at eleven thirty, and we're only ten minutes from the airport, so make it thirty minutes," Lane said before going to make two more waffles.

Zack laughed. "OK, thirty minutes, then."

DAN WAS PACKED and ready to head to the airport. If all went well, he would be in New York early and could get settled in at the hotel. He had wanted to make one more trip for beignets, but it would have to wait until his next trip to New Orleans. Dan stood waiting for the shuttle to the airport when the clerk that had given him information on Zaveen Keens walked in through the front door.

"Good morning!" he greeted Dan.

"Morning," Dan replied curtly and tried to ignore him.

"Did you get to talk to your partners?"

"Yes, thank you," Dan replied.

"Did you know that they checked out of the hotel last night?" the clerk asked curiously.

Dan look puzzled. "No, they didn't call to let me know."

"I heard they went to a hotel closer to the airport."

"Thank you," Dan said and turned away.

The clerk frowned and walked away briskly.

Dan was still confused as to why they had left the hotel in the middle of the night, but he didn't care. He knew he could have killed both Zaveen and her partner. But Caydon had made it clear to the team that only he would be the one to kill her. The last thing Dan ever wanted to do was to disobey an order or anger him. The information he had given Caydon was all that mattered, and now he simply needed to focus on finishing the job at hand.

LANE DROVE TO the airport, where they dropped off the rental car and headed to the security office to check in before heading to their gate. Their bags were not secure, so both would remain armed. Their letters of official travel with weapons were taken and copies were made. The sergeant then made a call to Bevan for further confirmation.

"Thank you for your cooperation," the sergeant said, and he shook hands with both of them.

"We're all working on the same team," Lane replied.

The seargent nodded. "Have a good flight," he said and walked both of them out of the office.

"That went smoothly," Zack mused as they headed toward their gate.

"When we get to LaGuardia, I want to buy a hard-shell case that we can lock the guns in and check them through to Dublin," Lane said.

"Why do we . . ." Zack stopped midsentence and froze.

Lane knew that look; he pulled her out of the stream of human traffic. "I'm getting used to this, I think. What now?"

"He's here," she whispered, looking up at Lane.

"Who?"

"Dan; he's here in the airport," she answered urgently.

"Close?" Lane inquired and started to look around them.

"Ahead of us by three gates, and across from ours."

DAN ARRIVED AT his gate, hoping the morning would continue to go as nicely as the previous night had, but his flight had been delayed, and it would be one in the afternoon before he could leave. Dan waited for his boarding pass and new gate assignment, then headed toward the new gate. He stopped at one of the bars on the way and sat down.

"What can I get you?" the waiter asked.

"Irish coffee with an extra shot," Dan answered.

"Whiskey?"

"Jameson."

Dan waited until the waiter left, then took out his file on Taylor and Jace Shaw. They had been gone for a month and would be arriving back anytime. Aaron had given him several names of individuals who could update him on their arrival time and location. He was feeling good after having found the information on Zaveen Keens. Once he got a schedule on Taylor, he would go back, and Aaron could begin to finalize his plans.

Dan knew that once the ransom was paid, he and the others would be set for life. He would disappear, like Aaron was planning to do. He would live the rest of his life on a beach, drinking champagne and enjoying the finer things in life: artwork, expensive meals, and fine wine. He might return one day to New Orleans and purchase a home within walking distance of his favorite café.

⦿

LANE AND ZACK watched as Dan walked away from his gate. They then made their way to their own gate and checked in. Both were seated in the early boarding area.

"That was interesting. Any idea where he's going?" Lane asked.

"Well, according to the sign at the gate, New York, but his flight has been delayed. He's flying into JFK," Zack answered.

"Any chance you can get anymore information?"

Zack rubbed her head. "There's too many people. I'm getting bombarded; it's . . ." She didn't finish.

Lane put his hand on her shoulder, and she relaxed. "Not a problem, partner."

The flight crew arrived, and the agent walked down the gateway with them. He returned shortly with one of the flight attendants, and they were taken on board. They were introduced to the pilots and crew, seated, with their locations noted for the crew's reference.

Once they were settled in, Zack questioned, "You said we need to buy a case for the guns. Why?"

"We can carry inside the States, but once we get overseas, we won't be able to carry our guns. The case will just make our lives easier. I have a friend with the Gardaí who is going to meet us when we land in Dublin. I had Bevan send a letter to his superior a week ago with proper introductions and a request for my friend to assist us. I translated it into Gaelic for extra brownie points for us."

"That was a smart move. I hope it makes our arrival easier," Zack said.

"Speaking of easier, I had some flyer miles, so I upgraded our seats to business class for the flight to Dublin. I refuse to fly coach, packed like a sardine for eleven hours or more." He grimaced at the thought. "Can you buy the case for our weapons when we land at LaGuardia? Just don't buy a pink one. I would never be able to live that one down," Lane teased.

"Black it is, and thanks for the upgrade."

"No problem. I knew the job wasn't going to cover it, and since I'm going to see some family while we're there, I felt it was justified," Lane explained.

"Ladies and gentlemen, please take a moment and give your attention to our flight crew as we show you our safety features," a female voice announced.

"I've heard this one too many times." Lane closed his eyes.

Zack turned and looked out the window, trying to calm the storm building inside her. She was frustrated because she felt the need to stay and protect her family. Zack knew she had to focus mentally, as one missed sign or mistake could be fatal to her or Lane. She had to trust her papa, brothers, and uncle. They would protect her mama, and if anyone could outsmart Aaron's men, it was her family.

Once the plane leveled after takeoff, she took out her earbuds and plugged them into the console. She went through several channels until she found music that would allow her to relax and center herself. Zack slowed her breathing, and she listened to the music, allowing her body and mind to come together. She remembered a conversation she had had with Mr. Joe.

"Zack, focus! Your abilities are above any I have ever encountered. What has happened to your ability to connect over distance?" Mr. Joe's frustration had begun to show.

"I'm not sure. It seems that since I've begun to control my abilities instead of just letting the dam flow, I can't reach out to others over distance like before," Zack had answered.

"Ridiculous! You're setting limits that do not exist. I believe your abilities may possibly be endless," he'd told her sternly.

"Is that possible?" she had asked.

"Yes! You must simply focus on one thing, one person, and regardless of how far they are from you, you will be able to connect," he had said with confidence.

"I'm afraid that if I go back to the way I was, I won't be able to tolerate the flood again. At times, it was just too much. It was like being on a ride at an amusement park where things fly at you from all directions," Zack had told him.

"You must continue the exercises I have given you. Take one thing at a time. Find what is most important. Triage your thoughts when you're in a crowd. To reach across the distance, you will have to let go again. Trust yourself; you can do it. Let go, Zack." He'd put his hands on her shoulders. "Let go."

"Let go, let go, let go," Zack repeated softly.

Lane shook her. "Zack, are you alright?"

She opened her eyes. "What?"

"You were saying 'let go' over and over again. Were you dreaming?" Lane asked.

"I guess. I was trying to meditate. I was thinking about Mr. Joe and my last training session before we left DC."

"Well, we're about to land. I'm ready to get out and walk around," Lane said impatiently.

"We have what, a two- or three-hour layover?" Zack asked, stretching in her seat as much as she could.

"Three, with the time change, if there's no delay. You buy the case; we'll go to security and pack the guns, then check it," Lane told her.

She nodded. "I want to grab something to eat, and I would suggest you load up on PayDays unless they have something similar in Dublin."

"I already have four boxes in my bag. But I do want to eat during the wait. They'll probably feed us on the plane, too, but it's never enough for me," Lane said, and his stomach suddenly growled.

Zack let out a chuckle. "At least I'll be able to sleep on the next flight, and we'll be getting there in the morning, so to speak. I'm dreading the jet lag."

"It's going to take me a couple of days for my mind to adjust. Sometimes it gets unpleasant to be around me," he cautioned.

Zack began to laugh as they got up to leave the plane. "Unpleasant in the fact that you can't stop talking?"

"That and I can't focus, so we're going to go see my family for a few days until I adjust. Sorry, that's my curse when I travel, and why I asked Bevan to give us plenty of time for this assignment," Lane said.

"Whatever it takes. I'm going to need a day or two, also. We need to be at our best," she agreed.

They exited the plane and stopped at the first restrooms. Then Zack headed to find a case, and Lane headed to security. Twenty minutes later, their weapons had been unloaded, secured, and checked for the flight to Dublin with an officer at the airport.

"Thank you, Sergeant Robinson," Lane said and shook his hand.

"Mr. Benjamin had contacted the office earlier about your arrival. Your decision to secure your weapons and check them through has simplified your plans. I certainly appreciate that decision," the seargent said with a smile.

"And we appreciate your time," Zack said, returning his smile.

"Have a good flight; looks like it's on time. You two should have time for a nice meal on me," Sergeant Robinson said and handed them a Visa gift card.

Lane looked at Zack once they left security. "Steak?"

He licked his lips. "Sounds good to me."

They headed to find a place to eat before boarding the long flight to Dublin.

New York, New York
4:30 p.m.

DAN WALKED THROUGH JFK International Airport and down to the baggage claim area. He travelled light and always used a carry-on. If he needed something, he could buy it. Too much time at the baggage claim allowed cameras to scan, and that was something he didn't need. He walked to the curb and was directed to the limo service. Dan used another prepaid phone and called the number Aaron had given him before he left.

"I'm here," Dan said.

"Mr. Caydon's guest?" the trembling voice inquired on the other end of the line.

"Yes."

"Number fifty-nine."

"I see the car," Dan said.

The young driver got out and opened the door. "Can I take your bag, sir?"

"No. Just get me to the hotel," Dan answered, stepping into the limousine.

"Right away, sir. By the way, I have something for you," the young man said and pointed to the back seat.

Dan sat and opened the envelope. A key and a note fell out.

This is the key to your room at the Marriott. You need not register; simply go to your room. Order anything you wish, and simply mark an X on the ticket. I hope all is acceptable and that your stay will be reported so to Mr. Caydon. If there are any issues or needs, call this number, and all will be arranged to your satisfaction. I have also left in your room what information I was able to obtain on the individuals requested. My people are still attempting to obtain additional information.

L.

Dan smiled, leaned back into the soft leather seat, and watched as the lights of the city grew closer. He was driven to the Marriott Marquis on Broadway. The driver stopped and started to get out of the car.

"It's fine. I can take it from here," Dan said, attempting to tip the driver.

The driver waved him away. "No, please; it was my pleasure. Be sure to let Mr. Caydon know you were happy."

Dan nodded his head. "I will."

"When you're ready to go back to the airport, call anytime."

Dan watched the limo disappear. Aaron's reach was vast. Dan had experienced this type of service on many occasions. He took the appropriate elevator in the hotel and then walked down the hall to his room. The key opened a door to a room with an excellent view of Times Square. There was a bottle of chilled champagne, chocolate-covered strawberries, and vouchers for any shows he wished to see while in New York. Dan hoped he would have time for at least one show. He ordered a sumptuous meal to go with the champagne.

He then picked up the large envelope on the bed and opened it. It contained about twenty pages of information, which he spread out on the king-size bed. There was information about the wedding and where the newlyweds had supposedly gone for their honeymoon. The other papers contained information on individuals who worked at the *White Daily Journal*, most of which was useless. He would have to do a lot of footwork to make sure that what he had was correct. The last thing he wanted to do was give the wrong information to Aaron.

A knock on the door ended his studies for the night. The waiter entered and set up the tray with the food that Dan had ordered, and Dan marked an X on the bill. The man's eyes widened, he bowed and left the room, not waiting for the tip Dan had planned to give him. Dan sat down and enjoyed his meal. He could not imagine what the men in this city owed Aaron for him to be treated as a VIP. Dan would certainly give a positive report on his treatment if things continued as they had thus far. He left his room and took a walk outside, enjoying the lights and sounds of the city.

CHAPTER ELEVEN

Dublin, Ireland
Thursday, December 5, 2002
6:30 a.m.

Cian Hely had been at the airport for over an hour with paperwork from his superiors, requesting a quick expedition through customs for Lane and Zaveen. Cian had been with the Gardaí for eight years. He had worked hard and had been promoted into a position of inspector. The last time Cian had seen his good friend Lane, he had still been a garda. There would be much to talk about over food and beer.

Lane and his partner would be met at their gate by airport security when they arrived, and would be brought directly to the office. Customs officers would be there to go through their bags. He knew that Lane would have brought that damn candy with him, too. Cian hoped it was still in its original wrappers or the customs agents would be eating them as a snack later that day—the bastards!

He'd planned to take possession of their weapons upon arrival, and that was where all the argument had begun when he'd arrived at security. The official at the airport seemed to believe that *he* had the right to keep the weapons, but Cian would win out on this issue. He would not have his best friend's service weapon misplaced in a back room, never to be found again.

"They've landed, so now it's just a matter of getting them off the plane. My people are on their way to the gate," the official told Cian.

"Good. I'm anxious to see my friend," Cian replied.

ZACK LOOKED OUT the window as the plane landed. She could already feel the time change, and she knew that Lane could, too. Once the attendant had woken them, he had not stopped talking. Their breakfast had been nice, but she knew that they would have to stop and eat once they left the airport.

"I bet airport security is waiting for us at the gate," Zack said.

"Shit; those assholes are going to give us trouble," Lane said.

"But you said there's someone waiting for us in the office. Kayon?" Zack asked, trying to remember how to say the name of Lane's friend.

"Cian; you pronounce it like KEY-in. He's probably been arguing with some dumbass for at least an hour, trying to get us through all the political crap. I bet they're trying to keep our weapons, but that isn't going to happen under Cian's watch. He'll win that battle, and will end up being responsible for them."

"Sounds like your twin," Zack said, grinning.

"Close, just not as handsome as me."

As the plane approached the gate, one of the flight attendants walked to their seats. "Airport security is waiting for you. We're going to have you leave the plane first," she said.

The announcement came over the intercom soon after that. "Ladies and gentlemen, we ask that you remain seated. We have two individuals that need to depart the plane first. Your cooperation is appreciated."

"Well, we just pissed a few people off," Lane said as they moved swiftly down the aisle between rows.

"Actually, no. Most of them are OK with it," Zack told him softly, scanning thoughts as she passed. Lane just rolled his eyes.

Zack and Lane exited through the Jetway. A tall woman in uniform walked up to them. "Lane Brigham, Zaveen Keens, please follow us. Your weapons?" she asked.

"Checked."

They were escorted to the security office. Zack could feel Lane becoming anxious, but when the door opened, he relaxed. "Cian!"

Cian embraced Lane and patted him on the back. "Fáilte abhaile, mo chara," Cian said. ("Welcome home, my friend.")

"Go raibh maith agat. Tá sé go maith a bheith ar ais," Lane responded. ("Thank you. It's good to be back.")

"Cén chaoi a bhfuil do theaghlach?" Cian asked. ("How is your family?")

"Tá mo theaghlach go maith, agus do mhuintir?" Lane said. ("My family is well; and yours?")

Zack stood for a moment, listening to the chatter, then finally cleared her throat noisily and looked at Lane. "And?" she said, notching an eyebrow.

Lane turned and smiled at Zack. "Is é seo mo pháirtnéir, Zack ." ("This is my partner, Zack.")

"Zack, it's nice to meet you," Cian said, switching smoothly to English.

When Cian turned, Zack heard his thoughts, betraying his impression of her. "Nice to meet you, too, but please don't call me one of the 'little people,'" Zack said.

Cian stood with his mouth hanging open, shocked. "How did you . . ."

Lane started laughing. "If you think it, she knows it. Something not to be discussed right now."

"My apologies, then," Cian said with wide eyes.

Another officer entered with their weapons case, and Cian opened it and nodded in appreciation. "Nice." He looked up as the customs officers finished their search of Lane's and Zack's bags. "Done?"

"Yes," the customs officer said curtly.

"Good. Then we thank you, and we'll be on our way," Cian said briskly, gathering up their possessions.

As they walked out, Lane said, "You already know where I want to go. I'm starved, and I think Zack could probably eat, too."

"Old Harbor Bar?" Cian asked.

"That or your Máthair's house," Lane said.

"You and your partner are in luck. Máthair is cooking today."

Reston, Virginia
12 p.m.

BEVAN AND E. usually didn't take off work, but the wedding was as good an excuse as any to stay home for a private meeting. Laura and Deanna were completing the final touches on the plans. The men had no wish to be a part of the planning and simply needed to be told a time and place to be on the fourteenth of February.

Unfortunately, due to the publicity building around the event, there were going to be a few more guests invited—or rather, security personnel who Bevan felt would be needed besides the usual off-duty officers. Deanna had objected at first, but with Taylor and Jace coming, she had agreed in the end that it would be necessary. Bevan had asked E. not to tell Deanna that Eric had been kidnapped. Bevan and E. would make some excuse for Eric not being at the wedding if he hadn't been located and rescued before then.

"Bevan, we're going out for a while. Can you watch Sarah?" Laura asked.

"Sure, I'll be on daddy duty," Bevan said and picked his daughter up, kissing her.

"E., help Bevan with Sarah, we'll pick up something for dinner," Deanna added, then kissed him.

Bevan took Sarah to the kitchen. "E., time to eat lunch." He fixed sandwiches for them and opened a jar of carrots and peas for Sarah.

"What time are they calling?" E. asked.

"Later this evening, around four, which will give us some time after our call with Ron," Bevan said as he started to feed Sarah.

Just then, the house phone rang. Bevan handed E. the spoon to continue feeding Sarah, then accepted the call on speakerphone.

"Ron, thanks for calling. We're here," Bevan spoke up loudly. "Sorry you had to call the house, but we needed to do this away from work."

"Zack and Lane are in Ireland?" Ron asked.

"Yes, they arrived after six o'clock this morning, Dublin time. I'm expecting a call from them in about an hour. Lane called last night before they got on the plane in New York. They almost had a face-to-face with one of Caydon's men, but they were able to avoid him."

"Did they recognize him?" Ron asked.

"Yes, he's the same man we had an issue with last year. Zack said he wears an American tie, and that his name is Dan, but we don't have a last name or any other information on him. I'm doing some searching through older paper files to see if I can find him. He has to have been associated at one time with Caydon, possible special forces. What have you found out on your end?" Bevan hoped for a better lead from Ron.

"The agent found the temporary worker from the real estate office. She wasn't any help. She described a heavyset man with long grey hair," Ron said.

"What about a sketch?" Bevan asked. He smiled as Sarah spewed green peas on E.'s shirt.

"No. She wouldn't even try."

"Great," E. said with exasperation. He handed the spoon back to Bevan, attempting to wipe the veggies off of his shirt in the process. Bevan pointed to the carrots, and E. handed the jar to him.

"What about you, E., anything?" Ron asked.

"Nothing. They've disappeared off the face of the earth again. I've been checking on all major ports and entries here, but I haven't found anything solid. But I do have information that inquiries are being made about Zack and her family."

"Where is that coming from?" Ron asked.

"Three places where I'm sure someone has hacked into websites and phone lines. But I need to do a more in-depth check before sending out the men in black. I don't want to waste any time," E. said.

"What news on Eric?" Ron asked.

"Nothing. Taylor and Jace won't be back until the first of the year. Ron, keep that quiet. Besides Zack, we're the only ones who know that," Bevan cautioned as he continued to feed his daughter.

"What about the people at the newspaper?"

"Not even them. Alfred Prichard handles everything at the paper," E. answered.

"Bevan, I need to know about it the moment contact is made on the ransom. I'll have direct control."

"It's difficult knowing that Eric has been taken, but being unable to prove it," Bevan said, trailing off into his own thoughts.

"So E., how many weeks left till the wedding?" Ron asked, changing the subject.

"About ten," E. answered.

"We can't make it, but you and Deanna are welcome here anytime. We're sending something off the registry," Ron said.

"Thanks, and we might stop by on the way back from the honeymoon to see you guys," E. said.

"Just give me a day's notice," Ron said.

Bevan jumped in again. "Ron, I'll keep you updated, and you do the same."

"Will do."

After the call ended, E. commented, "Well, we didn't learn much more than what we already knew. Any idea how to get peas out of this shirt?"

"Where are these places you're checking? And you'll have to ask Laura about the peas," Bevan questioned, and began to laugh.

"A winery outside of Bowie, Texas, called Brushy Creek; Café Du Monde in New Orleans; and a restaurant in Amarillo, Texas, called the Big Texan."

"All of these were recently used?" Bevan asked.

"Yes, all in the last two weeks."

"Those are really odd locations."

"If I'm right I think these are user points. Places he sent updates to Caydon. The one in New Orleans will probably be where he began to gather information on Zack," E. told him.

"Keep after it; be sure to get me the managers' and owners' names. This sounds like more footwork," Bevan said.

"I might be able to get what we need. Let me have a few days to make some connections and see what I can find," E. said.

"Do I need to know what you're about to do?"

"No," E. said, taking his soiled shirt off. "Where's the washer?"

CHAPTER TWELVE

Dublin, Ireland
Thursday, December 5, 2002
8:40 p.m.

Zack was exhausted, but she knew they had to make a call to Bevan in about twenty minutes. Once that was done, she was going to go to bed. Since their arrival that morning, they had had an early lunch at Cian's mother's house, where she'd eaten until she thought she might explode. Then they had gone on to the office, where she had met Cian's superior and watched the political games began. He had been quite surprised when neither of them had argued about storing their case in the office safe. She knew they would not be able to carry their guns. Actually, she was fine with that, as knives would be just as good for both of them.

Cian had given her a list of things to do: banshee hunting, the Hell Fire Club, the Black Cat of Killakee, and going out into the woods to find the "little people." The last place they had stopped was the Guinness Storehouse. Zack thought it would only be a place to drink, but she found the menu had much to offer, and was very pleased with her choice of beef and Guinness stew.

Cian had then dropped them off at Lane's aunt and uncle's house on St. James Avenue and Upper Basin Street. When the door had opened, they'd been welcomed with more Gaelic, hugs, and introductions to Zack. "Lane, we don't have a lot of time before we have to call," Zack told him after an extended time of introduction and chatter.

"We should have gotten here sooner, but I'll take care of it," Lane said, and he asked for their rooms.

They followed Lane's aunt upstairs to the bedrooms and were shown where the bathroom was located. She then told both of them what time breakfast would be ready the next morning.

Zack thanked her, then turned to Lane. "I'm so tired, and I want to take a shower. Can you give Bevan an update on your own?"

He nodded. "Sorry about today, but Cian and I haven't seen each other in a while."

"It's fine. You put up with my family; I can do the same," Zack said with a smile.

"I'll call. Go shower, and I'll fill you in," he said and started to open his cell, then stopped as he remembered something. "Zack, wait a minute." Lane ran downstairs for a minute, then back up to her.

"What?"

"The heating systems here aren't like in the States. It can take up to an hour for water to get hot, so I checked to see if they had warmed any for us yet."

"And?" Zack asked, irritated by the prospect of having to wait.

"You're good. I'll wait until the morning."

"Thank you," Zack sighed, and headed to the bathroom.

Lane made his call to Bevan. "We're here. We're tired and ready for some sleep. Zack's in the shower. She's worried about her family. We avoided a face-to-face confrontation with Dan at the airport. He was taking a flight to New York, JFK. Dan now knows the name of her uncle.

"Do you think Caydon's man saw her uncle?"

"No, but we're pretty sure Caydon now knows who Zack is and where her family can be found," Lane told him.

"It was inevitable; I just wish we would have had more time. How did it go with Cian's boss?"

"We left our weapons at the office, which made Cian's superior very happy. Besides, there are other things we can use that are acceptable to carry. But we're going to need a couple of days for downtime to adjust before we get into the thick of it. Anything new we should know about before then?" Lane asked.

"Not a lot right now. E. is checking on some leads in Texas and Louisiana. He thinks Dan has hacked servers to check on Zack's family. But we found nothing useful from Wyoming. Has Zack been able to connect mentally with Eric?"

"No, not yet. And by the way, I owe you some payback for not telling me more about her 'abilities.' I'm still shaking from the shit that I found out she can do," Lane said.

Lane heard Bevan chuckle on the other end. "Best learned by experience."

"That's bull, and you know it."

"Keep me informed. Take time to recoup, as long as it's only a day or so," Bevan told him.

"You're too kind," Lane said sarcastically. "Check back with you in a few days." He disconnected.

"Nothing new, huh?" Zack said as she entered Lane's bedroom. "Did you leave any hot water?"

"I think so."

"Then I'll go ahead and shower, hot or cold. Bevan said we need to do whatever it takes to settle."

"Two days and we should be OK. I'm going to bed. If I'm not up when you are in the morning, wake me," Zack told him and went toward her room.

Lane turned back as Zack closed her door. *Up before her? I'm more likely to find a pot of gold with a leprechaun sitting on it,* he thought.

ZACK LAY DOWN under homemade quilts and fresh linens. It brought back memories of another time with family in Georgia, and it began to ease the stress of the day. She missed Eric, his arms wrapped around her, and his dry sense of humor. She looked around the room at the few pictures that were on the walls, and made a mental note to view them closer the next day. Zack could hear Lane's aunt downstairs putting away dishes and laughing. Zack wanted to get a better feel for Lane's family, and she hoped their thoughts weren't all in Gaelic.

She looked at the crucifix hanging above the door and could hear her mama. *"Zaveen, don't forget your prayers!"* She smiled and took a moment to pray for her family and friends. She was worried about her family and was concerned for Jace and Taylor, but Eric weighed the most heavily on her mind. The thought of his smile, terrible jokes, and sarcastic humor made her smile and shake her head. She missed him, the way he held her at night while they slept, the words he whispered in her ear after making love. Where was he? Why was her gift failing her?

She was tired, physically and mentally, and she needed to rest. There was so much they needed to do—and quickly. But it had been impossible that day for her to focus, to let her abilities run free. "I need to sleep," she told herself. She closed her eyes, and a few moments later, the smell of fresh tortillas filled the room.

"Zaveen, Zaveen; come, my college graduate. We have work to do," Papa told her.

"*Oui*, I'm coming," Zack responded. She kissed her mama, then followed her papa out the back door of their home, where she stood in total darkness. "Papa?" There was no answer, and the smell of fresh tortillas had changed to something old and musty.

She reached out, searching for something familiar, and a chill ran down both arms. Cold—she was cold. Zack looked at her feet and saw snow beneath them. She touched something that felt like a wall covered in velvety wallpaper. She could hear voices arguing, then men laughing. Zack turned away from the wall, and she could see four men sitting at a table. The darkness was growing lighter, like a sunrise, with each laugh. "Eric?"

Zack turned back, praying there would be a window so that she could see where this place was, but there was none. *Focus! Where are you? Pay attention to your surroundings,* Zack told herself, but Eric's laughter drew her thoughts away from what she needed to do. Why was he laughing? He should be trying to leave, escape, and come home! Didn't he know how worried she was?

The anger was building inside her as Zack walked up to the table, ignoring the other men sitting with Eric. She looked into his face, and waved her arms, trying to get his attention. "Help me, Eric. I'm here; all you have to do is look up!" That didn't seem to be working. "Look at me, damn you! Why won't you look at me?" she screamed and slammed her fists on the table.

There were pieces of paper with writing on them on the table. Zack drew back with her fists once more and slammed them down, breaking the table and scattering papers and cards. "Look at me!" she screamed.

Lane felt like it had only been a few minutes since he had lain down in the soft bed he knew so well when screams and the crash of wood breaking. The noise woke not only him but the rest of his family. He jumped out of bed, banged his knee, and fell over a small chair, destroying it. He hit his head on the foot of the bed as he fell. When he regained his footing, he stood and felt what could only be blood running down his face. "Íosa, Joseph agus Muire, cad an ifreann?" Lane said. ("Jesus, Joseph, and Mary, what the hell?")

He got up off the floor and ran across to Zack's room. He opened the door and looked at the destruction. The small table next to her bed was in pieces, and she was on the floor, pounding it with her fists and screaming. He was glad they didn't have weapons, as his next move could be extremely dangerous. Lane could see that she was asleep. When he felt the moment was right, he pounced, holding her. Lane could not believe how strong this small woman was, but he could see that there was anger in her face. "Zack, wake up! Zack! Zack!"

Zack broke one arm free and reached out, swinging at dead air. "Look at me, Eric! Damn you!"

"Zack, wake up!" Lane repeated. He felt her body relax and then begin to shake as she awoke.

"Lána, cad a bhfuil ar siúl suas anseo?" Lane's aunt asked, peering into the room. ("Lane, what is going on up here?")

"Níl sé ach tromluí. An féidir leat roinnt uisce beatha a thabhairt chugam?" ("It's just a nightmare. Can you bring me some whiskey?")

"What did you say?" Zack asked as his aunt retreated.

"That you needed a drink. What the hell were you dreaming about?"

"My family and Eric, but something isn't right."

Lane looked up as his aunt brought a bottle and two glasses. He smiled, and she left the room, shaking her head.

"Did I do that?" Zack asked and pointed to the table.

"Yep, but don't worry; I also destroyed a chair in my room. We'll go shopping later this week," Lane said and poured them both a drink.

"Your head," she said, reaching up to wipe the blood off of his forehead.

"I was a bull in a china shop trying to get out of my room. Cheers!" Lane said and downed his drink. "Now tell me more of what your dream was about."

"Mama, Papa, home, fresh tortillas, and then blackness. I was in a room with no windows. I heard laughter, Eric laughing. He was sitting with three men, playing cards. I was so mad at him for worrying me, and he wouldn't look at me. I lost it."

"OK, the family thing is your worry; I understand that part. Could you tell anything about the room you were in? Were there any clues to the location?" Lane asked.

"It was old, it had a musty smell, there was velveteen-type wallpaper, and I was standing in snow."

"What about the men?"

"Nothing. I lost focus because I was mad. All I wanted was for Eric to look at me, for him to know that I was there."

Lane poured them another drink. "You're worried and tired; you're displacing it on him."

"It's more than that. It seems like he's on vacation. He wasn't trying to get away."

"Zack, we know he's been kidnapped. If there were three men with him, that means he's being guarded. Don't you think he would try to escape if he could?"

"You're right. I don't feel like I have any control over anything right now," she said.

"We've got to rest. I think we're going to need more than two days to recover. No running or work-related stress for the next few days. I have some things in mind for us to do, a place to go. My mind is in overdrive, too."

"I'm really sorry about all this mess," Zack said, looking around.

"Don't worry, my family has seen worse. If it's OK with you, I'm going to head back and try to get some sleep. Do me a favor and sleep in; I'll feel better."

Zack raised her glass. "One more drink before you leave, and I just might be able to do that."

Lane poured both of them one more drink, then left Zack's room. He stopped in the bathroom, cleaned the blood off his face, and looked at the bump above his right eye. He headed back to his own room, picked up the pieces of the chair, and put them in the corner. He found his cell phone and dialed Cian's number.

"Lána, féadann duit a bheith i dtrioblóid le bheith ag glaoch orm comh déanach," Cian said. ("Lane, you better be in trouble to be calling me this late.")

"You remember the problem I have?"

"You mean the one where you can't stop thinking or go to sleep?" Cian asked.

"Yeah, that one. I need you to make some arrangements for Zack and me for the next week. We both need some downtime to adjust, and two days aren't going to do it."

"I have a couple of places in mind. Give me a day," Cian said.

"Fine, and can you get us some knives and hunting bows?" Lane asked.

"I don't even want to know. Talk to you later." Cian hung up the phone.

Lane smiled, then walked across to Zack's room and opened the door quietly. He watched for a moment to make sure she was asleep, then noticed that the raven fetish was lying on her pillow. *We all have our demons—and the things that keep us grounded.*

CHAPTER THIRTEEN

Bevan sat in his office, checking all the messages that had come in since his meeting with the president that morning. The latest reports on the new class of agents were sitting on top of their files. He had been asked to review four of the files, as there seemed to be issues arising. He would look over them later. E. had left the information he had obtained from his investigation on the three servers that had been hacked. He felt that there might be some need for someone to go to Brushy Creek Vineyard and to Café Du Monde. There was nothing new at the Keenses' farm.

Bevan looked up when his private line lit up. "Business or family?" Bevan asked after answering.

"Business; what else?" Ron returned the question.

"I have a couple of things I need you to check out."

"Where?" Ron asked.

"Texas and Louisiana, ASAP. Check to see if there was anyone that seemed out of place: a large sale at the winery, possibly, or a big tipper at the café. Maybe there's someone who might be able to give us a description this time," Bevan said.

Ron agreed. "You're thinking that this is Caydon's man, Dan. I'll get someone on both places today."

"I'm trying to figure why they're hitting up these out-of-the-way places, other than the fact that there's not much security in some of the small-town airports. I don't believe he flew into Dallas. I'm thinking it was Amarillo," Bevan continued.

"He's here on what we can only assume is some type of recon for Caydon. Anything at Zack's home?"

"No, the report this morning shows nothing new, but we know they've identified her and her family."

"Well, then what I have to tell you just adds more bad news. Taylor and Jace arrived back in Hawaii this morning. I got a call from Milton; he said Jace had some type of premonition about Zack," Ron told him.

"Damn it! Does anyone else know?"

"No, not right now. They took a private jet home, which helped to keep them out of the public eye—for now. I'm heading over there this afternoon to meet with them. I told Milton to keep their arrival and all information about them quiet. I asked him to meet me there, too," Ron said.

"I don't envy what you have to tell them. Get back to me once you've seen them. See if you can get them out of Hawaii, at least for a few more weeks."

"What about Lane and Zack?" Ron asked.

"They left Saturday morning for a place in Clifden. It seems the jet lag hit both of them harder than they thought. Lane promised they would stay focused on the job, but they needed the time," Bevan said.

"If we can keep Jace and Taylor's arrival quiet, we'll gain a few weeks' advantage. It would be nice to get ahead of this bastard for once. I don't know about you but I'm damn tired of eating his dust. I'll talk to you tonight."

Bevan leaned forward and rubbed his head. Things were now even more complicated, and his two agents were down for at least a week. His only hope was that Caydon was still a patient man and that he didn't have information on Jace and Taylor.

New York, New York
2:30 p.m.

DAN HAD SPENT more time than he had wanted checking on information at the newspaper and local hot spots for gossip. If anyone knew when Jace and Taylor were returning from their honeymoon, they had been warned or paid to keep quiet. Dan had a couple of places to go and individuals to talk to before he left Friday. Cash travel arrangements had been made by several individuals for his return back to Austria. He would take Amtrak out of New York to DC before making a final stop in Boston for Aaron.

Dan sat at the desk in his room at the Marriott, thinking about his relationship with Aaron. He was the only person in the squad who knew that Caren was Aaron's daughter, not his sister. The trip to Boston would be to contact one of Aaron's many attorneys regarding her. He would deliver the package and advise him to expect one more. Dan was not privy to the contents, nor did he care to know. His knowledge of Aaron's true genetic makeup and age was a secret he would keep to the grave. Dan's ability to keep those secrets would make him a very rich man.

He leaned back in the leather chair and thought about the long trip back to Austria. It would be via smaller airports before taking a major carrier, a long and tedious process, but it was necessary. But Dan would certainly give a positive report to Aaron on his treatment in New York.

The room phone rang. "Yes," Dan answered.

"Sir, a package has just arrived for you. May we send it up?" the clerk asked.

"That will be fine," Dan said.

A few moments later, the package was delivered. He knew there was a phone inside it. He opened the package and took out the note wrapped around the phone. On it was written the time and date he was to call Caydon. He looked at his watch and headed out to see if he could find any information to make his boss happy.

◉

Honolulu, Hawaii
12 p.m.

THIRTY-YEAR-OLD Taylor Shaw stood on the balcony of the penthouse he'd inherited from his uncle. He stretched his tall frame and looked out over the blue waters of Honolulu. He was happy to be back at what he now called home, but he wished his honeymoon had continued through the first of the year. Jace had suddenly changed their plans when she woke from what he had called a bad dream, but she'd corrected him, saying, "No, it's a premonition. Zack's in trouble. We need to go home *now*." So here they were, back in Hawaii, hoping that it truly *was* just a bad dream.

His usually bright green eyes were tired and bloodshot from the long trip home. The call that morning from Bentwood, his attorney, and Ron Edwards of the FBI had given more credence to Jace and less to bad dreams. Taylor was also worried that no one had heard from Eric during his job in Wyoming. They had had enough tragedy since the loss of their older brother, Sherman, over a year previously in the Twin Towers. Taylor also remembered the maniac who had kidnapped Jace. He had almost lost her.

A call from the intercom startled him out of his thoughts. "I'll get it, Taylor," Jace called from the kitchen.

"It's Ron Edwards and Bentwood."

"I'll send the elevator down for them," Jace said, looking over at Taylor on her way to the door.

"I hope you're wrong about Zack," he said as she began to walk away.

She looked back at him sadly. "I'm not, and it's not just her who's in trouble."

RON EDWARDS STOOD before the doors with Bentwood Milton, waiting for the elevator to take them up. Ron had come without another agent, as he felt that having fewer people involved would help to protect everyone. If word got out that Taylor and Jace were back, the media circus would begin. Taylor was now a huge public figure with the inheritance he had received from his uncle and from the family business.

But both Taylor and Jace were not what one would expect, given the huge fortune at their fingertips. Both Jace and Taylor had been thrust suddenly into the world of the rich. Jace was a nurse, and she intended to continue working in her profession and to donate her time where it could be used best, such as at free clinics. They were giving people, and Milton had given him the list of charities he had requested. Ron needed to be sure none of these were not associate with Caydon as the donations would be substantial. Their notoriety was not something either wanted, but they had made the decision to use the money for those in need.

"I assume that your request for me to be here, and the press release you want, mean that you don't have good news," Bentwood said.

"You would be correct," Ron responded.

"I was contacted by the media this morning. They were asking if the newlyweds had returned. I told them that the rumor was false at this time."

"Thank you," Ron said and allowed Bentwood to enter the elevator first.

The ride to the penthouse seemed to take forever. When the door finally opened, Jace met them. She had her blonde hair up with a clip, and her tan was glowing in the light blue sundress she was wearing. Ron understood why Taylor had fallen in love with this beautiful twenty-eight-year-old. She had eyes that were as blue as the Hawaiian sky, but today he saw a furrow between them, and concern was showing in her face.

"Welcome, gentlemen. I hope you're hungry; we'll be eating soon. But first I need you to tell me what has happened to Zack and Eric," Jace said as they walked into the penthouse.

"Well, that was to the point," Ron said.

"Ron, Bentwood, good to see you, even under circumstances where my wife feels that you're not going to have good news for us," Taylor said as he shook their hands.

They walked out to the balcony, where Jace had set lunch for them. "She is correct, but maybe this information will be better after lunch."

"Then let's sit," Jace said.

The conversation during lunch was kept light, and they mainly asked questions about their honeymoon. Ron looked at Jace as they concluded their meal. "Thank you for lunch."

She nodded graciously, then jumped right into the matter at hand. "Something has happened."

Taylor agreed. "This must be serious or both of you wouldn't be here."

Jace looked at Ron with a steady gaze. "I think that Eric's been kidnapped and Zack's gone to look for him."

"Is it Caydon?" Taylor asked.

Ron took a deep breath at the flurry of their questions and looked at Bentwood. "Yes, on all accounts."

Jace looked at Taylor with anger in her eyes. "Money. It's about the money."

"No one but a few people knew you had planned to extend your honeymoon until after the first of the year. We were expecting Caydon to attempt to contact you at Christmas. What I need now is for you both to leave again and go somewhere until New Year's Day. Zack and her new partner need time to follow the leads on Caydon and Eric. This means we need you two out of sight. Can you do that?" Ron asked, looking from Taylor to Jace with hope that they would agree.

"There are only two places I can think of that will keep us out of the public view and that will have people there who we can trust to keep our presence a secret," Jace started.

"Galveston at the B&B or Waynesboro with family," Taylor completed.

"Do you trust your pilot?" Ron asked.

They both nodded.

Brentwood jumped into the conversation. "I have a press release prepared to be put out here and with the newspaper in New York later today. It says that you've extended your stay in Europe and will return January 3."

"We'll have everything prepared for you here once you come back, and we'll be waiting for Caydon to contact you," Ron told them.

"What about Zack's family?" Jace asked.

"They're prepared, with monitors over their entire property."

Jace shuddered. "He found her?"

Ron nodded slowly. "It wasn't in our plan, but Caydon's reach is far. It was only a matter of time."

"Do you have any idea how this happened?" Taylor asked and stood up, walking to the railing to look out to the ocean.

"It happened through planning that took the better part of a year. Bevan and I feel that Eric was his objective from the beginning. He had to wait until legalities were completed after the death of your brother. Caydon is a patient man, and he has people that are loyal even to death." Ron watched as Jace sat back in her chair and shot a worried look at Taylor.

"Well, we need to pack for a little cooler weather, regardless of our choice," Jace said, preparing herself for the weeks ahead.

Taylor turned around and looked at his wife. "The airport in Waynesboro is smaller, and I feel we can better keep our presence secret there for a few weeks, staying with Daniel and Denise at the

Long-Bowe. I'll send the plane and pilot to Galveston until we're ready to return."

"Our friends in Galveston can be trusted," Jace reassured Ron.

"Is there any chance that anybody saw you at the airport when you arrived?" Ron asked.

"It was late; the pilot brought us home, and no one was in the lobby when we arrived here. I would have to say no, at least for now," Taylor answered.

Brentwood nodded, pleased to have at least one advantage. "I'll contact your family in Waynesboro."

"Ask for the house down the road, and tell them to meet us alone at the airport," Jace said.

"When do you want us to leave?" Taylor asked.

"Actually, now. I had Bentwood contact the airport, so your plane is fueled and waiting for you."

They blinked in surprise, but they agreed to go. "I assume you've talked to the pilot and explained the situation here," Taylor said.

"Yes, and he is agreeable to whatever will be best for you," Ron said.

Jace stood up. "I need an hour to repack."

Ron nodded. "I'm going to ask for one more favor when we leave. I need both of you to wear pilot uniforms. We just don't want to take any chances that someone will recognize you. Your pilot will be in a suit and will stand outside the plane in full view, just in case someone is watching. I'm mainly concerned about the media."

"Bentwood, I would appreciate you keeping an eye out here in case Caydon doesn't buy the extended honeymoon story," Taylor said.

"Of course. I may spend a couple of nights just for the view."

Jace looked at Ron. "And Zack?"

"As far as I know, she's OK. She has a new partner who Bevan handpicked."

"That's where you're wrong. She's in trouble, but it's with herself."

Ron looked at Jace, not really understanding. She didn't explain further; she simply walked back into the penthouse.

Bentwood made the call to the Long-Bowe B&B in Waynesboro, explaining what he needed and the necessity to keep the visit private. Jace was true to her word. In an hour, she had repacked two suitcases, and both she and Taylor were dressed in uniforms that Ron had brought for them. It was time to leave.

"Bentwood is meeting us out the side door," Ron said, picking up the two suitcases.

"Ron, are you planning on having any agents at the B&B?" Taylor asked, straightening his tie.

"No, I think you'll be better off with just your family, but if at any time you feel there's an issue, call and I'll have someone there."

Twenty minutes later, Jace and Taylor were entering the jet, while their pilot stood outside for another fifteen minutes. Ron and Bentwood waited at the airport until the jet disappeared.

"Well, that went better than I thought," Bentwood said.

"They're reasonable. They've already been through enough in the last year. What else could they say? It's family," Ron said.

Brentwood nodded. "Please keep me informed, and I'll do the same for you. I'm going back to the office to send out the press release. I hope you're right and that this gives you and the NSA the time you need."

"Me too," Ron said, and he headed back to his office to call Bevan.

CHAPTER FOURTEEN

Reston, Virginia
Tuesday, December 10, 2002
1:00 a.m.

Bevan sat in his home office, waiting for Ron's call. Laura was used to his all-night meetings, but Sarah had changed their lives, and he didn't want to wake either of them. He was interested in hearing what Ron had planned, and he hoped Taylor and Jace had been amicable. Bevan's phone buzzed.

"Tell me things went well," Bevan said.

"They're on their way to safety, but they're worried, of course. The information in the press release going out today will be general knowledge in a few hours."

"Good. Anything else?" Bevan asked.

"Yeah, Jace is worried about Zack. She told me Zack was in trouble, but that it was 'with herself.' Make any sense to you?"

"Yes."

"Weird family."

"If only you knew," Bevan said, chuckling.

"No thanks, I'll pass. I already know more than I want to. Kiss Laura and Sarah for me," Ron said.

"Will do. Talk to you in a few days," Bevan said, and hung up.

He hoped the time Lane had asked for would settle both him and Zack. He knew they were capable of finding Caydon together. Bevan hoped they would be able to save Eric and take Caydon into custody; however, he knew that Caydon would not go down without a fight. He turned out the office light and checked in on the nursery. He kissed his daughter, then smiled when he passed his chocolate lab, General Lee, who protected Sarah better than any alarm system. "Good boy."

New York, New York
1:30 a.m.

DAN SAT DRINKING and looking out on Times Square from his room, celebrating his luck in obtaining information about Taylor and Jace Shaw's return. The press release sent from Hawaii stated that Mr. and Mrs. Taylor Shaw would be returning to their home in Honolulu on the third of January after a two-month honeymoon. Any changes in their plans would be released through their attorney, Bentwood Milton.

Aaron had been pleased with this and the other information that Tomas had delivered. Dan would have loved to have been there when Tomas delivered the package. Aaron had known very well that he would not be at the castle when Dan had instructed Tomas to deliver the information in person. Aaron delighted in causing that man to sweat and worry. It was a nerve-racking five-hour drive that Tomas would have to make again once the wine arrived for Aaron.

Plans that had been on hold could begin moving again once Dan returned to Austria. Aaron had told him to enjoy his last night in the States. His trip into DC would be quick, and then he would stop to see the attorney in Boston. There was a knock on the door. Dan opened the door and smiled at the well-dressed young man who stood holding a small suitcase.

"I'm looking for a Mr. Jones. I was told he would be in this room," the young man said.

Mr. Jones was the name that Dan used when looking for personal entertainment. Aaron was the only other person alive who knew this. He smiled, knowing that this was one of his rewards for the information he had obtained on the trip. Dan was beginning to get excited.

"Yes, come in. Mr. Jones is certainly in, and he needs some of your special treatment. I hope you've been advised of my special tastes."

"Why, of course; bondage is my specialty," the young man said, walking to the bed. He opened the case and removed a number of leather straps and handcuffs.

"Perfect," Dan said as he locked the door behind him.

CHAPTER FIFTEEN

Fort Meade, Maryland
Monday, December 16, 2002
7:00 a.m.

Bevan was at work early that morning for several reasons. The new class of recruits were having issues: they were unhappy with their living assignments and their work load, and two fights had already happened between three individuals (including two women) who felt that they should be the alpha of the group. He had assigned extra work and gym time as punishment, plus mandatory time with counselors for anger management for those three. They had been warned that any further issues would mean dismissal from the program. He sighed. At least there was no meeting that morning with the president, who was gone for the holidays.

It had been almost two weeks since Lane and Zack had left for Ireland. He hoped their downtime would be advantageous, but they needed to get back to the job at hand. It was important that they trace Caydon's movements in Scotland. He looked at his watch and waited for his top line to light up. It flashed, right on time, as always.

"Please tell me you have something."

"For once, I do," Ron responded. Bevan could hear the grin in his voice.

"What is it?"

"There's information coming to you as we speak," Ron told him.

"Hang on." Bevan went to the fax machine and took all the papers that had arrived.

"We hit the mother lode with the information your computer guru sent me on Brushy Creek in Texas and Café Du Monde in New Orleans. It seems there was a large purchase of wine made at the winery on a Sunday in November. The only reason they remember it is because the man who made the purchase asked that each bottle be double wrapped. They thought that was an odd request since they're limited as to where they can mail or ship out their wine."

"Did he ask them to mail or ship the wine?"

"No," Ron answered.

"Then that means he shipped it himself. How much wine did he purchase?" Bevan asked.

"Four cases."

"Any chance they can describe the man?"

"Better; they had a picture, which we were able to use to find information about him in our FBI database. It's in the papers I sent you, along with his full name," Ron said triumphantly.

"Got it. Daniel DeJonghe: he's one of Caydon's men, ex-military, and a medic. His file is gone from our records, along with any pictures. How did they get a picture of him?" Bevan asked.

"Just by luck. He happened to be standing in the right place at the right time—right for us, at least. There were several group shots taken that day during some type of get-together, and he just happened to make it into one of them. I'm sure he had no idea," Ron said.

"Any idea which direction he had come from?" Bevan asked.

"I had agents check the smaller airports just to be thorough once I got this picture: Lubbock, Amarillo, Wichita Falls, and even Clovis, New Mexico. A rental car agent in Amarillo recognized him and gave my guy the type of car he had rented and the name that was used. It was an alias, of course, but it's information we didn't have until now. Then we followed up in New Orleans, where he stayed at the Inn on Bourbon."

Bevan perked up in recognition, remembering what Lane had reported to him after their run-in with Aaron's man named Dan. "This all makes sense now."

"That's where things pretty much end. He spent a lot of time at Café Du Monde eating his weight in beignets, drinking coffee, listening to music, and tipping big to the waitresses. I tried to get in touch with Ernest, but it seems he and his wife have left town," Ron said.

"I'll have E. check with Zack's father, but I bet it all has to do with DeJonghe finding out about Zack and her family. We know that DeJonghe was headed to JFK next, but our trail runs cold there. Any further information on him or the shipment of wine?"

"No, that's pretty much where the trail dies off. The wine shipment could have gone out anywhere; it probably went through a larger city where he could pay to keep things quiet. DeJonghe's rental car was left at the hotel and picked up by the rental company. The desk clerk said he took a cab to the airport the morning of the fourth. My agents checked with the airports in both New Orleans and New York, but the alias in Amarillo hadn't been used at either. It also seems he was able to avoid security cameras at both airports, and that's alarming. So right now, he is either back with Caydon—wherever that is—or he's still running errands somewhere on the East Coast. Any activity at the Keenses' farm?"

"Nothing, and I hope it stays that way. My agents haven't reported in, either. One more week and I'm going over there if I don't hear something positive," Bevan grumbled.

Ron laughed. "You know the children need playtime."

"Playtime is over; I need positive reports—and soon," Bevan said.

Ron laughed again, then changed the subject. "Oh, good news: Liz and I will be able to come to the wedding after all. Can you tell E. for me? Liz is sending an RSVP, but I want to make sure we make the cut."

"You can stay with us. What about the kids?"

"The grandparents are coming for a long visit and said for us to leave," Ron said.

"Thanks again for the good news. I hope I have some of my own, and *soon*," Bevan said, then hung up.

He sat for a moment and opened his cell, but he quickly closed it, deciding to give Lane and Zack a few more days. He pushed too hard sometimes, but time was running out. Jace and Taylor would have to make their return in about two weeks.

Bevan had called his parents, who lived in Waynesboro, and had asked his dad to keep an eye on them. Jace and Taylor had already gone over for dinner several times since they'd arrived. There was nothing out of the ordinary at the B&B. There had been no unexpected arrivals or requests for the house where the Shaws were staying. It seemed Ron's idea had worked. Bevan wondered how Caydon would eventually contact Taylor. He was sure of one thing: it would not be traceable.

Darlene walked in with an envelope. "There's a delivery for you."

Bevan looked at it and saw that there was no return address. "Darlene, did this go through the regular channels?"

"Yes, sir. Why?" she asked.

"Just checking. There's no return address. Can you call E. and tell him to come now?"

"Right away," Darlene said, leaving his office.

In what seemed like just a minute, E. arrived at Bevan's office. "Whatcha need, boss?" E. asked.

"Something's not right. I may need you to take this and check the barcode," Bevan said as he opened the envelope. Three pictures fell out on his desk. His face went pale. "Take this envelope and go *now!*"

E. left the office, running. Bevan picked up the photographs to examine them more closely. The first one was of E. and Deanna at a local restaurant, having dinner. The next was of Laura and Sarah outside her law office. The last one was of Eric, lying in a coffin. He turned each one over and saw a warning written on the photograph of Eric. *Last chance.*

"Boss," E. said, out of breath when he returned in a few minutes.

"Where did this come from?" Bevan asked him.

"Here in DC; it was paid for with cash five days ago and set to be delivered today."

"Not a word to anyone. Can you fire a weapon?"

"Did you forget that I was raised in the country?" E. returned, with rolling eyes.

"I'll make arrangements for you to carry once you've passed qualifications. You need to go today. I'll call the range master," Bevan said and picked up the phone. "Now, E.!"

"I'm gone," he said, starting to walk out briskly.

"E.—when you're finished, I want you to get two of your trusted geeks to go over video from the airlines, the border entries, everything. Search it all and find these bastards!" Bevan yelled.

"I'm on it, boss."

Bevan made his call to the range, then made arrangements for security for his wife and daughter, has hands shaking with rage as he dialed the numbers.

CHAPTER SIXTEEN

Clifden, Ireland
Monday, December 16, 2002
12 p.m.

Lane looked out the window of his room in the manor house and thanked the saints that the last few days had been peaceful. Their arrival at Abbeyglen Castle had been a blessing for both of them. Cian had called in some favors to obtain rooms for the three of them at the manor house for as long as needed. It must have been a huge favor; they had choice rooms at the manor, and they were able to roam the grounds as they wanted, even for target practice.

Lane had to admit that their special abilities needed some downtime, and with Abbeyglen being so close to the Connemara National Park, Zack was in heaven. The first night when they'd arrived, she had asked for a map of the grounds and park. The next morning before dawn, she had set out, disappearing for two days. When Lane had checked her room, the only thing missing had been her backpack and jacket. At first Lane had been worried and had started to search for her, but then he'd remembered her upbringing. Her time on the family land, and the report he'd read on her survival training in the desert, had made him realize that she could take care of herself. When she'd returned, Lane had given her several knives and a takedown bow with twenty arrows that Cian had obtained, with instructions to not kill anything unless she was threatened with bodily harm. He wasn't really sure that she needed the bow, but it made him feel better.

He finished his coffee. His mind had been in overdrive when they'd first arrived in Dublin, but that had changed after a few days at the castle. Lane hoped that Zack would soon be ready, too. They needed to get back on track. He knew that Bevan understood, but understanding could only go so far with agents out of the country who seemed to be on vacation rather than on assignment.

Lane changed into running clothes, sheaved his knives, and headed to the area set aside for practice. After three hours of running on the grounds and completely destroying another target with his knives, Lane walked back to the castle. As he entered, Cian called to him.

"Lane! I have information."

"Follow me. I need to shower, and then we can talk," Lane said.

"Where's Zack?" Cian asked.

"Out there; not sure when she'll be in, if at all. She seems to have found solitude and enjoys the company of animals over that of people right now," Lane said as they entered his room. He began to shed his clothes, heading to the shower.

"After being around you, I can totally understand," Cian chided playfully.

"It's a good thing we're friends or I would have to remind you who truly is the better man here."

Cian jabbed at him, then asked, "How much longer do you think you'll need here?"

"Why? Is your favor running out?" Lane questioned and laughed.

"No, you can stay forever if you'd like, but I have a lead from Oban," Cian said, his eyes gleaming with excitement.

"Hold on to that thought for a moment. I'll make this quick."

Lane quickly washed away the sweat and dirt from his workout. "Lane, you do know that I can't release your weapons, right?" Cian said as he heard the shower stop.

"Not a problem; at this point, Zack and I will make do with what we have. Knives and bows don't seem to be at the top of the dangerous-weapons list. We can get them through security a little easier and avoid the political crap. Want to get a drink?"

"As long as you're paying," Cian answered.

Lane looked at his watch. "Let's make it dinner, and yes, I'll pay."

Cian and Lane headed downstairs and were seated in the restaurant. They placed their orders for food, along with drinks.

"So, what's the lead?" Lane asked as they waited.

"I have information about a passenger who boarded a ship in Oban around one of the times from last year that you gave me." Cian noticed the restaurant getting crowded, and he lowered his voice. "And this is a cargo ship that doesn't usually take on passengers."

"And?"

"The passenger had limited amounts of luggage, and he was dropped off by a woman," Cian said, toying with his friend.

Lane looked bored. "And?"

Cian looked around the restaurant to ensure no one was listening to their conversation. "We had an informant working on the ship. He just happened to take down the number of the tag on the car." Cian paused dramatically. "An old family of friends of yours."

Lane sat forward in his seat suddenly. "The MacNiels?"

Cian nodded, smiling coyly. "But it wasn't the brothers he was there to see."

"Their sister: Kirsten . . . Karliene . . . no, wait . . . *Kyliegh*. Kyliegh MacNiel," he mused, then whistled lowly.

"It seems she was driving the car that brought the man to the dock," Cian boasted proudly.

Lane thought for a moment. "You're using Kyliegh as an informant, aren't you?"

"She has been helpful with information on her brother's arms dealings."

"How are you keeping her safe?" Lane asked.

"We use local constables to help us run raids on their locations knowing she is present to help keep suspicion away from her." Cian responded.

"Do you believe Caydon is part of the arms dealings?"

"Guns, drugs, probably all of it." Cian replied.

"Do you believe they are involved? That has been our thought from the beginning."

"Kyliegh has indicated that Caydon may have some feelings for her, but nothing serious," Cian reassured Lane.

"Guess we were wrong about a lover." Lane looked up in hungry anticipation at the waiter as their food was delivered. As soon as the plate hit the table, he started shoveling the food into his mouth. Cian laughed at his friend's appetite as he sipped his beer.

Before beginning his own meal, Cian commented, "You know I'd like nothing more than to go with you two, but my last encounter with the MacNiel brothers ended badly. My boss wouldn't be able to defend me if I was to get involved in another shootout with them. So I'll pass. But you two need to be careful."

"It's not a problem," Lane replied between bites.

Cian waved the waiter back to their table. "Two more drinks, please."

THE WEEK AT Abbeyglen had been exactly what Zack had needed: spending time out in nature, listening, focusing, and being at peace with all that was there. She had built a hunting blind to conceal her presence. There, she could center and try to connect with Eric, Jace, and possibly even Caydon. She could hear the movement of smaller animals and their larger predators. They passed her by, leaving Zack alone, as she did them.

She took the raven fetish out of her bag, held it tightly, and began to center. She breathed slowly and steadily, concentrating on all that was around her. She had to go back to that scene from her dream. There were clues to where Eric was being kept; she just had to find them. Zack let the light of day, the fresh air, and the scent of pine fade to a place of darkness, age, and mustiness. The laughter, the snow at her feet, the wallpaper with a velvet quality.

Zack turned: Eric laughing, men playing cards. *Focus. Calm the storm; he is a victim.* The voice of her trainer echoed. *"Your abilities are limitless!"*

She walked to the table and, this time, looked at each man. They were ex-military—mercenary, well trained. They were dressed casually, with no weapons, a Caucasian, an African American, and a Hispanic. Where was Caydon? Not there, at least not at that moment in time. *Listen Zack; listen to what is being said.*

"And now, gentlemen let's play a little five-card, jacks or better to open," Eric said, dealing the hand.

"I'll open," the African American said as he threw $200 in the middle of the table.

"I'll see that and raise you $200," Eric replied, throwing four pieces of paper into the middle.

Zack reached out and picked up one of the papers; it had Euro written on it with a mountain and Austria across the bottom. She turned it over and a castle was roughly drawn. She looked at Eric, and he smiled.

"Very good, Zack," a familiar female voice said.

Zack looked up at the woman standing on the other side of the table. "Jace?"

"Taylor and I are home from our honeymoon, and we're at the Waynesboro B&B. We're safe there until the New Year. Now go; you must help Eric," Jace said urgently before she faded away.

Zack opened her eyes and smiled. It seemed she was not the only one in her family with limitless abilities. "I'm back. I've found my control."

She looked down; sitting in her lap was a small gray rabbit. She shooed it out of the blind, picked up her weapons, and ran toward the manor. Zack looked back toward the blind and could see dark clouds building.

LANE AND CIAN had finished dinner and were waiting for another round of drinks. Lane sat back in his chair, remembering the day Cian had saved his life. Lane had been on assignment, attempting to take down the MacNiel brothers for arms and drug sales shortly after he had been made an agent. Cian had been in the right place at the right time. He had killed the older MacNiel just as the criminal had been about to shoot Lane. Lane's life was owed to Cian, now and always, but that incident would also keep Cian behind scenes, gathering information for them, instead of being part of the hunt.

"What's on your mind?" Cian asked, already knowing what Lane was thinking.

"Nothing, just old ghosts creeping in," Lane said.

Moments later, they both heard a commotion at the front of the restaurant. Lane looked up as Zack pushed her way in, bow and all. "Something is wrong—or maybe right. I can't tell. Either way, it's big."

Zack walked over to the table and sat down abruptly. "I know."

"You know what?" Cian asked, completely confused.

She looked at Lane intensely. "I know where Eric is possibly being held: he's in a castle somewhere outside of Innsbruck. It's being guarded by a small contingency of men. They're loyal to Caydon and, as we thought, are military trained."

"Are you sure?" Lane asked seriously.

"Yes, but we have another problem. Jace and Taylor returned from their honeymoon early. They're in Waynesboro, hiding until the New Year."

"How can you know all this?" Cian asked, completely flabbergasted.

Lane attempted to explain. "Cian, Zack has a gift. I told you when we arrived that if you think it, she knows it."

"Smoke and mirrors," Cian spouted. "She's in touch with someone who's feeding her information. Lane, I know you, I've seen what you're capable of, but what you're talking about is just not possible."

Zack knew where this was headed, and there just wasn't enough time to argue. "I know about this the same way I know . . ."

"Zack, no!" Lane said, fearing what secret she was about to expose.

"The same way I know about the diamond and emerald ring for Cara that's in your coat pocket: a claddagh, size six. She's pregnant, and you two are getting married this weekend. It's going to be a private ceremony at St. Teresa's Church on Clarendon Street."

"Íosa, le gach a bhfuil naofa," Cian said, turning pale. ("Jesus, by all that is holy.")

At that moment the lights began to flicker and thunder roared, shaking the windows in the restaurant. He stood up, knocking over his chair. "Cailleach!" ("Witch!")

"We need to go upstairs to figure all of this out. Zack, order something and have it sent to my room. We need to make plans and head out by the weekend. It appears your time out in the park was helpful," Lane said approvingly.

"I'm ready. I've found the control I've needed," Zack told him with a determined smile.

Lane waved impatiently to the waiter. "She needs to order, and can you send it to my room, please?"

Lane took their drinks from the waiter, signed the ticket, and he and Cian went back to his room to wait for Zack.

"I tried to tell you, but until you experience Zack for yourself, it doesn't seem possible. But she is for real," Lane told Cian.

"Cailleach, cailleach!" he said, still shaking from the shock.

Lane rolled his eyes impatiently. "She's not a fucking witch, OK. She's my partner, and she's a damn good one, too. Zack's special. You need to try to understand." Then he grinned. "Is Cara really pregnant?"

The door opened. Zack entered with a tray of food, along with two more drinks for Lane and Cian. "I'm really sorry about what just happened, but sometimes I just have to blurt it out to speed things along," she said, handing the men their drinks.

"What are you?" Cian asked warily. He backed slowly to the window, never taking his eyes off of Zack. Lightening lit up the sky, followed by a clap of thunder. Cian trembled and made the sign of the cross for protection.

"I'm not a witch, but my abilities have been passed down for generations. I just haven't had control over them, but it's coming," Zack answered before eagerly diving into the bowl of soup she had ordered.

"We need to call Bevan. I'm sure he knows about the Shaws. I need to see if he wants us to go to Scotland or to make our plans for Austria. Do you have any more information about the location?" Lane pumped.

"No, I could just see the room where he was being kept."

"That's not a lot of information. I'm sure there are numerous castles for rent," Lane said.

"Yes, but what they need is isolation," Cian interjected. He slowly moved to a chair, keeping his eyes on Zack.

Zack could feel Cian's suspicions. "Cian, I understand your reactions. But I'm still human. I'm Catholic. I go to mass, say my rosary. My mama is Hispanic, so that's where my black hair and dark eyes came from. I was blessed with something special. Although you may not understand it, please know that I'm not a witch."

"Cian, you know me. I trust Zack with my life. Can you help us? Do you know anyone that can get us more information?" Lane asked.

"I may, but he's not always reliable," Cian said, starting to relax.

"Do what you can. We're going to have some issues traveling due to the holidays, too," Lane said.

"If the weather continues to be bad, it could delay you here," Cian said.

"I'm going to call Waynesboro," Zack said and left the room.

Lane turned back to Cian. "So, you didn't answer my question. Is Cara really pregnant?"

"Yes, yes, and yes to everything Zack said."

"Comhghairdeas, mo dheartháir," Lane said and hugged Cian. ("Congratulations, my brother.")

"Go raibh maith agat. An dtiocaidh tú agus an seasfaidh tú liom?" Cian asked. ("Thank you. Will you come and stand with me?")

"Tiocaidh mé," Lane joyfully agreed. ("I will.")

The door opened, and Zack entered. "Jace said they're hiding until the third of January. They'll go back to Hawaii then and wait for Caydon's ransom demand. Oh," she said, turning to Cian, "and I'll have to buy a dress for your wedding. Thanks for asking us to attend."

"Jesus, how do you deal with this, Lane?" Cian asked, rubbing his temples.

He shrugged. "You get used to it."

"Give me a few days to see if I can get the information from Austria that you need. I would rather you have solid leads to check before you go there," Cian said, getting back to business.

"What about information out of Scotland?" Lane asked.

"Nothing from the constable; no strangers in town. He was more interested in the MacNiels. I haven't heard from Kyliegh," Cian said.

"We need a couple more days for scenarios," Zack said.

"OK," Lane allowed, "but we need to be on our way by next Monday. Vacation is over."

"I should have what you need by the weekend. And, since you know the place, be at the church on Saturday at noon. Don't be late," Cian said with a smile before he left. "Oh, and don't forget to wear a kilt."

Zack was going to enjoy seeing this.

CHAPTER SEVENTEEN

Austria
Wednesday, December 18, 2002
5:00 a.m.

The sound of feet running down the hallway woke Eric out of a deep sleep. He stood at the door, attempting to listen. He surmised that Caydon and his henchman Dan had returned. It had been a month since he had heard from the psychopath, and he guessed that Dan was the asswipe who had doped him up for shipment. He could only assume that report time and planning would be the topic of discussion among the troops. It could also mean that the ransom request had been sent. Now what? More drugs and packing him off? But to where? As far as he knew, this place was about as secure as it could get.

The knock on the door made Eric stumble back and turn on a light. "Mr. Shaw, good morning. Would you join me for an early breakfast?" Caydon asked as he came in.

"My pleasure. Do you mind if I get my smoking jacket first?" Eric returned mockingly.

"Please. Proper dress is necessary," Caydon replied seriously. "I'll wait."

"I hope you will regale me with the story of your time away from the castle. I so wish to hear of your adventure." Eric waved his hand above his head as a flourish.

Caydon smiled. "Let's discuss the terms of your return."

"As long as it doesn't involve being shipped in a box."

Both men entered the dining hall, where the table had been set. This was the first time Eric had seen everyone together. They were a small company of men, six total, including Dan. The demeanor at the table was all business. There was no conversation, just stoicism and attentiveness.

"Caydon, you really should find another color besides black for your men to wear. A royal blue or light green would be nice," Eric said.

Caydon ignored him. "Gentlemen, our time starts now. We depart for training in fifteen minutes."

Eric looked around the table; not a word was said. Breakfast was eaten, then each man stood and followed Dan into the next room.

"Eric—I hope you don't mind me calling you Eric," Caydon said.

"Of course, as long as you don't mind me calling you Aaron. I feel we have a connection—one I would like to sever," Eric responded.

"The time is coming when I will be contacting your brother. I need you to pick a lens from your equipment and place your thumbprint on it for me."

"Well that's a relief. I was expecting to loose a finger or ear," Eric said and wiped his head.

"You are so dramatic."

"Is Taylor home?" Eric asked.

"You don't know?" Caydon said in surprise.

"What—they're alright, aren't they?"

"Oh, yes. They just extended their honeymoon to the first of the year."

"Taylor will give you whatever you want."

"I'm planning on it. In the meantime, you can continue to use the gym, and I'll have Dan take you for a run off the property. Please, don't try to escape."

"I hadn't thought about escape since I have no money, no passport, and not exactly sure which side of Austria this castle is located. Why would I want to run away from this awesome vacation you've arranged for me?" Eric's sarcasm was in full swing.

"Good, I thought you might see things reasonably. Now, excuse me; I have arrangements to make. Dinner will be a six sharp," Caydon said before rising from the table and leaving him along in the room.

Dan entered the dining room shortly afterward. "Mr. Shaw, if you would like, we can take that run at eleven."

"Sure. Can we run into town for a coffee?" Eric asked jokingly.

Dan didn't miss a beat. "Maybe tomorrow," he said and left the room.

I think he's serious, Eric thought. *Something is definitely wrong.*

AARON LOOKED UP as Dan entered the library. His second-in-command stood silently until he finished looking over the information that Dan had brought back. There had been no problems in DC or Boston with the deliveries Dan had made. The trip back to Austria had been long and tedious, but uneventful. *Things seemed to be in order—a little* too *orderly,* Aaron thought.

"Something wrong?" Dan asked. He proceeded to the window and opened the curtains, checking on his men. The last thing he wanted was for Aaron to be disappointed in their performance.

"This seems a little too neat to me," Aaron responded bluntly. He sat musing behind the huge antique desk.

"I may have to agree now that I'm back. I seemed to have problems in New York obtaining any information, and then word was everywhere that Taylor Shaw was returning after the New Year."

Aaron leaned back in the large leather chair. "This smells of Bevan—and the FBI."

"Is that the reason for our departure?" Dan asked.

"That, and some issues that came up before I left Scotland."

"What kind of issues?" Dan walked up to the desk.

"Kyliegh's fucking brothers thinking they can't be touched. I had a short conversation on my feelings about their recent activities, explaining what would happen if they involved their sister," Aaron said with irritation, cracking his knuckles slowly.

"That wasn't the only thing, was it?"

"No. The local constable seemed to be showing up a little more than usual in town. I made a night run and checked his office. There was a letter from the Gardaí in Dublin," Aaron said.

Dan rubbed his forehead. "About you?"

"Me and her brothers."

"What made you suspicious?" Dan asked.

Aaron walked over to the book shelf and picked out *War and Peace*. "Kyliegh's younger sister works in one of the local pubs and mentioned the constable being in the pub three times in one day."

"We can have the area here sanitized in two or three days," Dan said.

Aaron nodded. "When we leave, I only want what can be carried. Everything else should be destroyed and placed where it will never be found," he instructed without turning around.

"Then we're leaving sooner than you announced?"

"As soon as I have the lens and print. Arrangements have been made for a personal delivery to Taylor Shaw the day he arrives home. For now, contact the pilot and schedule a false flight plan. I'll need one van. Get rid of the car and . . ." Aaron trailed off.

"Kill the guards," Dan finished, without batting an eye.

Aaron picked out two more books. "No loose ends."

"And Eric?" Dan asked.

"Just use a light sedation," Aaron answered.

"What about your wine?"

"It arrived. It was one case short," Aaron said.

"And Tomas?" Dan asked.

Aaron turned back around to face Dan. "He has already met his well-deserved fate."

"Then the extra week before you came back wasn't spent in Scotland?" Dan asked.

Aaron nodded. "Tomas was becoming a huge liability. He continued to think he would never be responsible to me for his debt. That was most troubling."

"What made you go to his house?"

"I'd received word that the boxes had arrived."

"I assume his response to your arrival was one of surprise," Dan said, chuckling at the thought.

"You might say that. He had called his entire family to come for an early holiday celebration to enjoy the spoils of his corruption, which included my wine. You know how I feel about someone taking things that belong to me," Aaron said softly, sinisterly.

"There was something else, wasn't there?" Dan prodded.

Aaron walked back to the desk with his books and sat down. "It seems his corrupt life had caught up with him. In exchange for his freedom and continued lifestyle, he was willing to deliver an internationally wanted criminal," he said with meaning.

"He told you that?"

"No, his wife did—just before she died." Aaron looked at Dan. "Don't you have work to do?"

"Yes, sir, I do."

"Dan, I need you to discover who is responsible for disclosing this location to Eric?"

"I'll find out." Dan responded.

Aaron sat back and looked at the photograph of Zaveen Keens lying on the desk. He picked it up. "And your lover's fate is in my hands."

◉

Dublin, Ireland
Saturday, December 21, 2002
10:30 a.m.

ZACK STOOD OUTSIDE St. Teresa's Church, thinking about Eric and how time was slipping away. The last days at the manor had been put to good use. Targets had been destroyed and then remade, over and over. The night training scenarios were harder; each one came with additions of new targets and possible complications they might face. But they were ready. She could anticipate Lane's next move, as he could hers. Bevan had been correct; Lane was the partner she needed. Now they needed to stop Caydon. Cian promised he would give them all the information that he had been able to obtain that day at the church. Later that night, once all the wedding celebrations were over, they would make a plan and call Bevan.

"Did you get the gift?" Lane asked, and then took a moment to look at his partner. "Zack, you look very Irish. You seem to have been busy."

"Yes, I got them a bell, just like you told me to. I thought I would do a little checking on my father's name, and to my surprise, I found some history and a tartan to wear. The lady at the shop helped me with a blouse and broach, too. I hope this is OK," she said, twirling.

"The red, black, and yellow look nice on you. It's more than OK—it's appropriate for today. Cian and Cara will be as impressed as I am," Lane said.

"And don't you look nice in your kilt. This must be your family or clan tartan," Zack said, returning the compliment.

"Yes, but things change over the centuries."

"I assume this is your mother's tartan. What is her family name?" Zack asked.

"Gre`go`ir."

"The colors are striking: light blue, dark blue, red, and white."

He smiled. "You're going to see something very traditional today. I'll explain it later."

Just then, Cian walked over to them. "Dearthàir!" Cian shouted. ("Brother!")

Lane hugged Cian and patted him on the back. "Did you think we wouldn't show?"

"Tá mé chomh neirbhíseach." ("I'm so nervous.")

"English, Cian. Zack is going to have to sit through this ceremony in Gaelic."

"I think I'll be able to follow. Mass is mass, no matter where you are," Zack told them.

Cian looked at Zack in her tartan. "An bhfuil sí gaol?" ("Is she kin?")

"At this point, anything is possible," Lane said.

Cian turned to Lane. "Do you have the ring and the binding? And don't forget to be the first to congratulate her. I know this is simple, but traditions still need to be followed." His voice was shaking with nervousness.

"It's all taken care of; just because I don't live here doesn't mean I've forgotten my heritage," Lane reassured him.

The church bells began to ring, and Lane looked at Cian. "It's time, my friend."

"I'll meet you inside," Zack said. As she entered the church, she stopped to place her hand in holy water and made the sign of the cross. She smiled as family memories flooded her mind. The voice of Zack's mother spoke softly in her mind: *Remember to say your prayers.*

Zack sat alone and watched Cian, in his tartan of blues, yellow, and rust, take the hand of his bride, who was dressed in a tea-length cream dress made of what could only be Irish lace. The priest began the ceremony and mass in Gaelic. Though the ceremony was simple, Catholic doctrine was followed, including the sacraments. Lane had given her a copy of the traditional vows they would repeat, and when those were finished, Cian placed the ring on his bride's left hand with the heart turned toward Cara. The binding of lace and red-and-blue ribbon was wound and tied around their hands. The final blessing and announcement of marriage ended with a sweet kiss.

Lane walked up to Cara immediately after the ceremony. "Comhghairdeas," he said. ("Congratulations.")

Cara smiled. "Chuimhnigh tú." ("You remembered.")

Zack walked up to the couple. "Please forgive me if I miss a word," she said, then began to recite the blessing.

D'fhéadfadh go mbeadh tú i gcónaí	May you always have Walls for the wind
Ballaí do na gaotha	A roof for the rain
Díon le haghaidh an bháisteach	Tea beside the fire
Tae in aice leis an tine	Laughter to cheer you
Gáire chun áthas a cur ort	Those you love near you
Coimeád iad siúd is breá leat, in aice leat	And all your heart might desire.
Agus gach b'fhéidir do chroí ba mhian.	

Cara looked at Cian with tears in her eyes. She walked over to Zack and hugged her. "Thank you."

"This is from Lane and me," Zack said, giving Cara the gift. She noticed the sprigs of shamrocks in the bridal bouquet.

Cian looked at Lane in surprise, who responded, "Not me, brother. She did that all on her own, and it looks like she may have learned another language. We'll have to be more careful now."

"I have something for you, but we need a few more moments of your time for pictures first. After the wedding celebrations, Cara and I must go," Cian said.

Zack watched the wedding party exit to the garden. She knelt and began to pray, asking for the guidance and protection of St.

Michael. They were going into battle against evil, and could use all the help they could get. She knew from the first run-in with Caydon that he would not go down easily, and she felt that someone could die this time.

"I guess I should be asking for a favor, too," Lane said, coming up behind her.

"I asked for both of us," Zack reassured him, then stood and looked at the envelope. "Time to go back to work, I see."

Lane nodded. "By the way, my aunt said she would have our rooms ready again. I promised her there would be no nightmares this time."

Austria
2:00 p.m.

ERIC AND DAN returned from what had become a daily run since Caydon's return. He had even been allowed to have coffee in the small village. Caydon had been right. Where would Eric go? He couldn't speak the language, and he had no money or means to escape. Eric knew they would be leaving—and soon. That was the only reason he had been allowed this freedom. The lens with his fingerprint on it had been taken, and it was on its way to the States.

He only hoped that Zack had somehow been able to connect to him. He kept thinking she would break down the door and save him. *Wow, that's a sappy idea,* he thought. In the meantime, he would continue to work out, and if the time came, he prayed that his strength and nerve would not fail him. He wished that he'd taken some gun safety classes and learned to shoot, but that was all water down the drain.

"Eric, gym," Dan said, interrupting his thoughts.

"Right behind you," Eric replied, following Dan.

Everyone was in the gym that day, including Caydon. For the first time, he saw the scars, scars that Zack had inflicted. He knew Caydon must hold a deep anger for her, and that horrified him. It was becoming apparent that this kidnapping had progressed to a vendetta.

Caydon looked up as Eric walked by. "Eric, did you know that the Internet is becoming the way of the future?"

Eric picked up a set of weights. "It's inevitable, don't you think?"

"I can find anything or anyone I want if the right information is fed into the blanks," Caydon said as he increased the weight on the vertical leg press.

Eric did not like the tone of this conversation. "Being connected at one time to the military, I assumed you've always had that ability."

"True, but the public has become my best and most reliable source of social information," Caydon stated, beginning his workout.

"I'm not sure what you're trying to say." Eric gripped the weights harder.

"I think you do; but let me continue, if not for your pleasure, then definitely for mine. When your brother got married, it was quite the dog and pony show, even though he tried to keep it private," Caydon continued, barely breathing hard or breaking a sweat.

Eric remained steady, knowing that there were pictures of him and Zack from the wedding. Maybe he could play it off.

"The photographs that I've been studying are very interesting. Bevan Benjamin hid her very well, but as I have always told him, I am the better man. Did you know that you talk in your sleep? 'Zaveen' seems to be a word you speak often. But do not worry; I have known for a while who she is, but what I didn't know is how much she meant to you—until now. I saw you looking just now at the scars she left me." Caydon stopped and stood up, facing Eric. "She is very special to you, as she is to me—but for a different reason."

Eric was shaking; he knew he would never be a match for this man. But he had to stay calm.

Caydon smiled. "You see, I took something from her that I intend to return. I hope you did not have long-term plans with her."

"You bastard!" Eric screamed, causing everyone to stop their workouts and walk toward him. "If you think those scars are bad, wait until she blows your fucking head off!"

"We will see, but again, I am the better man," Caydon said smoothly, returning to his workout.

Eric stormed away. He looked up and saw that Caydon's men had surrounded him. "What! I'm not allowed to get pissed off?"

"Relax, everyone," Caydon commanded.

Eric began his workout, and the shaking in his hands decreased. Caydon might have been the better man, but Zack was the better *woman*. She would not walk into a trap; she would set one. He only hoped she had a partner that could hold his own in a fight.

"Eric," Dan called to him.

"What?" he blasted back.

"We're done; you need to clean up and come to the hall for dinner by six," Dan instructed him.

Eric shook his head and left the gym. He avoided looking at Caydon.

As Eric exited the gym, Dan looked at Aaron. "Tonight?"

"Yes; just sedate him to a light sleep. We won't have the luxury of a two-week recovery this time."

6:00 p.m.

Eric showered and dressed for dinner. He pictured Zack's face. *I must have faith that she'll find me, and when the king is dead or gone, we'll live happily ever after.*

Eric was confused about everything that had taken place since Caydon had returned. He had been given more of his personal belongings back, including his watch and cameras, and he felt physically better now than before he'd been packaged and shipped.

Eric opened the case holding his cameras. From the moment he had been allowed to leave the castle, he had begun to leave bread crumb trails for Zack. He'd left items that would not be missed should anyone go through his camera case: two lanyards and several lens covers that he'd licked, like he had seen on crime shows. They may not have been worried about him escaping, but they still watched him closely, which had made dropping those items a little tricky at first. But nature calls and cooldowns had helped to get ten items away from the castle.

A knock on the door meant that it was time to go. "Eric, you need to come," Dan said, opening the door.

"Damn, did I miss the news that the Queen was coming, or do you guys just really like me?" Eric asked him.

"Funny."

When he arrived at dinner, it seemed to be quite the celebration. He was served steak, lobster, wine, bread, cheese, and a dessert so decadent the taste of it made him shiver. There seemed to be lightness at the table that night. Eric looked around the room and noticed that two of the men had left before dessert was served. Eric could tell that this was their last meal at the castle—it had to be— but before he could say anything, his eyesight blurred.

"Oh shit! Not again . . ." he said as darkness took him.

Aaron stood. "We leave now."

Dan watched as all the final plans he had made with his men progressed quickly and without fanfare. Miguel and another man carried Eric to the van. His room had been cleared during dinner. There would be nothing left to indicate that anyone had stayed in the castle.

Dan walked past Aaron, who was standing at the front door of the castle. "Done and clear." He took his place behind the wheel, waited for Aaron to get in, and then drove out the front gates.

"Stop," Aaron instructed. A moment later, an explosion and fireball filled the night sky. He looked back at his men. "No loose ends."

Their arrival at the private airfield left only one item to be discarded. Soon the men and their captive were aboard. Dan set a timer for twenty minutes.

Aaron walked to the cockpit and handed the pilot their destination. He gave no explanation to his men; this was something they were accustomed to, working for a man who had secrets. "Dan, keep him out, just not in a coma. We will make two stops before reaching our final destination."

"He'll need to wake up if we're boarded," Dan said.

"I'll handle any issues as far as anyone trying to board," Aaron said smoothly.

"I'll do what I can, but he might get sick again."

"Just keep him quiet and compliant."

Fort Meade, Maryland
5:00 p.m.

BEVAN HATED WORKING on the weekends but this case was important, the clock was ticking and this meeting necessary. He was with E. and his team, sitting in the conference room and going over all the information they had been able to find. The information—or lack thereof—was frustrating. The past five days of searching had produced a possible location for Caydon's hideout in Austria, but the lack of cameras in the surrounding towns made the chance that Caydon or his men had been captured on film a zero chance. The fact that one man and a small contingent could come and go unchecked meant that the US was still vulnerable to more terrorist attacks. This was not something the president would want to hear about, but it would need to be addressed at his next meeting.

"Boss, we haven't found anything at the manned borders in and out of the US. My team and I feel that they are using small unmanned airfields or possibly private ones on personal property," E. summarized.

"I don't understand how they're doing this. New guidelines to prevent this type of action are in place."

"If they're setting up flight plans that are probably false, and it will be some time before they're discovered. Another possibility is that he's had the plane repainted and the identification numbers changed each time he moves. His finances are endless, and money keeps lips sealed," E. said.

"Any information on the package delivered here?" Bevan asked.

One of E.'s team handed him a folder. "The original package was sent locally, as we know. The person making the arrangements was a college student. The package arrived at his school with a note from his grandmother, asking him to have it delivered here by courier. This student's grandmother is a retired NSA agent. She, of course, knows nothing about any of this, etc., etc." E. said, holding his hands up in resignation.

"Jesus Christ, these men are using our own tactics against us," Bevan said with exasperation.

"And they're good at it," E. said.

"Do you have anything else that might be helpful?"

"Actually, I think we do. We obtained information this morning about the death of the mayor of Innsbruck. There is a report of the destruction of a castle and a van about two hours away," E. told him.

"Show me," Bevan said.

E. pulled up a map of the area on a large screen, and circled the areas where the mayor had been murdered, the castle destroyed, and the van burned. "There's quite an acreage associated with this property."

"Plenty of room for them to hide. Who was the mayor?"

"A man named Tomas Waldburg," E. said.

"Can the family help us with who may have done this?" Bevan asked.

E. looked at his team grimly. "The information we obtained said that everyone in the family was killed."

"What about family not living there?"

"This man's entire family—children and grandchildren—were all slaughtered. His lineage is no more," E. said solemnly.

Bevan rubbed his forehead. "Do you have photographs of the scene?"

E. took out another folder and handed it to Bevan. Several photos slid out. "We found something a little odd." He pointed to the wine bottles sitting on the table in one of the photos.

Bevan looked up at him after squinting at the scene. "Does that say 'Brushy Creek'?"

"Yes."

"How many boxes were found there?"

"One."

Bevan paused for a moment before speaking again. Finally, he asked, "What background information do we have on this man?"

"It's all in the folder with the photographs," E. said.

"E., you stay. The rest can go. Thank you and nice job, everyone," Bevan said, watching the others leave the conference room. He was proud of E. and his team, and he would be sure to place letters in their files.

Bevan picked up the phone and dialed Ron Edwards's number. "In about ten minutes, you are going to receive some photos and information that we obtained today."

"Hope it's something we can run on," Ron said.

"Well, it's a good start. We found the wine," Bevan said.

"What else?"

"The man who was in possession of it was murdered, and his entire family is dead, with no survivors: men, women, and children," Bevan told him gravely.

"Caydon's work, I assume."

"This is something he would do," Bevan confirmed.

"Over a box a wine?"

Bevan looked at E. "Anything else in the house to indicate why this was done?"

"Nothing that we were able to obtain. It appears that he killed everyone over drinking his wine," E. said, shaking his head in amazement.

"I know he's a crazy, psychotic bastard, but this is beyond that," Ron said.

Bevan agreed. "It wouldn't surprise me, but I feel that this goes beyond the wine. What little amount I have read on this Tomas Waldburg leads me to believe that he was involved in some way with Caydon. The wine just set off the fuse."

"We need to find him—and soon."

"Working on it. I'll keep you informed." Bevan ended the call and looked at E. "No word of this to anyone, and keep yourself armed."

E. raised his eyebrows. "You don't have to tell me twice."

"Go home. See you tomorrow." Bevan watched E. leave, then began to read over the rest of the report. He looked forward to his call with Lane and Zack that night, hoping that they would have better leads than his.

CHAPTER EIGHTEEN

Dublin, Ireland
Sunday, December 22, 2002
1:00 a.m.

Since their return to his aunt's home after the wedding celebrations, Lane had noticed Zack pacing. She had gone out twice that night to run, and she had barely eaten at dinner. He had been trying to focus on all the information that Cian had obtained for them. They would need to find and interview the mayor of Innsbruck, a Tomas Waldburg, and see if he could give them information on any property rentals from Americans over the last month. The information on Walburg was passed to Cian from Kyliegh. He looked up as Zack entered his bedroom. "What's wrong with you?"

"I'm not sure. I feel as though something has happened to Eric again. I can't connect; that's why I've been going on all the runs," she said.

Lane shrugged. "We need to call and make final plans with Bevan."

"Go ahead."

Lane opened his cell and made the call to Bevan's home. "Boss, time for updates. You're on speaker here."

"I was about to send out agents to find you," Bevan responded sarcastically.

Lane ignored the comment, continuing on with his report. "Cian gave me information about a mayor in Innsbruck."

"Tomas Waldburg," Bevan said immediately.

"You seem to be ahead of us," Lane said with surprise.

"He was the provincial governor, wealthy and corrupt, and he had a lot of enemies," Bevan told them.

"We want to go and speak to him to see if we can get possible locations where they may be holding Eric," Zack said over Lane's shoulder.

"Zack and I feel he'll be our best contact for information on Caydon. We received his name from one of Cian's informants," Lane added.

Bevan was silent for a moment. "He's dead."

"Waldburg?" Lane asked, not sure he was hearing correctly.

"Yes, he and his entire family—and I mean *everyone*," Bevan said.

"Jesus. When?" Lane asked.

"The information that came to the office said that the family had been dead for about a week. They wouldn't have been discovered until after the first of the year if it hadn't been for a caterer who found them. There was something a little odd at the house. A box of Brushy Creek wine from Texas had been opened, and all but two bottles had been consumed. I knew that there were four boxes related to Caydon that had been shipped. Now I know where they arrived."

"What about the other boxes?" Lane asked.

"Not in the house," Bevan said.

"Cause of death?" Zack wondered.

"Undetermined at this time due to the decomposition of the bodies. It will be weeks before we know what the real cause of death was," Bevan answered.

"Any reason we should go to Austria, then?" Lane asked.

"Yes. We also have information of two explosions several hours away."

"The castle," Zack surmised.

"And a vehicle—or what's left of it—on a small private field not far from the property," Bevan told them.

"We found someone who we thought was a love interest for Caydon: Kyliegh MacNiel. She was seen dropping a man off at the docks in Oban, which we know was Caydon. The license on the car leads back to her, but as it turns out she is Cian's informant. She told Cian that Caydon was associated with her brother's interest and had tried to start a relationship with her. Kyliegh said she blew him off," Lane shared.

"MacNiel, you said?" Bevan asked.

"Yes. I've had issues with the brothers, but you know about that. I'll send Cian's information on Kyliegh to you," Lane answered.

"She's important, but I don't feel that you need to go to Scotland at this time, especially if there's a chance of you possibly coming in contact with the brothers. If Caydon attempts to make contact with Kyliegh in the next week I need to be notified immediately," Bevan told them. "Zack, I'm hoping you'll be able to find something on the property in Austria. I don't want you to spend more than a few days there, though. I want both of you back here in the States by the third."

"Any idea where Caydon may be going?" Lane asked.

"The possibilities are limitless. Zack, how are your abilities?" Bevan asked.

"Where they need to be, but I want to meet with my trainer. Can you have him there when we get back?" Zack asked.

"I'll make arrangements," Bevan told her.

"Bevan, we're as ready as we can be. The time here has not been wasted, I promise you." Lane looked at Zack, and she nodded in agreement.

"How long will it take you to get to Austria?" Bevan said.

"I may have a favor I can call in to get us dropped directly to the locations. Can you make a call and clear the path for us?" Lane asked.

"I'll do it once we're finished talking," Bevan assured them.

"We should be there Monday afternoon," Lane said.

"Keep me informed daily." He hung up.

"Do you really think you can get us dropped into the area during the week of Christmas?" Zack asked Lane.

"Yep, and I think we should stay on the property. I'll make arrangements for the equipment we'll need."

"I'll take my bow," Zack said, twanging the string.

"No, leave it; I have something better for you. What you have is OK for targets, but you need something with a little more punch and distance."

"Compound bow!"

He laughed. "You must have been a real downer at Christmas—you ruin the surprise! It will be here before we leave. I'll have to make the adjustments for you once you have the chance to practice with it."

"Let's go to the airfield first, then to the castle."

"My plans exactly." He noticed that she was wrinkling her brow. "Zack, what's bothering you?"

"I'll know more once my feet are on the property, but I know that Eric left me something. I just have to find it," Zack said.

"You sure about that?"

She nodded.

"Then I'll follow your lead. Now, I need to make some more calls," Lane said.

"You have some strange late-night friends," she teased.

"If you only knew—but then I'd have to kill you," he joked. "Go to bed and try to sleep, and no fights with the furniture, please."

Zack headed to her room. Just before she went to sleep, she heard Lane say, "Remember that favor you owe me?"

"HIDE AND SEEK, Zack, hide and seek." Eric's words ran over and over like a recording in her head. She'd had a restless night, and had risen just before dawn. Zack dressed, waiting for sunrise so that she could go on one more run.

"Where are you going?" a female voice asked.

"For a run," Zack answered, and she turned to see who was asking, not recognizing the voice.

"Hide and seek, Zaveen, hide and seek." The voice began to fade.

"Wait, wait . . . Martha?" Zack asked.

"Mack," the female said before it disappeared.

CHAPTER NINETEEN

Monday, December 23, 2002
11:30 p.m.

Eric Shaw sat on the edge of his seat on the plane, vomiting into a large plastic bucket. His head was killing him, and his eyesight was blurry. He was able to make out a bandage on his right hand with something sticking out of it. That must be where Dan was shoving medication to keep him in a haze. The plane dipped, and his head went back into the bucket. He looked up as Caydon sat down in front of him.

"I really fucking hate you," Eric said before hurling into the bucket again.

"It will pass."

"I guess I should be grateful that you didn't pack me like furniture this time," Eric said, then looked at Dan. "And you, asswipe—if I ever get my hands on that needle, I'm gonna stab you in the heart with it."

"I told you this might happen again," Dan looked at Aaron.

"We'll be landing at our final destination soon," Aaron said.

"I hope it's on some island where it's warm. I need to work on my tan," Eric said weakly.

Dan reached for Eric's hand and pushed medication into the port. "That will help with the nausea and let you have a better sleep."

"I fucking hate both of you," Eric said and closed his eyes.

Aaron stood and looked down at Eric. "I want this to go without a problem."

"We've been cleared; the airfield is isolated and private. I made the arrangements myself. Equipment and provisions are waiting for us," Dan said.

"I'll stay for a few days until everything is set up. You and I will be leaving on the thirty-first for Honolulu. Miguel will be in charge during Eric's stay in Hawaii."

"He *did* say he wanted to work on his tan," Dan said, chuckling.

"Welcome home, Eric," Aaron said and walked to the front of the plane. He took out the picture of Zaveen Keens. "Just a little more time, because if you are a patient man, all things will come to you."

Austria
2:00 p.m.

ZACK WAS CONSTANTLY amazed at the endless connections Lane had when it came to calling in impossible favors. He had secured the transport, equipment, and supplies that they would need for the next few days and nights. It was nice that no one had questioned her new compound bow, but she felt they may have objected had they known about the arsenal of knives she and Lane were both carrying. There was a jeep, courtesy of Bevan, waiting for them at the private airfield where they'd landed. It appeared that the Austrian military had control of the area.

Lane turned to one of the pilots who stood near the jet's door. "One more favor and we're even."

"Screw you, Brigham," the pilot said.

"It's your own fault," Lane said airily before turning to exit the jet.

"Do I want to know why he owes you?" Zack asked, following him down the airstairs.

"Probably not. It could make you an accessory."

She shrugged, then motioned below. "Looks like our welcoming committee is waiting."

She watched as Lane descended to the group waiting at the bottom of the airstairs and, without missing a beat, introduced both of them in perfect Austrian German to the man in charge at the scene.

"Impressive, but English will be fine," Lieutenant Feist told them.

"We appreciate your cooperation," Zack said.

"There isn't much left here, but you are welcome to look around. I do ask that you not remove anything," Lieutenant Feist instructed.

"Of course," Lane replied. "What about the castle and surrounding area?"

"You will be permitted to stay and camp for two or three days. Again, I ask you not to remove anything, and if you find something that will assist in our investigation, please speak with the sergeant in charge, Karl Manz. You have no weapons?" Lieutenant Feist asked.

"Just my bow," Zack answered.

"No side arms?"

"No," Lane responded.

"Then you can proceed to the area."

Zack and Lane walked over to the area where the vehicle had been destroyed. It was obvious that the military had processed and taken most of the larger pieces away.

"Probably a C-4 with a timer. That would cause the most destruction and distribution of parts," Lane said, surveying the wreckage.

Zack knelt down to examine the wreckage more closely. "What the bomb didn't destroy, the fire did."

"Can you sense anything?" Lane asked.

"Not much, other than they were in a hurry."

"That's pretty obvious, isn't it?"

"No, you don't understand. What I feel here is more than a quick exit. There's a feeling of urgency," Zack said.

"We need to go. I want to get to what's left of the castle and find a place to set up before dark," Lane said.

Zack and Lane packed the jeep and followed Lieutenant Feist to the castle. As they drove up to the gates leading to their destination, Zack reached and grabbed Lane's arm. "They killed the guards. No loose ends."

"Don't say anything yet. Let me ask when we stop," Lane said.

There was a small number of men waiting for them, and they guided Zack and Lane to a spot where they could camp. Lieutenant Feist made the introductions to Sergeant Manz.

"Sergeant Manz will be checking in with you during the day. You will be safe here; there are some deer around, but that's about it."

While Lane continued to talk with the lieutenant, Zack went to ask for assistance from two men who were speaking French.

"D'ailleurs, qu'est-ce que ces Americains pensent qu'ils vont trouver?" the first man asked the other soldier. ("What do these American's think they will find?")

"Et il a apporté avec lui une fille de petite taille, miniscule on pourrait dire." the second soldier responded. ("And he brought a little girl.")

She waited for the two men to cease their conversation, then spoke to them. "Surement, j'aimerais de l'aide, si possible avec les approvisionnements. J'apprécie enormément. " ("If you two are finished, I would appreciate some assistance with our supplies.")

Their faces turned red. Both men apologized and followed Zack to the jeep. They quickly set up the tent. She had expected two tents, but they would get by with one; Lane was a gentleman, and they were partners. There were standing cots and cold-weather sleeping bags, which they would need in the Austrian winter.

"Chère demoiselle, autre chose que nous pouvons faire pour vous?" ("Miss, is there anything else we can do for you?")

"Non, merci," Zack said. ("No, thank you.")

She watched as both men walked away, then saw Lane walking toward her. "Well, that's nice. How did you get them to help?" Lane asked.

"They made the mistake of thinking I only knew one language."

"I see. I assume you had a pleasant conversation. French?" Lane asked.

"*Oui.*"

Lane smiled. "Two men, the gate guards, were executed. Their bodies were dumped in a lake about two miles from here."

Sergeant Manz walked up to the campsite. "My men were helpful?"

"Yes, thank you," Zack answered, smiling brightly.

"Good, good. Do you have water and food?" Sergeant Manz asked.

Lane confirmed that they did.

"Then you are all set with equipment. Now, the lieutenant said that there are only deer around, but he hasn't spent much time here; there are wolves in this area. If you keep the food contained and have a decent fire, you should be fine, but I regret that I cannot give you a weapon. Now, on to the ruins. We have not been able to check and clear the entire castle. The building may not be stable—be cautious when you enter," he told them.

"Sergeant, we'll be fine, and thank you for everything," Lane said.

They watched as the small group finally left. He turned to talk to Zack, but she was standing at what looked like the front door of the ruined castle. He waited a moment, then slowly approached her. "I know you want to go in, but we need to secure the area and get a fire going."

She nodded. "Bevan sent a satellite phone. We need to call him and check in. I wasn't sure at first why we needed to come since they're gone, but now I know why we are here," Zack said confidently but sadly.

"Why?"

"There are three bodies in there that they haven't found, staff that became expendable," Zack explained.

"Damn it! This is not going to be easy to explain to the sergeant."

"I hate to extend their time down there, but we need a day before we notify him. Be sure to ask Bevan if we can stay the full three days. I need time to connect with the dead, and I believe there is evidence we need to recover," Zack said, wiping away the tear running down her face.

Lane nodded. "Fine. Get your bow; we need to adjust it to the amount of pull you can handle."

Zack had to get something else off her chest before they began work on the bow. She closed her eyes, said a silent prayer, and crossed herself. "I had a visitor last night at your aunt's home."

Lane stopped in his tracks. "What? Who?"

"One of my dead ancestors." She picked up her new bow and several arrows, then walked down the road.

"Íosa, cabhair liom," Lane said under his breath. ("Jesus, help me.") He picked up his tools and went after his partner.

CHAPTER TWENTY

Reston, Virginia
Tuesday, December 24, 2002
12:30 a.m.

Bevan sat in the family room, holding Sarah, who just wouldn't go to sleep that night. She was curled in his arms, looking at the blinking lights on the tree. He thought about how his life had changed from that of a bachelor to one of a father and husband. It had been a good change, one that he would not trade, and he would do anything to prevent harm to his wife and daughter.

Laura was in the kitchen, continuing to bake late into the night. He could hear the hum of the mixer, and each time she opened the oven, it filled the entire house with the smell of cookies and pies. He wished this moment would never end. He looked down at his daughter. Sarah smiled and moved her hands up and down, making gurgling noises.

Laura walked into the room from the kitchen. "Waiting for a call?"

"Ah, you know me so well," Bevan responded, smiling up at her.

Laura picked up her daughter. "Well, Sarah and I are finally going to bed."

Sarah looked at her mother and drooled. Laura wiped Sarah's mouth. "I wish someone had told me about teething."

"So, are you finished baking for the night?" Bevan asked.

"Yes, and I left a few of your favorites on a plate for you: chocolate chips cookies."

"Cookies fresh out of the oven: how can I resist?" Bevan said and started toward the kitchen for his treat.

"Come, General." Laura watched as the chocolate lab rose and wagged his tail. "Bevan, try not to be up too late; we have company coming."

Bevan walked back with his warm cookies and kissed his wife. "Promise."

He proceeded to his office to wait. As he sat down at his desk, the phone buzzed. "I hope you have good news."

"Good news, bad news, Zack's dead relatives visiting her, you know, the normal stuff," Lane told him breezily.

"Good news first."

"The military said we could stay for up to three days. Zack said that Eric left some bread crumbs for us to find, and she feels that she'll be able to locate most of them. Bad news: Zack feels that there are three dead individuals that the military hasn't found in the rubble of the castle. She is asking for one day before we contact the recovery team. And last of all, I may need an exorcism when this case is over," Lane said.

"Any idea who they are?"

"Staff assigned to the castle, casualties of Caydon's quest," Lane said.

"Do what you need to, then contact the military ASAP. I want to keep our relationship with them in good standing. You can forgo a report tomorrow—your time, that is. It'll be Christmas Day, after all. Be sure you and Zack contact your families. Work or not, take a moment to let them know that you're thinking of them," Bevan said kindly.

"Thanks."

"What's your plan for today?"

"It's just after six-thirty here, and the skies are starting to lighten. Zack is already dressed for a run, and after that, we'll be digging through the castle."

"I'll have arrangements for you to be picked up later this week. One more thing. Has Zack been making any further connection to Eric?"

"No. She said it seems like he's not answering the phone. I'm thinking he's drugged," Lane said.

"Keep me informed, just not on Christmas."

Bevan hung up the phone, then walked into the bedroom where Laura and Sarah were sleeping. General Lee was lying on the king-size bed, and he wagged his tail at the sight of Bevan. "Oh well, just this once. After all, it's Christmas."

Austria
7:00 a.m.

THE SILENCE OF the camp was disturbed by the whiz, thump, whiz, thump of arrows being shot, one after another, directly into the center of several targets. Zack had made each target more difficult to hit than the one before. In just the short amount of time she'd spent with her new bow, she felt at ease and confident using it. She stopped and listened as a deer walked by her next target. Zack loaded the arrow; she had to be sure, needed to be on the mark. She let the arrow go, hitting the target and missing the deer by only inches. She smiled as it ran off in the fresh snow and deadfall of the area.

"That could've meant venison for dinner if you had missed the target," Lane told her.

Zack smiled. "I had to know I could do it. There may come a time when my aim must be true."

Lane rubbed his hands together and shivered. "Looks good to me. Want to have breakfast? Then we're off for run."

"Crepes and espresso?" Zack asked playfully.

Lane smirked. "Power bars and shitty instant coffee."

"Guess it'll do." Zack walked out to retrieve her arrows. As she picked up the last arrow, she froze. "Lane."

Lane walked out into the woods to where she was standing. "What?"

Zack reached up with her bow and could barely reach the item she'd spotted that was hanging from a tree branch. "This is Eric's."

Lane took the lanyard off the end of her bow and looked at it. "Are you sure?"

"You're really going to ask me that? Wasn't our conversation about Mack enough for you?" Zack asked him.

"OK, let's eat something. Then we'll go see what else you can find."

After finishing breakfast and spending an hour and a half scouting, they returned to the camp. Zack had been able to locate a second lanyard and a lens cover. "I would've liked to search longer, but we need to get into the castle and locate the bodies," she told Lane.

"You remind me of a bloodhound," he said. He handed her a PayDay.

"I thought you ate all of these."

"My friend who dropped us off got some for me on short notice—he owes me big-time," Lane said.

She rolled her eyes. "I'm going to change."

As she changed, she heard a jeep pull up and knew it was Sergeant Manz. She exited the tent quickly in overalls, heavy boots, gloves, and a helmet with a light. Their boss had thought of everything when he had sent their supplies.

"Good morning. I wanted to check on you and make sure you had no problems during the night," he said.

"No problems. It was actually a peaceful evening," Lane said. "Excuse me; I need to change so we can get started in the castle."

Zack walked up to Sergeant Manz. "Coffee?"

"No, thank you. I'll let you get to your search. But please contact me if you find anything," Sergeant Manz said.

"I promise we will." Zack watched him leave the area, then looked up as Lane exited the tent.

"You ready?" he asked her as he picked up ropes, handheld floodlights, and harnesses.

"Yes. I want to find those bodies and see if there's anything left inside the castle that might help us," Zack said.

They headed toward a pile of rubble that was once a regal castle with a place in history. "We need to take this slow. Watch your footing. I'll anchor," Lane said.

He checked Zack's harness before letting her enter, then found a steady wall and anchored the ropes. She made her way about fifty feet in when the floor beneath Zack suddenly gave way. Lane held tight to the rope. "Zack! Are you OK, Zack?"

Zack was suspended in the air, swinging and turning on the rope. "I'm fine! I'm about a hundred feet above the floor below. Let me down—slowly."

"What are you seeing?"

Zack took out her light and shined it below her. It appeared to be a formal dining area. "Lane, lower." Zack finally reached the floor. She looked up and saw Lane searching for her below in the darkness.

"I'm going back for more lights; don't move."

She stood looking at the beauty and destruction around her. *Such a waste*, she thought.

"We're here," a male and female voice called in unison. She turned to where the voices were summoning her and started to move.

Lane saw the movement below. "Zack, don't move; wait for me. I'm sending down lights, and then I'll follow."

Zack felt such a pull to go search for those waiting to be found, but Lane's yelling had stopped her. If she fell again, he would not be there to save her. "I'll wait."

Lights were sent down, and she watched Lane descend to her location. "Damn, going back up may not be so easy," Lane said, looking back up through the gaping hole they had come through. Then he saw that look on his partner's face. "You found them?"

"No, but they're close. They're calling to me."

"We need to get these lights up so we can see. Then we should find them first, out of respect, before we look for clues," Lane said.

They both worked quickly and together to get the lights situated where they would get the most coverage for safety and searching. Lane took a quick look at their surroundings once the lights were all on. "He dropped the roof, pancaking the building, so it would take longer to go through. Bastard!"

"They're back this way," Zack said. She began to slowly make her way to what she believed was the kitchen.

"Christ!" Lane could see a woman and two men. Their bodies were crushed beneath a wall. Zack continued to move toward them, beginning to remove the rubble that was on top of their bodies.

"Thank you," a female voice said softly. Zack turned; before her stood an apparition of the woman who had been killed.

"Peace to you," she said gently to the phantom.

"The tall young man, there is still something of his here," the woman said. She pointed to a far corner where the ceiling had caved in.

All the while, Lane watched Zack speak as if someone else was there. The hair on his arms and neck rose straight up. "Do I even want to know?"

Zack ignored his question, beginning her trip to the far corner of the room. She struggled over the rubble. "Help me look."

"OK, but take it slow."

When they reached the corner, they found that there was a wall still standing. As Zack touched it, the scene of Eric playing cards resurfaced. "This is what I saw; this was part of his room."

She began to pull rocks and wood away. Slowly, the corner of a piece of clothing appeared. When it was pulled away from the rubble, she sat down.

"Eric's?" Lane asked.

"Yes. It's the jacket I gave him before he left for the job in Wyoming."

"Zack, the smaller items we can hide, but Sergeant Manz is going to want this."

"I know. I have a feeling that what I really need to find is still out in the woods. Let's go back up so that you can call to have the bodies removed," Zack said. She held the jacket close.

The ascension proved to be more difficult. Zack anchored while Lane basically had to pull himself up the ropes. The ruins were too unstable for him to use. Once he was on stable ground, Zack was easily brought up.

Zack watched Lane make the call to Sergeant Manz, and she sensed his frustration as he hung up. "Can't make it tonight, huh?"

"It'll be tomorrow afternoon probably, due to the holiday. He asks that we not go back inside," Lane told her.

"Can you make up some kind of story that we need to go back in once the bodies have been removed, so we can have the time we need to search the woods?" Zack asked.

"It may be difficult for a good Catholic boy to lie, but I'll try," he teased.

She gave him a small smile, then said, "I want to clean up."

"Sorry, no shower," Lane chided.

"Maybe not, but I can warm up some water over the fire and at least wash off some of this dirt and dust. I'll leave a little for you," Zack said.

"Are you saying I stink?"

"Yes, and I prefer not to smell you all night in the tent."

As the day ended, a silent meal was eaten by the two weary souls. Lane made a quick sweep of the area on his nightly bathroom run, then they zipped themselves up in their mummy bags for what would be another very cold night. Zack had placed Eric's jacket inside her sleeping bag, holding it tightly. She hoped that the coat wasn't needed wherever he was.

CHAPTER TWENTY-ONE

Niihau, Hawaii
Wednesday, December 25, 2002
7:00 a.m.

Eric opened his eyes and reached for the plastic bucket, expecting to vomit, but nothing happened. He sat up on the side of an army cot. "What the hell?" he said out loud. He rubbed his forehead and realized that there were beads of sweat on it. He guessed his suggestion on improving his tan had been taken seriously. As he stood up and took a deep breath, the smell of the ocean was present. The only sounds besides the waves were the voices of Aaron's men. He opened the flap of the tent and stumbled out into the light.

"Good morning, Eric," Miguel said.

Eric looked in all directions. The only thing besides water and a few mountains in the distance were the three Zodiacs anchored on the beach. "So, can we start twenty questions as to where the hell I am today?"

Miguel smiled. "You have free range."

"I assume this is not the Four Season on Tahiti," Eric said dryly.

"Correct," Miguel answered.

"Is there a restroom?" Eric inquired.

Miguel handed him a small shovel and a roll of toilet paper.

"Rough," Eric said, then took the implements he would need and stumbled off to a somewhat private bush.

When he finished, he walked to the water and washed his hands. He could smell coffee and what he thought was bacon. When he stood up, he noted that the temperature was maybe in the mid-70s.

Since he had been asleep most of the trip again, he had no idea where he was or if there was any hint of civilization.

"Breakfast, Eric," Miguel called.

Eric counted the men: four. The king and his jester were nowhere to be seen. "So, where is our host, and what day is it?"

"Gone, and Christmas Day."

"You gentlemen will have to forgive me, but I seem to have left your gifts at the castle. I'll be most happy to run into town and get you something, though," Eric told them.

No one said anything; they just laughed.

"I guess that would be a no then," Eric said.

"As I said, you have free range," Miguel told him, spreading his arms wide.

Eric sat down and drank his coffee, wishing that he had never left the loving arms of Zack.

Austria
2:00 p.m.

ZACK SAT AT the campsite, thinking of the conversations that she'd had in French and Spanish with her parents on the phone earlier that day. The conversations had been short, but heartfelt words had been spoken on both sides. She'd promised to come home when possible, and had told them that next time she would bring Eric. She'd noticed that Lane's conversation with his mother in Gaelic had included the same feelings as hers.

Zack walked back to the castle, hoping that the recovery of the individuals' bodies would bring peace to their families. Their run through the grounds that morning had produced the discovery of a clear lens with saliva and two film canisters with notes in them. They would check the coffeehouse in the village the next day. Zack hoped it would be open. She wanted to confirm her thoughts that Eric and Dan had been there several times before their departure.

She heard the satellite phone rang, and knew it would be Sergeant Manz. A few minutes later, she heard Lane's footsteps as he came up behind her. She looked up.

"They're on their way," Lane said.

"Tomorrow I want to spend the afternoon in the woods," Zack said.

"More training scenarios?"

"Yes. We need to work together before we leave here."

"The notes we found in the canisters: your fiancé has quite the sense of humor," Lane told her.

"That was done so we would know it was him," Zack replied flatly.

"'Caydon's a king and Dan's a medical jester' is pretty specific. Plus, the dates are helpful," Lane said encouragingly.

"He's just letting us know who's been drugging him, but what worries me is that he's calling them by name."

"What else are they going to do? It's not like he doesn't know who Caydon is," Lane said.

"Something else is at play here. Caydon wants more than just the money."

"Like what?" Lane asked.

"Revenge on me." She looked up at the sound of tires on gravel. "Manz and his men are here."

Lane and Zack walked up to the vehicles. They had brought more lights, and every man had his climbing gear.

"Thank you for your call," Sergeant Manz said, shaking Lane's hand.

"It's time for these people to be taken care of properly and not discarded as trash," Lane said solemnly.

"I have something you'll want," Zack said, walking to their tent and returning with Eric's jacket. She handed it to the sergeant. "This belonged to my fiancé."

"Is he in there?" Sergeant Manz asked hesitantly.

"No, and I'm surprised it was left. Eric must have hidden it."

"Then he is a prisoner of whoever did this?"

"Yes. He's possibly being held for ransom. His family—his brother—is very wealthy," Lane explained.

"Then I hope he is returned quickly and unharmed. Please, can you show us where we need to begin? It will take us some time to complete the recovery and identification," Sergeant Manz told them.

"We left our equipment down there. The brighter light will help you and your men. The explosion dropped the roof and top floors, sandwiching them. When we entered, one of the sections gave way, providing an opening to what appears to be the dining area," Lane said.

"And causing us to have to take a longer time to search and find the bodies," Sergeant Manz finished. "C-4?"

"I believe so."

"Have there been any inquiries about people missing in town?" Zack asked.

He shook his head. "No."

"Well, if we can be of any assistance, please let us know," Zack said.

"Thank you, but we must do this on our own. But Lieutenant Feist will be here, and he may have some questions for you."

"We'll make some coffee, then. And sergeant, I have a small request," Lane said.

Zack walked back to the campsite, allowing Lane to talk to Manz alone. She put a few more pieces of wood on it so that there would be a little warmth for those in the castle when they emerged. She knew it would be a long afternoon, and that the search might even extend into the night. She was starting the coffee when Lane sat down beside her.

"He bought it?" she asked. He nodded. "Thanks."

"I don't know why I bother, but you're welcome. Have you heard anything else from the servants?"

"No, their spirits have moved on now that they have been found."

"I'm afraid it's going to be a long evening," Lane said, picking up a cup of coffee.

CHAPTER TWENTY-TWO

Austria
Thursday, December 26, 2002
2:00 a.m.

L ane and Zack sat outside in the cold, watching the last body being loaded onto a truck. It had taken longer than expected to extract the bodies due to another section of the roof caving in, causing injuries to two men. Sergeant Manz had had to call for more supplies and men. Lieutenant Feist's early visit at the beginning of the job had been short, which had made the sergeant happy. It had been a solemn day for everyone at the castle.

Lane stood up as Sergeant Manz walked up to the fire. "Coffee?" Zack asked as he sat beside them.

"Have anything stronger to go in it?" Sergeant Manz asked, rubbing his neck.

"As a matter of fact, I do," Lane said. He disappeared for a moment into the tent.

"I want to thank you for contacting us so quickly about the bodies," Sergeant Manz told Zack as they waited. She nodded graciously.

Lane emerged from the tent. "Here you go: Irish whiskey." He poured it into the sergeant's cup.

Sergeant Manz took a long drink, then looked at both of them. "The people in the castle were locals: a husband and wife, and their son."

"No!" Zack got up and walked away from the fire, outraged.

Lane shook his head. "You knew them?"

"Yes; they were good people, and they will be missed in the village. I would ask of you one favor, man to man," Sergeant Manz said, motioning him closer.

"You don't need to say anything; it's already understood." Lane filled his cup one more time.

The sergeant toasted to him, then finished his drink. "There is something else. I was advised not to say anything, but I feel this is of importance. We found what was left of possible gun crates."

"Military grade?"

"ARES Shrike."

"It seems his reach is far," Lane said to himself.

Sergeant Manz stood. "I should go. Please give my regards to your partner, and our thanks, again. When will you be leaving?"

"We should be able to finish what we need tomorrow—I guess it's today, actually—and depart for the airport by the afternoon," Lane told him.

"It's been nice to meet both of you; come back when you can stay longer and under better circumstances."

Sergeant Manz shook hands with Lane and walked to his jeep. Lane waited until he could no longer see the lights of the jeep, then turned around and observed Zack back at the fire. "We need to turn in."

"I know about the weapons. The Shrikes weren't the only things they found. They had upgraded sidearms for every man: Beretta M9A1s," Zack told him.

"I need to call Bevan, but the last thing he told me was not to call him on Christmas, which it still is in the States. I'll wait to call until morning his time. He needs to know about the weapons, and I can tell him we're pretty much finished here," Lane told her.

"When you do get hold of him, ask if we can get out of here tomorrow night," Zack said, shivering.

"I'll see what he can do, and I'll ask him where we're going after that. For now, I'm heading in."

"Be there in a minute."

Zack sat down. She began to focus on the flame, and then she closed her eyes. She pushed away the anger and listened to the popping of the wood, focusing. Slowly, dark turned to light. There was sand beneath her feet, and the smell of fish and the ocean.

"Zack!" Lane called, unzipping the tent.

"He's near water," she responded with her eyes still closed.

"Where?"

"Not sure."

"This has been a long day. We need to rest," Lane said, and he zipped the tent back up. She finally went in, beginning to feel hopeful again.

Reston, Virginia
6:00 a.m.

LAURA WAS UP early, cleaning the house and tending to a daughter whose internal alarm wouldn't be silenced. She had left Bevan sleeping, something he rarely did these days. She placed Sarah in her high chair and made cereal and fruit, a morning favorite. Sometimes these moments between girls were the best. She looked around at their home: peaceful, warm, and, for the moment, safe.

Mother, wife, and attorney: these were titles she had never thought would describe her, but she was so glad that they did. She worried for her husband and the scenario that was playing out with Aaron Caydon, who she hoped to never meet again. His intrusion into their home and lives had left its mark. After the incident, Laura had begun gun safety classes, conquering her fears by becoming confident in her abilities with a weapon. She would not be a victim ever again, and no one would harm Sarah.

Sarah cooed as Bevan entered the kitchen. "Good morning, princess," Bevan said, then picked Sarah up and kissed her.

"Breakfast?" Laura asked.

"Hmmm, OK."

Laura quickly made them crepes. Cooking was another skill she now added to her resume, and she loved it. She knew it would be a long day for him as he worried about his people searching for Caydon. He sat at the table, staring out the window, clearly miles away in his mind.

"Bevan . . . Bevan!" Laura's voice increased as he remained lost in thought.

"Sorry."

"I'm going to take Sarah and run to the office for a few hours," she told him.

"And I thought this was our holiday," Bevan said with a smile.

"Please—you'll be in the office the minute I'm gone. If we both take a few hours to tend to business now, I feel like I'll have you until Monday. I have some papers that need to be filed next week. My partners will handle that, and then I'm off the rest of the year," Laura said. The phone in Bevan's office began to ring as she finished speaking.

Bevan got up and kissed his wife. "Love you."

"I know your other children will be checking in. I'm taking General Lee with me," Laura said, rolling her eyes, and watched her husband head to his office. "General," she called, and she smiled as the he came running with his leash in his mouth.

General Lee had been a constant with her and the baby after Caydon's home visit. He too had suffered at Caydon's hands, being drugged. He was a good companion and warning system, and Sarah loved him as much as he loved and protected her.

BEVAN HAD ASKED Lane and Zack not to contact him on Christmas Day, but they were never far from his thoughts—and that included Caydon. He knew their holiday had not been like his, and he would see that they would have extra time off once all of this was finished. He sat down at his desk and answered the phone. "How are things there?"

"Cold, and it snowed last night, so we're ready to leave," Lane said.

"What did you find yesterday?"

"It's not good. Caydon has a crate of ARES Shrikes and several Beretta M9A1s. Any idea how he got those?"

Bevan was shocked; he would have to make some calls immediately to find who knew about the weapons, and how the hell Caydon had been able to get them. "I'll look into it and update you once you two are back."

"It's a major issue that needs to be tended to—and fast. I made a call to my buddy for information about these weapons, and they aren't even going to be integrated into the military for another year," Lane said.

Bevan reached in his desk, took out a bottle of antacids, and put two in his mouth. "Do you have any good news?"

"Eric seems to have been able to use his walks to leave us items that prove he was here: lanyards, a camera lens, lens covers, and Zack found two film canisters that he left messages in, including dates," Lane reported.

"Smart man."

"We sort of 'forgot' to tell Sergeant Manz about those. Zack located three bodies, a family that Caydon killed when he destroyed the castle. She also found a jacket that Eric apparently hid that survived the explosion. We turned that over to the military. Bevan, can you get us out of here, either tonight or first thing in the morning?" Lane asked.

"I'll need a couple of hours, but I might be able to arrange something for this evening your time," he told Lane.

"That's good news," Lane said.

"Pack up, and I'll call you back within the hour."

"We're on it. Oh, and one other thing," Lane said as Zack waved for his attention.

"Hurry."

"Zack asks that you send Mr. Joe to Waynesboro, since she says that's where you're going to send us from here."

"I won't even ask how she knew that, but tell her it's done."

Bevan had a chill run down his back. The reports he had received from her trainer were wrong; Zack was getting stronger. He'd made arrangements several days ago for the trainer to meet Zack in Waynesboro. Bevan wanted to be sure that she was still in control and focused. He picked up the phone and began to make the calls necessary to get them out of Austria and on their way to Georgia later that night. The next call on the weapons was something he dreaded, but he needed to find how that maniac had gotten them.

Austria
1:00 p.m.

LANE TURNED AROUND after hanging up and saw Zack breaking down their campsite. He couldn't always understand her gift, and, for the most part, it fucking scared the holy Jesus out of him. He was glad she was on his side, and he hoped her abilities would strengthen before the confrontation with Caydon. They had to be on the same page.

For the next two hours, they worked in silence, loading all the equipment into the jeep. "Anything else you want to do before we leave here—another run-through to check for more items from Eric?" Lane asked.

"No, I'm good, but what about our weapons?"

"They should be waiting for us when we leave; it was another favor I called in."

The satellite phone rang. Lane answered and listened for a few moments, then hung up. "OK, private airfield 2100."

"Sergeant Manz owes you a favor?" she asked.

"It starts with Cian, then to my buddy who dropped us off, and then to Manz. It's a guy thing."

She shrugged. "Well, I want to go, even if we have to sit at the airfield for hours."

"Let's go then."

"It's going to be a long trip back, but you'll love where we're going," she said, excited about the prospect of seeing Jace and Taylor.

"As long as I can get some PayDays, I'm good."

Zack smiled as Lane started the jeep, and they headed away from the death and destruction caused by Aaron Caydon.

CHAPTER TWENTY-THREE

Waynesboro, Georgia
Monday, December 30, 2002
5:00 a.m.

Zack had been up and out on the land with her bow since just before daybreak. The wind and cold heightened her senses. Lane had set up ten targets late the previous night for practice, and she had already found six. She had sent arrow after arrow directly into the center of each target. Now, there were just four left to find.

Since their arrival at the Long-Bowe B&B, she and Lane had taken only two days to recoup from the long flight from Austria. They both had their own way to deal: she in nature, and Lane meditating and eating PayDays. She had been so happy to see Jace and Taylor, and had been ready to hear about their honeymoon, but she'd also been surprised that Jace had known about Eric's kidnapping. Zack had asked Jace to join her that day for her training session, and Jace hadn't hesitated to say yes.

She was pleased that Lane had settled in at the house like he had always been family. They were staying with Jace and Taylor, but her trainer was at the main house of the Long-Bowe. Later that day, they would discuss the plan for their return to Honolulu.

Hearing the break of one of the sticks she had left on the path behind her, Zack turned with her bow back and an arrow ready to release. "Damn, don't shoot—it's me," Lane cursed and stepped to the side.

"Sorry. I was busy finding your targets."

"How many did you get?"

"Six—no, wait." Zack loosed an arrow, centering it in the camouflaged target just to the right of where Lane had stepped. "Seven."

Lane closed his eyes and took a breath. "I knew that was coming. We need to go back; we have breakfast and a conference call with Bevan later."

"Jace is joining me this morning with my trainer. She seems to have picked up some abilities since she's been gone."

"Any idea what's happening to bring these on?" Lane asked.

"I have an idea, but I'll let you know later once I'm sure," Zack told him as they walked back to the guest house.

JACE AND TAYLOR were standing outside the guest house, waiting for Zack and Lane to return. The last day had been short and bittersweet there on the family land. Instead of it being filled with laughter and shared memories, there was silence and shared concern for all involved in this matter with Aaron Caydon.

Jace looked at Taylor, knowing the next story in their lives was going to be difficult. She leaned in and kissed him, then asked, "Can you see them?"

"No, but I can hear them, so they're close," Taylor responded, holding her.

"Denise and Daniel called and said they'd have breakfast waiting for us."

Taylor groaned. "I think I've gained twenty pounds since we've been here. It seems we're always eating."

"Family and good food go together. You should know that by now," Jace said, smiling.

"Bill called last night and said prime rib is on the menu for New Year's Eve dinner," Taylor said.

"Lane should love that. There they are—Zack, Lane, here!" Jace yelled as the two came out of the trees.

"Did you find all of the targets?" Taylor called.

"Seven. There are three more left to find," Zack yelled back to him.

"So, why don't I smell food coming from the house?" Lane asked when they got closer.

"Because Denise has it waiting in the main house," Jace answered, rolling her eyes in good humor.

"That woman is slowly becoming a huge part of my heart," Lane said with a grin.

Taylor shoved him playfully. "Well, if you like her cooking, wait until the killer prime rib tomorrow night at the Benjamins'."

"Bevan's parents live in the area, too. His dad is a physician; he's planning to retire, but he hasn't quite yet," Zack explained.

"Interesting," Lane said with surprise.

"He's an excellent cook, and he has an outstanding wine cellar," Taylor raved.

The four walked up the road to the main house where Zack's trainer was waiting for them. The man was small in stature with black-rimmed glasses and a signature bow tie and sweater-vest. His pants were just a little high-water, and he wore plaid socks and red Converse high-top tennis shoes.

He got right to the point, saying, "Zack, I want to start . . ."

"I know, right after breakfast. Lane, Jace, Taylor, let me properly introduce all of you to my mental trainer, Mr. Joe."

"Pleased to meet all of you. Alright then, if we don't hurry, Denise is going to be most offended," Mr. Joe told them.

As everyone entered the house, the smell of pancakes, blueberry muffins, and bacon filled the air. Zack looked at Lane. "Down, boy; there's plenty."

"Good morning, everyone! Please sit down. Coffee, milk, and juice are all on the table. It's family style here," Denise said.

Lane started to reach for the food, and Zack grabbed his hand. "Grace."

Daniel stood at the head of the table. "Lord, we ask for your blessing and continued love. Keep all safe who share this table. Amen."

Zack smiled. "OK, now."

Jace looked up with wide eyes as Lane filled his plate and ate as though he had been starved. She looked at Zack. "Does he . . ."

"Always eat like this?" Zack finished smoothly. "Yes."

"I'm a growing boy, and all this peace and quiet has really stirred my appetite," Lane said as he shoveled food into his mouth.

"Lane, when is Bevan's call expected?" Taylor asked.

"After my morning session with Mr. Joe. He wanted me to have extra time," Zack answered.

"She has the direct line, not me," Lane said between bites.

"What can you tell us about Eric?" Taylor asked.

"He's around water. That's all I know right now," Zack said, then looked at Mr. Joe.

"When did you make this contact?" Mr. Joe asked.

"While we were at the castle."

"Mr. Joe, would you mind if we do Zack's session at the family cemetery?" Jace asked.

"Is there some reason for that setting, Mrs. Shaw?" Mr. Joe returned.

Jace touched the heart necklace that had belonged to her ancestors. "Please, call me Jace; and yes, there is a reason. Family ties are strong here on our land, and we should be with those who can help us."

"Then I look forward to the session with great enthusiasm," Mr. Joe said happily.

ZACK TOOK TWO blankets out of the jeep and started toward the family cemetery. The morning was cold, but the air was fresh with the smells of winter on the land. She couldn't understand why Mr. Joe had been so hard on her in the beginning of their sessions, but now she understood. That day, she needed to attempt to make connections with both Eric and Caydon. Zack looked around at the cemetery. The family was keeping the grounds and graves clear of weeds and trash; traditions remained strong there.

She watched Jace enter the gate and walk toward Martha Keens Bowen's grave. Jace turned and smiled. "I think this will be the most appropriate place for us to start," she told Zack.

"Mrs. Shaw, I noticed that you always wear that heart necklace. Was it a gift?" Mr. Joe asked.

"It's a family heirloom. It belonged to Sarah Bowen and, before that, to her mother, Elise. It has special meaning to me."

"How long have you had your abilities, Mrs. Shaw?" Mr. Joe asked.

"They have always been there. She just ignored them," Zack responded for her.

"It seems you have now embraced what you have. Why?" he asked Jace.

"Because Zack needs me, Eric needs me, and I'm tired of Aaron Caydon's interference in our lives," Jace answered.

Zack placed the blankets on the ground, and all three sat down. She reached in her pocket and pulled out the raven fetish.

"Since I have not had the pleasure to sit with you, Mrs. Shaw, I am going to ask that you close your eyes and breathe slowly and deeply. Begin to focus on what you feel and what you are searching for, and push past any obstacles that you may encounter. Since there are three of us here, our energy will multiply," Mr. Joe said.

"I ask that those who surround us, those whom we love, come and assist us today. Sarah, Susan, Mack: your family is asking for your help," Jace said powerfully.

The air was cold, but Zack didn't feel it. She focused on the raven and pushed deep, harder than she ever had before. The sounds of the wind blowing through the trees faded away. It was replaced by the sounds of water breaking on the beach, the smell of dead fish, sunshine on her face, and the voices of men. Zack was standing inside a tent; there were military cots, Eric's clothes, and his equipment. She walked toward voices outside, heading to the center of the campsite. There were Zodiacs beached and weapons, and one man was cooking on a grill. There were generators and coolers, all the comforts needed for roughing it. She looked around in all directions. He was on an island. There was no civilization; it was isolated.

"Hey, Miguel, I'm going for a run on the beach." It was Eric! He looked well, and he was tanned, but he needed a shave and a haircut. She smiled.

"Zack," a woman's voice called.

"Jace?"

"No, it's Martha."

Zack turned to look at the woman, who could have been her twin. "Are you here to help?"

"Turn and walk away. Go and find the enemy. He knows you are coming. He is preparing for you. Be strong," Martha told her.

Zack didn't want to leave, but the pull to go was greater than the need to stay. She walked back to the tent and went inside, but now there was only darkness, dread, arrogance: Caydon.

"Welcome, bitch; I am waiting, patiently waiting," he said, then reached out and pushed her. She was falling, falling, falling . . .

The last words she heard were his: "Patiently waiting."

"Zack! Zack!" Jace yelled. Zack had gone pale, lifeless. "I heard him, Mr. Joe!"

"I know, Mrs. Shaw. I heard him, too," Mr. Joe said and took Zack in his arms. "Come back. You're safe, you're safe, we're here, Zack. Come back."

Mr. Joe placed his hand on her forehead. Zack opened her eyes, looked at Mr. Joe, and then looked at Jace for a moment. Jace smiled and nodded her head, relieved to have Zack alive and responsive.

"I'm OK," Zack said to reassure Jace and Mr. Joe. She looked at the sky above them and ran her hand in the dead grass, grasping it to make sure she was truly back. She slowly sat up.

"Zack . . ." Jace began.

"I want to go back now. I need to tell Lane about all of this before he calls Bevan," Zack said and stumbled as she tried to stand.

"Slowly; we have time. You were only gone for a few minutes, Zack." Mr. Joe reached for his backpack to get some supplies.

Zack sat, looking at the raven. How was that possible? It had seemed she had spent hours away. She took a breath and started to get up again, when Mr. Joe stopped her, stern with his care for Zack. He handed her and Jace water. "Sit, rest, recover, and center."

Zack lay down and closed her eyes. "He's preparing for us."

"I know. Mr. Joe and I heard him," Jace told her.

Zack suddenly turned and smiled up at Jace. "Jace, does Taylor know you're pregnant?" Jace looked at her in shock.

"Mrs. Shaw, is this true?" Mr. Joe asked with delighted surprise.

"Yes." She blushed and smiled, but her eyes still looked at Zack in wonder.

Zack continued. "When I first sat up, I saw Sarah and Susan standing behind you with blue roses. It's a boy!"

"Amazing, simply amazing. I have not ever had the honor to be around such strong women with abilities like yours," Mr. Joe said in awe.

Twenty minutes later, Zack stood up, fully recovered, and insisted that they return to the B&B. But as they started back to the jeep, Zack thought she heard her name. She turned back and looked toward the cemetery. "Wait a moment, please, Mr. Joe. Jace, you need to see this."

Jace turned around, and tears began to run down her face. Mr. Joe actually knelt down in shock, trying to grasp what he was seeing. Standing at the gate of the cemetery were three women, arms around each other.

"Martha," Zack said in greeting.

Martha Keens, the smaller woman, reached out and spoke softly. "Be strong." The three then turned and walked away, fading from sight.

Jace walked over to Mr. Joe, who was still kneeling, and placed her hand on his shoulder. "And that, Mr. Joe, is family."

◉

LANE SAT OUTSIDE on the steps of the guest house, drinking beer and trying not to think or worry about what might be taking place in the family cemetery. He looked up as Taylor sat down next to him on the porch. He wanted to ask Taylor if he had been privy to any of the family ghosts or Zack's abilities, but he was afraid that Taylor would think he was crazy.

"Lane, you seem to be a level-headed man," Taylor began.

"I try to be."

"Have you had any issues with Zack's dead relatives since you two have been partners?" Taylor asked without batting an eye.

Lane dropped his beer and choked. "Jesus, don't tell me you believe, too."

"Let me give you a little history of our families. The Bowens have been on this land since before the Civil War. Sherman's army went through and burned the original home to the ground. The White-Shaw family was tied to the Bowens long before marriages and children. It seems that one of Jace's ancestors saved the life of one of mine long ago. A year ago, our families were involved in solving a hundred-year-old love story. My search for answers then, and my marriage and fortune now, have brought our families back together. Ghosts, premonitions, and Zack's abilities have made me change my thoughts and beliefs to a more open view of the world around me," Taylor explained.

"You believe that the dead brought you together?" Lane asked.

"Yes. It all began with the death of my aunt and the will of my uncle, who had amassed a fortune after World War II. He left it to me, along with his controlling share in the newspaper. This didn't sit well with my older brother's lust for greed and power. I would have sold him the newspaper, but he couldn't wait, and he brought Aaron Caydon into our lives. I now have been thrust into a life I never wanted."

"Do you have any regrets?" Lane asked.

"The loss of my older brother, and Eric being kidnapped. I wish that Zack had killed Caydon when she had the chance. But I have been blessed with a wife who I love and the ability, with this vast fortune, to help those in need," Taylor answered after thinking for a minute.

"Well, I haven't personally witnessed any ghosts, but I have seen some creepy shit that makes me wish I was a better Catholic."

"You two know that Caydon isn't going to just let you arrest him, don't you?" Taylor asked.

"Yeah, but we're as prepared as we can possibly be, and I couldn't ask for a better partner," Lane said.

"I'm worried for everyone," Taylor confided to him.

"I understand. Caydon is a dangerous foe, but I have confidence in Zack and her special . . . whatever you call it."

Taylor looked up as the jeep drove up to the house. "Well, let's see what happened this morning."

Lane and Taylor watched everyone get out. Lane could see that Zack was pale. He didn't have to be psychic to know something big had happened. Mr. Joe stumbled as he exited the vehicle, and he stood for a moment, steadying himself. The only person who seemed to be glowing was Jace.

"So, how went the training?" Taylor asked.

"I have information on Eric, and I made contact with Caydon," Zack said weakly.

"If you'll excuse me, I'm going up to the main house to rest," Mr. Joe said once he had deposited Zack to Lane and Taylor.

"Mr. Joe, can we drive you to the house?" Jace asked.

"No, thank you. I believe the walk will be just what I need at the moment," Mr. Joe answered shakily.

"What's with him?" Lane asked.

"The strain of a mental connection with Caydon, and visually seeing our dead relatives," Jace answered smoothly.

"*What?*" Lane asked.

"I hope they were nice," Taylor said with a grin.

"Nice and helpful—but Caydon is preparing for us," Zack responded.

"Then I'll make the call," Lane said.

Reston, Virginia
3:00 p.m.

BEVAN HAD PROMISED his wife that the check-in with Zack and Lane would be his only call that day, and that he would spend the rest of the year focused on them. But he had become very troubled over the information on the shipment of ARES Shrikes that Caydon had obtained. He would have to do the check on this alone. If what he suspected had actually happened, he knew the internal leaks were even closer to him than he'd first imagined.

"Bevan?" Laura called, and then the phone in his office rang. "Never mind. But keep your promise . . ."

"I will," he replied before picking up the phone.

"You're on speaker," Lane said.

"What's the update?"

"Zack says that Eric is with Caydon's men on an island, but she's unable to locate him because Eric has no idea where he is. But Caydon is preparing for us," Lane reported.

"How's Mr. Joe?"

"A little shaken by this morning's training session. The connection with Caydon was stronger than he had expected, and seeing my dead relatives in the cemetery caught him off guard, but otherwise OK," Zack said.

"You two are to remain with Taylor and Jace. You'll fly back with them to Honolulu and wait for Caydon to contact them with his demands. I want Mr. Joe to go with you. Keep trying to find Eric, and locate where Caydon is hiding. I'll have Ron contact you once you're settled at the condo," Bevan said.

Taylor cut in. "Bevan, money will not be an issue. I'll give Caydon whatever he wants in order to get Eric back home safe."

"It's all a waiting game, which Caydon is—and always has been—the very best at," Bevan said before hanging up.

"Now what?" Jace asked.

"We wait, like Bevan said," Taylor answered.

Lane looked as Zack picked up her bow. "Three more targets to find."

"Plus the one you didn't tell me about," Zack said. She left the house smoothly.

Lane shook his head. "Best damn partner ever."

CHAPTER TWENTY-FOUR

Honolulu, Hawaii
Tuesday, December 31, 2002
5:00 p.m.

Aaron stood on the balcony of his suite at the Kahala Hotel & Resort, drinking Dom Pérignon and waiting for Dan to return with information on the Shaws. Since his arrival on Oahu, he had obtained information on E.'s wedding in February, where Bevan would be the best man. Miguel had updated him on the status of his men and Eric. His men were used to hardships, and he had been surprised at Eric's ability to adapt to his surroundings. Aaron was pleased with the news, as it would be their home for another four to six weeks.

Aaron turned around as the door opened to his suite, and Dan entered. "Were you able to obtain clearance?" Aaron asked.

"Yes."

"Any change to their arrival date?"

"None that I can find. It will be January 3. I don't know the time frame, but I have been guaranteed an early notice," Dan told him.

"Excellent."

"Do you have anything else for me, boss?" Dan asked.

"Why, do you have plans for tomorrow night?" Aaron asked.

"Unless you need me."

"No, you're free for the next two days," Aaron told him.

"Thanks. I'm a phone call away if you need me."

Aaron walked back out on the balcony and enjoyed his view from the top floor. "If you are a patient man, all things will come to you," he said.

◉

Waynesboro, Georgia
10:00 p.m.

ZACK STOOD OUTSIDE Bill and Donna Benjamin's house, listening to the sounds of the night. She could see deer at the edge of the trees, and three coyotes were approaching the water, waiting for their next meal. She raised her bow and let an arrow fly, missing the big male by only inches, which encouraged the pack to leave.

"How did you do that?" Bill Benjamin asked, as he had observed the shot from the front door.

"Luck," Zack said modestly.

"I don't believe that. Did you forget that I've seen what you can do before this evening?"

Zack smiled. "My gift grows each day."

Jace walked out on the porch. "Your mama is on the phone."

Zack smiled. "She worries about me." She saw Jace resting her hands on her stomach. "You should tell Taylor," she said on her way into the house.

Jace moved her hands across her abdomen. "It won't be a secret for much longer."

"Congratulations!" Bill said with delight.

"Is it that obvious?" Jace asked, beaming.

"Only now that I see the same glow that Donna had when she was pregnant."

Taylor walked outside. "Well, it seems this is the place to be this evening."

"If you'll excuse me, I'll see to the champagne to toast the New Year—and I'll see what I can find that's less strong for you," Bill said with a wink, excusing himself to go inside.

"What was that about?" Taylor asked after he had departed.

"How do you feel about being a father?"

Taylor stood for a moment, trying to accept what Jace had told him. "Really? When?"

"Next September, or maybe early October at the latest."

Taylor grabbed and kissed her. "Who knows besides me and Zack?"

Jace laughed. "Bill; he said I have the same glow that Donna had when she was pregnant."

"Let's go tell everyone. I don't want to wait."

Jace and Taylor went inside and announced their joy for the coming year. Champagne and apple juice was toasted for a healthy addition to the Shaw family.

"What do you want, boy or girl?" Donna asked.

Jace looked at Zack. "Healthy."

Niihau, Hawaii
7:00 p.m.

ERIC SAT ON the beach, unshaven and needing a haircut, some new clothes, and a real shower. It wasn't exactly the New Year's Eve he had planned for, but it could be worse. It *had* been worse. He knew Zack was looking for him, but this time he had no idea where he was. Surely Taylor was home and the ransom would be demanded soon. Eric knew that Caydon would drag this out for a while. He just hoped Caydon wouldn't cut anything off—he did want children one day.

He began to pace along the shoreline. He had to keep busy, to plan, or he would go crazy. No one in Caydon's crew had left the island since their arrival. They obviously had enough supplies for now, but they would eventually need to replenish.

"Eric, come—movies!" Miguel called to him.

"No more reruns, please."

"No, we have new ones and cold beer for tonight," Miguel told him.

What the hell? There must be a drop point somewhere on the other side of the island. Time for a longer hike tomorrow—they said I had free range, he thought. "Coming," was all he said aloud, keeping his plans to himself.

CHAPTER TWENTY-FIVE

Waynesboro, Georgia
Friday, January 3, 2003
5:00 a.m.

Taylor looked around the breakfast table at everyone and tried to prepare for the long day ahead. It would be almost a twelve-hour flight back to Honolulu, plus stops to refuel. He had called his pilot and had had him arrive the day before so that they could load and be ready to leave between six and seven that morning. Taylor hoped that Lane and Zack could end this nightmare. It was time all of them had peace in their lives. He wanted his child to be safe, but as long as Aaron Caydon was alive, he would worry.

"Taylor, it'll be OK. Trust Lane and Zack," Jace said, jolting him out of his thoughts.

"Well, it's been wonderful to have all of you here," Denise told them.

"Jace, Taylor, please come back again. You're family, and this is your land, too," Daniel said, passing hot biscuits to Taylor.

"Lane, you're welcome here, too. It's been a delight to meet you. Zack, bring that tall man of yours next time," Denise teased.

"I will," Zack said gravely.

"Mrs. Long, it has been a pleasure to be here, and if it's not asking too much, could I have some of these wonderful muffins to take with me?" Mr. Joe asked as he put more butter on the one that he had on his plate.

"Of course," she answered, beaming at the compliment.

"Where's the pilot?" Lane asked, spooning more gravy on his biscuits.

"I took him out to the field about an hour ago; of course, Denise fed him first," Daniel answered.

"We should head out soon," Zack said pointedly as she noticed that Lane was adding more food to his plate.

"Restroom trips, then let's go," Lane said, shoveling down the entire plate in a few bites. He put the last bite of biscuit in his mouth with a smile.

Thirty minutes later, everyone was in the Long-Bowe van, heading to the private airfield. The pilot was waiting for them, ready to go. Zack and Jace held back for a few moments to say good-bye to Daniel.

"Denise sent this. She said it was going to be a long day for all of you." Daniel handed them a huge picnic basket and two gallons of sweet tea.

"She thinks of everything. Mr. Joe will be thrilled," Jace said and hugged Daniel.

Zack hugged Daniel, too. "Thanks for everything. Eric and I will come when we can."

The pilot closed the door after they entered the plane and turned to address everyone. "The flight will take about twelve hours, Mr. Shaw. We'll need to make at least one stop for fuel."

Zack looked over at Lane, who was already asleep. Mr. Joe was eating another blueberry muffin with his coffee. Jace had lain down to rest. She and Taylor were the only ones awake. They were both dealing with the same demon, which seemed to never rest.

Honolulu, Hawaii
2:00 a.m.

THE PHONE RANG in Aaron's suite. Before he answered, he knew that it meant the Shaws were on their way. "When will they arrive?"

"Sometime around noon," Dan said.

"Make the arrangements. I want to be there waiting for them as they arrive home."

"Yes, sir," Dan said, then hung up.

Aaron turned over in the bed. "You need to leave. The money is on the table."

"Your loss," the tall brunette said as she got out of bed and slowly dressed in front of him.

Aaron showered, dressed, and proceeded to the gym, where he spent the next two hours, then headed to the beach for a run before sunrise.

Niihau, Hawaii
6:00 a.m.

ERIC PACKED SOME water and food in a backpack and walked out into the sunrise. He looked around, knowing that Aaron's men would be awake. They had told him that he had free range of the island. He would now see just how far they would allow him to roam.

"Where are you going?" Miguel asked, standing up.

"Exploring. You said I had free range. Don't worry, I don't have enough food to last more than a few hours. Then I'll be back," Eric said.

"There are snakes and some ugly spiders, so watched your step."

"Always the bright star in the night for me, Miguel. Any chance I can get a machete?"

"You are such a funny guy. Don't get lost." Miguel threw Eric a compass.

"Thanks." Eric walked away from the camp.

"Think that's a good idea?" another of Aaron's men asked.

"Where's he going to go?" Miguel answered.

Eric walked slowly until he was out of sight from the camp, then took off at a steady running pace for the next hour. He made his way back to the beach, hoping to find something, anything, that would give him some idea of where he was being kept. Eric walked for another hour, then couldn't believe what he was seeing: seals! He had to get closer. Slowly, he walked and made it to an observation area where he felt safe. They were monk seals. Suddenly, he knew.

"I'm on Niihau," he said out loud. Eric now knew that Miguel had been lying about the snakes, probably to keep him closer to camp. There were people who lived on the island, and there was a landing pad for helicopters. This was a perfect hiding place: the Forbidden Island.

"Not a good move on your part, Eric," Miguel said suddenly from behind him.

Eric jumped; he hadn't heard anyone approaching. He adopted a cavalier attitude to cover his jumpiness as he replied. "A guy's gotta try."

"This is going to really piss Aaron off."

"Fuck him!" Eric said. He looked up as one of the Zodiacs pulled up to where he and Miguel were standing.

"You messed things up. Now we have to leave," Miguel told him.

"And just when I thought that you and I were bonding," Eric said, watching his chance to escape disappear.

Honolulu, Hawaii
9:00 a.m.

DAN STOOD ON his balcony at the Kahala Hotel & Resort, looking at the water and wishing he didn't have to make the trip up to Aaron's suite. He had always trusted Miguel. He had been able to smooth the mistake in Austria over with Aaron. The problem now of having to move everyone again due to his incompetence would be fatal. The call meant that the crew was already loading the Zodiacs to move to the landing pad. Aaron was always thinking ahead, and he had made arrangements in advance for a secondary location, should the original one be compromised. Dan had made the phone calls, and he had been assured that whatever they needed would be available when Aaron's men and Eric arrived at the new location.

He left his room and made the ride to the top floor. He took a deep breath and knocked on the door. Aaron opened it. "Is there a problem?"

"Afraid so."

"Who is responsible?"

"Miguel."

"That is his second, correct? I'll expect you to handle it," Aaron said.

"Yes, sir. I made all the arrangements for the second location. They'll arrive late tonight."

"Join me by the pool, won't you? We have a few things to go over before this afternoon."

Dan followed Aaron down to the pool. Over the years of service he had become accustomed to Aaron's attitude and demeanor when it came to the murder and disposal of another human. Dan was ready for all of this to be over so that he could disappear like Aaron and live the rest of his life in peace and luxury. He would regret having to kill Miguel, but that was the chance you took if you made a mistake in the service of Aaron Caydon.

CHAPTER TWENTY-SIX

1:00 p.m.

Zack, Lane, Jace, and Taylor stood waiting for the elevator to arrive at the penthouse. They were all tired, even Mr. Joe, who had been let off at a lower floor in a guest condo. As they got closer to the penthouse, Zack felt that something wasn't right. The elevator doors opened, and Taylor and Jace entered the penthouse before she and Lane could clear the way. Once the doors to the condo had been opened, Zack heard 1940s music. She looked at Lane and both began to draw their weapons as they entered the penthouse. The doors closed behind them suddenly, and Zack knew they were in trouble.

A man's voice behind them said, "Please, don't. I'll take those weapons. We don't want anyone to get hurt now, do we?"

Zack and Lane raised their arms in defeat, dropping their guns to the ground. He reached from behind them to gather the weapons. Zack then heard the sound of what she knew was a Taser, and she watched Lane hit the floor. She looked back at the man in anger, and she immediately recognized him: Dan DeJonghe. "Was that really necessary?"

"It was that or shoot him," Dan told her simply.

Zack walked into the main room, where Aaron Caydon sat drinking wine. This man was once again ahead of them. She could only stand by and listen.

"Please, everyone, sit down. I know you're tired after the long trip home. I am truly pleased that you brought two of Bevan's finest," he said.

"I assume you felt this face-to-face would be better than a note or a simple phone call," Taylor said, with no fear in his voice.

"And less of a chance for the FBI to trace your location," Jace added.

Caydon smiled. "We have a problem that is easily resolved. I have your brother, and you have money."

"Why is it always over money?" Jace asked.

"Mrs. Shaw, I am wealthy, even wealthier than your husband. I could never spend the wealth I have accumulated in my lifetime, even if I tried," Caydon answered.

"Then what do you want if it isn't money?" Taylor asked.

"Of course I still want the money," Caydon said spitefully.

"Then tell me what else. I'm sick of your inference in my life," Taylor spat.

"Getting to the point; I like that in a person. I want $50 million—*and her*." Caydon stood and walked up to Zack.

Taylor stood up, but Dan was quick to move between him and Caydon. Caydon turned and looked at Taylor. "Is your brother's life not worth the money and the cost of Bevan Benjamin's special agent?

"You're insane," Jace said.

"I've been told that by a number of individuals who are no longer alive to repeat it. I have plans for you, Zaveen Keens, to repay you for this," he said, running his finger down the scar on his face. "Mr. Shaw, think about my request. You have time. I've left my instructions on the table."

Caydon walked to the door and looked down at Lane. "Zaveen, be sure to tell him about your last partner."

Caydon and Dan exited and closed the doors to the penthouse behind them. "Be sure that they can't leave here for at least a few hours," Caydon commanded calmly.

"The doors will have to be removed in order for them to get out," Dan said, and he set the fuse.

◉

ZACK RAN TO check on Lane, who was beginning to move. She then tried to open the penthouse doors; they were locked from the outside. "Taylor, the doors won't open."

"The phones are all dead, even my cell. We're prisoners," Taylor said.

Zack ran out onto the balcony. A helicopter hovered; she could see Caydon aboard as one of the passengers. He smiled and waved, and she watched as he disappeared from sight. "Bastard!"

Lane slowly came to and crawled to a chair. "What the fuck just happened?"

"You got Tasered and hit the floor. Caydon wants $50 million and me in return for Eric's release. We're locked in the penthouse. Oh, yeah, and they took our weapons," Zack said bitterly.

"Think you could use that super-special ability you have and let Mr. Joe know we're screwed up here?" Lane said.

She nodded. "Jace, come with me." The two went out on the balcony and sat down. "We have to focus together. Think of Mr. Joe. We must get him to go to the ground floor and call us from the intercom."

MR. JOE HAD been enjoying his accommodations, and he loved the little balcony he was sitting on, drinking a nice glass of red wine. He closed his eyes and began to meditate to ease the stress of the long trip. It was only a few moments before he heard his name being called with some urgency.

"Mr. Joe! Mr. Joe!" Jace called.

He opened his eyes to see who was calling him. It sounded like Mrs. Shaw.

"Mr. Joe!"

"Mrs. Shaw?"

"Yes. Go down to the lobby and call us on the intercom. We're in trouble."

Mr. Joe put his glass down and went to the elevator. He was amazed at the psychic power the family possessed. He rode down to the lobby and buzzed the penthouse, waiting anxiously for a response from above.

THE BUZZ ON the intercom stopped the session on the balcony between Zack and Jace. They ran to the intercom.

"Mr. Joe?" Zack asked.

"What is wrong? How can I help you?"

"You heard us?" Jace asked.

"Indeed. Mrs. Shaw, I must spend more time with you," Mr. Joe responded with amazement.

"Mr. Joe, I need you to call this number first; it's Ron Edwards's. Wait for him there in the lobby. He'll know what to do."

"Mr. Caydon has visited you and left a mess," Mr. Joe surmised, understanding the situation.

"Yes, and we're all prisoners," Zack told him.

"I'll make the call." Mr. Joe said and then he sensed something different in Zack. There was calm, but firerceness he had not felt before in all their sessions. This quiet anger was all directed toward ending the life of Caydon.

CHAPTER TWENTY-SEVEN

8:00 p.m.

Ron Edwards, the Honolulu police, and two FBI agents were standing outside the Shaws' penthouse doors. The doors were being removed, and they would be taken as evidence in the now ongoing investigation into the kidnapping of Eric Shaw. Aaron Caydon's appearance at the condo was not what Ron had been expecting. He had called Bevan to fill him in on what he knew, then had left immediately to go to the penthouse. Ron would call Bevan again after the local police left, and he'd place the phone on speaker so all could be involved.

"We're ready," the officer said.

"Zack, Lane, everyone, step back until we get these down," Ron said, then watched as the two large doors were removed.

He and his men stepped inside and allowed the Honolulu police to interview the Shaws first. Before they began, he said, "Sergeant, if it's OK with you, I would like to speak with the agents while you take the report from Mr. and Mrs. Shaw."

"We'll have a few questions for them when you're done," the sergeant said.

"Of course," Ron replied.

He, the two FBI agents, and Zack and Lane went into the back guest bedroom. "First, we have replacement weapons for you two."

"Damn, and that was my favorite Glock that Caydon swiped, too," Lane said, shaking his head. He watched Zack follow through on checking her new weapon, adding the magazine and holstering it, and he did the same on his own replacement.

"These are Agents Jared and Billings. What were the demands that Caydon left?" Ron asked.

"They were left in an envelope, which we hid when we knew that the local police were coming," Zack said, almost whispering.

"Did you get a chance to read anything?" Agent Jared asked.

"No, we were waiting for you. Any idea how they got access to the penthouse?" Lane asked as Zack turned toward one of the windows in the room.

"The building manager is dead, and we found his body covered in money," Agent Billings answered grimly. Zack's shoulders and head dropped.

"Why would Caydon kill him?" Lane asked.

"He probably had been in Caydon's pocket for a while, and had likely asked for more money," Ron answered.

"What about the doors?" Zack asked.

"They were welded shut at the lock and anywhere else with metal. It's something I've not seen before," Ron said, looking troubled.

"What about the cell phones?" Lane asked.

"They used a signal disruptor of some kind, and it's probably still in the condo. We need to find it once the locals have left. They have jurisdiction over the murder downstairs. But my agents have been brought up-to-date on the case so far, and they will be assigned here to the Shaws."

There was a knock on the door. "Agent Edwards, a moment please," the sergeant said.

"It seems you have a kidnapping to deal with, and I have a murder scene to process. Please keep us in the loop, and we'll be happy to assist the FBI in any way that we can."

Ron shook his hand. "Thank you. I'll pass that on to my superiors."

◉

JACE WAITED UNTIL the police left, then began to make coffee and sandwiches. She watched the agents that had come with Ron begin to search the house for the cell signal disruptor and for any recording devices. She thought about the demand for money and a human life, made like it was nothing, and she shivered.

"Are you OK?" Taylor asked.

"I'm tired and really pissed off, but otherwise I'm good," she said and kissed him.

"I need to go get the envelope," he told her, and he left the main room.

"They aren't going to find anything other than the disruptor. Caydon just sat and drank wine, patiently waiting, just like he said," Zack told Jace.

"Taylor will give him all the money he wants, but not you," Jace assured her, then handed Zack a tray full of food to distribute. She brought the coffee and other drinks for everyone at the main table.

"I found it," Agent Jared said from across the room.

"Good. Let me call Bevan," Ron said. He hit the first button on his phone. "Bevan, you're on speaker."

"Everyone OK?"

"Fine, just tired. Let's see what this madman has planned."

Taylor opened the envelope with Caydon's demands. He read the demands out loud so all could hear.

$50 million total is to be transferred to several offshore accounts forty-eight hours before the release of your brother. You will be contacted with the account numbers and the amount to be distributed to each account.

The release will be February 14 at the Hilton Alexandria Old Town during the wedding reception of Ethaniel and Deanna Long. Eric will be released only when Zaveen Keens is in my custody. Further attempts to locate me or Eric until then will result in his death.

"That's pretty direct," Jace said.

"I'm concerned about his knowledge of the wedding. I know it's going to be quite a social event, but most of the details have not been made public. He's getting information that only a few people know," Bevan said.

"Aren't you the geek's best man?" Lane asked.

"Yes, and it will make me unavailable to help that day. These demands are going to make the release even more dangerous and to Caydon's advantage. There were plans for extra security due to Jace and Taylor coming to the wedding, but now we have an entirely different situation."

"Bevan, I'll see if I can come a little early so that we can coordinate with your people and the local FBI office," Ron said.

"Just so you all know, I will not allow him to take Zack," Taylor said.

"I've got that covered," Lane told him, cracking his knuckles.

"I need all of you, including Mr. Joe, back here by midweek. Lane, I need you to make arrangements and to turn in your expense reports from the last month directly to me," Bevan said.

"You don't want me to give them to Darlene?" Lane asked.

"Not this time. Ron, I'll call later," Bevan said, and he disconnected.

Ron and his agents rose from the table. "We're going to leave. Since you have to be buzzed in to get upstairs, I think you'll be safe tonight, even without the doors. If you want, I can leave these agents here," Ron said.

"Now that we have our weapons back, I think we'll be OK," Lane said.

"Caydon made his point and left. We won't see him until the wedding," Zack said.

"I'll call first thing in the morning for repairs, and it seems we'll need a new building manager," Taylor said.

"I have an idea about that, if you can authorize it. I'll drop by tomorrow, and we can discuss it," Ron said.

"I'm sure we can come to some agreement. Thank you for coming so quickly and freeing us." Taylor walked Ron and his agents to the elevator.

"Zack, I'm going to set you and Lane up out here, just because I know you won't sleep in the guest rooms." Jace handed both of them pillows and blankets.

"Thanks, we'll be fine," Lane told her.

Taylor walked back inside. "Can't say this makes me feel safe, but with you two out here, at least I can sleep."

Jace hugged Zack. "Good night. Try to sleep in if you can."

Zack watched Taylor and Jace leave, then smiled as she saw that Lane was already snoring. She moved closer to the front door area and lay down. Thoughts of that day turned to thoughts of Eric. She closed her eyes and tried to connect to him; she had to find him. But there was nothing but cold and dark. He had been moved again.

CHAPTER TWENTY-EIGHT

Fort Meade, Maryland
Friday, January 17, 2003
8:00 a.m.

Bevan sat in his office, looking over his usual reports from the week. He had other duties besides Aaron Caydon that needed his attention. His agents had returned, and they remained busy with their assignment. Their time was filled with the gym, the range, and sessions for both with Mr. Joe, which seemed to be going well from the reports he was receiving. His own investigation of the ARES Shrikes, Berettas, and the information on the wedding reception was becoming more disturbing with each inquiry.

"Boss, you called for me," E. said, walking into his office.

"Come in; we need to talk. I have information about the wedding and some things you are going to need to do in order for everyone to be safe," Bevan told him.

"I don't think I'm going to like what you have to say."

"Caydon plans to release Eric Shaw at your wedding reception. You know I'll keep you and Deanna safe, and plans are being made to keep the guests from knowing what will be happening. But I want you armed, and you can't tell Deanna until this is over."

"You aren't making my new life easy," E. said.

"Caydon isn't making anyone's life easy. I need you to make arrangements from now until the wedding to go to the range at least three times a week. You'll need gym time with Zack and Lane, too."

"I'm not an agent. What are you expecting from me?"

"For you to be able to protect Deanna and yourself if something goes wrong. Is there anything new?"

"Nothing. There is no information anywhere to be found; everything has gone cold," E. told him.

Bevan saw his top line light up. "Hit the range and begin the workouts starting today. Now go."

E. left the room, and Bevan picked up his phone. "Any news from your end, Ron?"

"No, nothing. I had my agents take over the manager duties at the condo. They seem to have settled into their new roles. Taylor and the other owners are going to have to watch who they hire a little more closely next time," Ron said.

"I assume they found other issues."

"Several. Some are minor, but a few not so much. He had failed to do scheduled maintenance, and some city taxes had not been paid; nothing that Taylor hasn't resolved. But it also seems that the late manager had been skimming and pocketing quite a bit of money. I had the manager's accounts checked, and it showed the increases matching up with what was taken from the property," Ron reported.

"No further contact from Caydon?" Bevan asked.

"None, and Taylor is making arrangements to have the money transferred once he sends the account numbers. Taylor and Jace are leaving here and flying to the B&B in Georgia a week before the wedding. Liz and I are going with them. I'll have people from the office in Virginia back me up once we arrive."

"I have two rooms reserved at the hotel. I want to have more of a hand in all of this, but I have a full schedule with the wedding and the security," Bevan told him.

"Right now, it's all in Caydon's hands, and we'll just have to wait."

"Keep me updated."

The next few weeks were going to be important if Bevan was to keep those he cared for safe. He had an appointment with the chief of police in Alexandria on Monday. The meeting would include information on the situation at hand and laying out the security plans for the wedding. Bevan had to put an end to Caydon and this madness. He would not allow his people or family to be harmed. He looked at his calendar and made a call to the range master, asking for special hostage scenarios to be set up for him.

Mathews, Virginia
10:00 a.m.

ERIC SAT IN his small basement prison, drinking coffee and listening to music. During this last transfer, he had not been drugged, only blindfolded. He knew it was cold where he had been taken, but the lack of windows added to the mystery of his location. This also meant that the ransom demands had probably been made, and it would just be a matter of time until his release.

He had asked for free weights so that he would have something to do; plus, he didn't want to lose what strength he had gained those past few weeks. He looked up as the door opened.

"Eric, you're a lucky man," Adam said, bringing in a number of free weights.

"Thanks, I need something to do. Where's Miguel?"

"Dan sent him on another assignment," Adam said.

"Hope he comes back soon. He and I have become buddies."

"Maybe," Adam said cryptically before leaving.

Eric had a bad feeling about Miguel being on another assignment for Caydon, but Adam had been with the group from the beginning, so why would he lie? He turned up the music and began to work out. He had to keep his strength just in case he would be needed in the days to come.

⦿

Fort William, Scotland
8:00 p.m.

KYLIEGH MACNIEL SAT at a small table near a window at the Ben Nevis Inn, looking at the envelope that had arrived for her two days earlier in Glenfinnan. Aaron had sent for her; inside the envelope was money and directions to his location. Aaron had given instructions for her to pack light, as he would buy her anything she needed from that point on. Kyliegh had known that this day would come, and she had been preparing for it. She had said nothing to her family or to her liaison with the police about her plans to leave for good.

Kyliegh thought of the life Aaron could give her. She was done with being an informant for the government. Each assignment becoming more dangerous than the next and Aaron was offering a better life. It had been difficult to keep that part of her life unknown to Aaron, but his absence from her for long periods of time had made it easier. All Kyliegh wanted now was to disappear with the man she loved.

"Will you be ordering now?" the waitress asked.

"Yes, and I'll have someone joining me soon," Kyliegh said before giving her order.

A few minutes later, the waitress brought her drink and food. Kyliegh was concerned that the message she had sent had not been received in time. She ate, listened to the music, and continued to look out the window for any sign of her associate.

"Feicim nár fhan tú liom," a male voice announced in Irish Gaelic. ("I see you didn't wait for me.")

"English, Cian! I don't want to draw any unnecessary attention," Kyliegh hissed.

Cian waved the waitress over and ordered quickly, then said, "You have information about a gun dealer in New York?"

"I do. And I needed to check in with you. I'm being sent by my brothers as a new contact. I will be making arrangements for shipments to be sent from the States to Scotland and Ireland," Kyliegh said.

"Hence the early meeting," Cian finished. He was never privy to Kyliegh's assignments or dealings until she contacted him with information. This just seemed to be another standard operation.

"I wasn't sure I'd be able to get away and meet any other time before I leave. There are some family issues you need to take care of." She handed Cian an envelope.

Cian looked at the information. "Drugs and guns this time?"

"Yes. I need to be gone before they're arrested. I leave on Monday."

"I'll make arrangements," Cian said.

"Cian, I need to be done after this. Every time I go on a job, it becomes more dangerous. When I return, I want to be relocated," Kyliegh said, knowing that she would not be returning.

"You know that isn't my call," Cian said abruptly.

She leaned in and said sternly, "It may not be your call, but your word carries weight."

"I might be able to help you. If you could give me more information on Aaron Caydon," Cian said.

"What kind of information?"

"Anything that will help the NSA, his location, associates."

"Why is he so important to them?" she asked.

"He has kidnapped the brother of an American socialite. The reward for his safe return could be your way out." Cian smiled.

She looked into Cian's eyes and coldly responded. "I haven't heard or seen him since the last time I contacted you. I do not expect to hear from him again."

Cian shrugged his shoulders. "I need to go. Have a good flight."

Kyliegh watched him leave. "And good-bye to you."

CHAPTER TWENTY-NINE

Alexandria, Virginia
Friday, January 31, 2003
9:00 a.m.

Zack and Lane stood on the roof of the Hilton Alexandria Old Town, checking for possible access points that Caydon's men might attempt to penetrate. The hotel's main door would be the focus point, and Zack would position herself at the back of the hotel while Lane would take the area overlooking the main entrance. They had two weeks to finalize and perfect the plans for the ransom exchange at the wedding. She knew that Caydon and his men would have to be eliminated in order for the plan to work. She would have a number of weapons with her, but she intended to add her bow to the repertoire.

"We may have an additional problem with the Wyndham being so close," Zack told Lane.

"Maybe we can get a couple of men over there," Lane said.

She nodded. "We need eyes on the roof or it could leave Caydon with an advantage."

"We need to go; Bevan and the Alexandria chief of police are waiting for us in the manager's office," Lane said.

"I'm hoping they'll let us handle as much of this as possible, along with Ron and his agents."

"I did some checking, and the police force here is not big enough to totally handle this, so I'm betting they'll be thrilled to hand it over," Lane said.

"We're going to have to dress for cold weather," Zack said, shivering.

"Don't remind me."

Zack and Lane made their way to the elevator, mentally continuing to check the stairwell and any areas that might be accessible from outside. All nonessential doors needed to be locked.

BEVAN SAT WITH the police chief and the manager of the hotel, waiting for his people. The atmosphere was cordial, and he hoped it would remain so throughout their conversation that morning. The door opened, and his agents entered.

Bevan got up to greet them, and the manager waved them in graciously. "Please, have something warm to drink. It had to have been cold on the roof."

"Thanks," Lane said, reaching for a mug of coffee.

"I'd like to get started, if possible, as I know you and the chief are busy," Bevan said, walking back over to the table where the chief of police was sitting.

"I obtained the schematics that you asked for, and based off of the information, I believe we can contain most of the entrances," the chief said.

"When the venue was booked, we knew this would be a large affair. The bride has made quite a name for herself with her clothing designs. There are a number of celebrities on the guest list, and most of the hotel's rooms are booked for people coming to the wedding. We've had to limit the media, and we have kept the information about Mr. and Mrs. Shaw coming as quiet as possible," the manager told them.

"What I have to tell both of you only complicates things. The social event itself is a nightmarish media circus. On top of that, Mr. Shaw's younger brother has been kidnapped, and he will be released from his captors at the wedding," Bevan announced.

"Mr. Benjamin, I assume that the FBI is involved in all of this," the chief said.

"They have been for quite some time, Chief. I'm aware of the limits of your force."

"I don't have the manpower you're going to need. I could possibly send five or maybe six off-duty officers, but that's all. That date is one of the biggest other than Christmas for my people," the chief responded.

"I usually hire off-duty officers and others from the surrounding area for security," the manager offered.

"This time, you're going to have to allow me, the chief, and the FBI to manage the security due to this situation with the Shaws," Bevan said.

"Are my people in danger?" the manager asked with concern.

Bevan was vaguely reassuring in his answer. "The focus on the night should be the bride and groom, as usual. I don't want your people to do anything out of the ordinary. Information of the situation need go no further than this room and to the officers on duty the night of the reception."

"My partner and I will be on the roof that night," Lane said.

"To answer your question, the man in question is a sociopath who will not hesitate to kill anyone who gets into his way," Zack said. She looked into the eyes of everyone in the room.

"I realize we can only do so much, and the number of people coming to this event makes it even more difficult, but our main goal is the safety of the guests and the people working here," Bevan said.

"We need to look at the blueprints again to make sure we haven't overlooked other possible entrances," the chief said.

"My day is yours, and I'll have lunch brought here," the manager told them.

The next six hours were spent going over the blueprints and floor plans, including those for the suites on the upper floors, all entrances in the back, and on all sides of the building. The manager contacted the Wyndham to see how many rooms had been reserved for the wedding. The list of employees, valets, and any outside caterers was given to Bevan to be checked. The chief promised to send only his men who were financially stable and who had been on the force for at least five years.

At the end of the meeting, Bevan felt somewhat comfortable with all that was coming together. As they finally left the manager's office, Bevan told Zack and Lane, "I need to see you two in the restaurant for a few minutes."

"Good. I could use some pie," Lane said.

After the three arrived at the foyer of the restaurant, Zack asked, "What's on your mind?"

"Just a minute. Can we get a table in the back, please?" Bevan asked the waitress, and they were shown to a corner booth.

"I'll have cherry pie and a vanilla milkshake," Lane said eagerly.

"Cherry pie and coffee," Zack said.

"Same, and a milk," Bevan said.

After their orders arrived, Bevan asked, "How goes E. and the gym?"

"The geek has surprised me. He's been working out. He's focused, and he improves each session," Lane said in approval.

"I heard you were a little rough on him the first couple of sessions. He complained about the bruises," Bevan said.

"I promised not to mess up his pretty face," Lane said jokingly.

"Deanna will appreciate it, that is, when she finally knows what has happened," Bevan responded.

"I went with E. to the range last week," Zack offered. "He's proficient with the revolver, but he needs to improve with the 9mm. But I think that with a few more sessions, he'll feel comfortable carrying the nine."

"I need both of you to meet with agents from the local FBI office on Sunday to check the Wyndham. I'll have Ron make arrangements."

"They'll need two, maybe three, to cover it," Lane said.

"Everybody, including E., should be at the range tomorrow morning for hostage scenarios. The next week before the wedding, continue with the gym and the range. Both of you, keep your appointments with Mr. Joe," Bevan told them. They both nodded.

"Jace and Taylor will be leaving Monday, the third for the Long-Bowe," Zack said.

"Ron and Liz are going with them, along with two agents."

"Waiting is not my favorite part of the job," Lane said, sighing.

"No one likes to wait, but it's what Caydon is best at, Lane. That is one reason he seems to be ahead of us: because he's patient," Zack said.

CHAPTER THIRTY

New York, New York
Sunday, February 9, 2003
12 p.m.

Kyliegh and Aaron sat eating a late breakfast at Junior's Restaurant. They watched the sea of people coming and going on the streets, as well as in the restaurant. They had been in New York, staying at the Marriott Marquis on Broadway, for almost three weeks. She had seen five shows and had eaten at both some of the finest and simplest restaurants in the area. Aaron had taken her shopping and had fulfilled his promise to see that she would never want for anything. He had given her diamonds and rubies, watches and jewelry, and today would be her third massage at the hotel. This life was all that she could ever hope for, now and forever.

"I have to leave today," Aaron said.

"And am I to stay?" she asked.

"Until Wednesday. I've made arrangements for you. Everything you need will be provided, and a package will arrive for you on Tuesday morning with further instructions."

"I have never asked about the work you do," Kyliegh started.

"After the fourteenth, you never will have to," Aaron cut her off.

Kyliegh knew not to ask any more. "How long before you leave?"

"As soon as we return to the hotel. The car should be waiting."

Aaron waved for the waiter and paid the bill with a hundred, not waiting for the change. They walked back to the hotel, where the limousine and driver were waiting. Dan was standing at the car.

"My love, I will see you soon, and then I'll never leave your side again." Aaron wrapped his arms around Kyliegh and kissed her.

She watched Aaron and Dan enter the car and drive away. Kyliegh returned to her room, where four dozen white and yellow roses filled the room. There was a box sitting on the table with a note.

For you, forever.

She opened the gift to find a ring with a large center diamond surrounded by sapphires. "Íosa, cabhair liom!" ("Jesus, help me.")

Waynesboro, Georgia
12:30 p.m.

RON EDWARDS SAT at the dining room table at the Long-Bowe B&B, trying to eat one more blueberry muffin. The last week had been more of a vacation than work. He had made a promise to Liz that they would bring the children and return to this peaceful place one day when all of this business with Caydon was over.

His men checked the area daily for strangers, but nothing appeared to be new or out of the norm for the B&B. Earlier that day, Ron had sat with Taylor and Jace, preparing them for the next week. He'd assured them that everyone would do what was necessary to keep them—and all involved with the wedding—safe. Taylor had been absent at lunch that day, and when he walked into the dining room, Ron immediately knew that something was wrong.

"Ron, if you have some time, I'd like to show you and your men some things out by the barn," Taylor said.

"Let me get my jacket, and we'll go," Ron said. A moment later, he and his two agents followed Taylor out to the barn. "You really don't have anything out here to show us, do you?"

"I didn't want to Jace to see this," Taylor said, pulling out an envelope.

"Caydon?"

"It arrived this morning in the mail. No one knew we were coming here but you, your men, and my pilot," Taylor said.

Ron looked at the note.

There will be instructions for you when you arrive at the Hilton.

Ron took the envelope and looked at it. "No return address. The postal mark is Atlanta." He handed it to his men to examine.

"The fact that he knows that we'll be staying at the Hilton is not surprising. Though we've tried to keep that information quiet, it just wasn't possible. We're fine with that, but this note is very troubling to me," Taylor said.

As they walked back to the B&B, Taylor hoped that Ron would discover how Caydon knew where they were. Ron had an idea about how Caydon might have gotten information about Taylor and Jace, but he kept the theory to himself until he could confirm.

"Did you guys have a nice walk?" Daniel asked, walking out to meet them.

"Very nice. Daniel, did anyone attempt to make reservations here for this last week?" Ron asked.

"As a matter of fact, a gentleman who has stayed here before called. His name is Bud Johnson, from Muleshoe, Texas. I had to tell him we were booked up with family from Hawaii this last week," Daniel said.

"Did anyone else call?" Ron asked.

"No, just Bud; he's a nice guy. I need to run to town. If you need anything, check the fridge."

"We'll be fine," Taylor said.

Ron looked grim. "I need to call Bevan and update him. Bud Johnson is one of the aliases Caydon used. He stayed here, and according to Bevan the bastard even ate dinner with his parents. He knows this area well."

"Ron, this needs to end," Taylor said.

"I agree."

Fort Meade, Maryland
4:00 p.m.

BEVAN SAT AT his desk, attempting to finish everything that he could before leaving the office. He had taken the next ten days off for the wedding and, hopefully, to close the case on Aaron Caydon. The call from Ron just verified that Caydon was still in charge, for now. Caydon's use of a known alias did surprise him, however.

He and Laura would be checking in at the Hilton on Wednesday. He still had best man duties to attend to, which included the bachelor party. Bevan and Lane would be E.'s bodyguards during the party, while Zack would be following Deanna and her party out on Thursday night, along with two female agents from the local FBI office. He had checked in with the manager, who had said that the media had gotten word of the Shaws coming. But Bevan had known that was inevitable. The door to his office opened.

"Boss?" E. asked, poking his head around the door.

"I thought you were off."

"Came in to check on a couple of things. We have a problem coming up."

"Besides Caydon and his men?"

"Afraid so, and this is something we can't fix," E. said.

"The only thing I can think of is the weather," Bevan joked.

E. nodded seriously. "There's a major storm heading this way. It should arrive sometime late on Friday night."

Bevan sat back in his chair, rubbing his temples. "How bad?"

"If it continues to intensify, record breaking."

CHAPTER THIRTY-ONE

New York, New York
Tuesday, February 11, 2003
10:00 a.m.

A aron's package arrived early on Tuesday, as he had promised, with instructions for Kyliegh. A car would arrive the next day at noon, and she would drive to a location in Mathews, Virginia. GPS coordinates would already be set in the car, and there would be a key to the property. The trip would be between six and seven hours, depending on traffic and her ability to drive in New York City.

She made a local call after Aaron's package arrived and was given an address where she could do some unauthorized shopping that Kyliegh felt was needed before her trip. She took a taxi to the address she'd obtained, arriving at a pub. A man opened the front door of the building and motioned for her to come.

"Wait here for me. I won't be long," Kyliegh told the driver as she handed him a hundred.

"Not a problem," he said, pocketing the cash.

She got out of the cab and walked up to the man at the door. "I have family issues that need your assistance."

He shushed her. "Inside," he said and then locked the door behind them. "I have what you be looking for, along with extra clips."

Kyliegh took the box and opened it. Inside were two guns: a Glock 28 .380 and a Kahr 9mm with high-capacity clips. "Are they clean?"

"Yes."

She took both weapons out and began to dismantle them. "What you be doing?" he asked.

"You dinna believe I would trust you?" she asked him as she continued to check both weapons for missing parts.

"I dinna sell junk."

"I dinna said you did, but a lass has to check," Kyliegh said. She put both weapons back together, satisfied.

"I see you be happy?"

She nodded, then handed the man a paper bag. "This should cover the cost."

He smiled as he examined the contents approvingly. "Let me know if I may be of further service to you."

"Possibly, in the future." She walked out of the pub and got back in the cab. "Back to the hotel."

"Yes, ma'am."

Alexandria, Virginia
12 p.m.

ZACK STOOD IN the lobby of the Hilton Alexandria Old Town, watching as family, agents, and strangers checked in to their rooms and suites. The information about a possible storm was making everyone nervous, but it hadn't dampened the spirits of the wedding party. Weeks of planning had come down to the next three days. She and Lane felt they were as prepared as possible for what Caydon had planned. Though she had tried over and over, she was unable to make any connection to Eric. But the sessions with Mr. Joe had heightened her connection with Lane, which was what she needed at that point. They couldn't make any mistakes or they would both die.

"This is a circus," Lane said, looking around.

"If you think this is bad, wait until the reception. I heard that two of Deanna's big clients are coming. Their bodyguards checked in with Bevan and the Alexandria chief of police," Zack told him.

"It hasn't made our jobs any easier," Lane said and opened a PayDay.

"The media has been better than expected. Taylor and Jace stopped to answer questions, and allowed some pictures. It seemed to make everyone happy."

"Whatever. Bevan wants to meet with everyone at two. He's turned our rooms into command center," Lane told her.

"Oh well. I wasn't planning on sleeping, anyway."

AARON SAT IN his suite at the Wyndham Old Town Alexandria, drinking champagne and waiting for Dan and his men to return. Eric was sleeping in a room across the hall from Aaron, and he would stay there until Friday. His plan was set. It could cause a slight problem that his company was one man short, but it had been too late to replace Miguel. A pity.

He had received word that the weather could possibly be turning against him, but if all went as he planned, they would be in, out, and gone before any storm could interfere. Kyliegh would be on her way to the house in Mathews the next day. Very soon, Zaveen Keens would be dead, his men would be paid, and he would be gone with his lover, never to be heard from again. He stood and refilled his glass as the door opened.

"We're ready," Dan told him.

"Any issues?" Aaron asked.

"None."

"I need Eric to be alert on Friday. The fog needs to be gone."

"Not a problem. The simple sleeping medication I've administered to him will be out of his system once I stop the drip," Dan said smoothly.

"I wouldn't want him to miss any of the show."

1:30 p.m.

TAYLOR STOOD LOOKING out the window of his and Jace's suite at the Hilton, worried for his brother, Zack, and everyone involved in this mess. He didn't care about the money; arrangements had been made for the transfer to occur as soon as the account numbers were received. The reach of Aaron Caydon seemed impossible. He was there at every turn, ahead of them, taunting them with his arrogance.

Jace handed him an envelope. "Taylor, this was lying on the bed."

Taylor walked over to the phone and dialed Bevan's room number. "I've been contacted."

"Damn it! When?"

"Not sure. An envelope was on the bed when we came in."

"Can you both come to Zack's room immediately?" Bevan asked.

"Yes, we'll be right down," Taylor said.

"Meeting at the command center?" Jace asked once he was off the phone.

"If you're up for it."

"Taylor, I'm pregnant, not sick. Please stop worrying. It's giving you wrinkles," she said and kissed him.

"Worry is something I will always do, my love."

TAYLOR AND JACE entered the command center, and Taylor handed Bevan the envelope. The thirteen men and women who would be involved in this plan were busy with weapons and equipment. Winter suits were stacked in one corner of the room for their use on Friday.

"You didn't open it?" Bevan asked.

"Why? I know what's in there," Taylor said pessimistically.

Bevan opened the envelope and read the note aloud.

Welcome to Alexandria. Transfer $10 million into each of these five accounts by four o'clock tomorrow, forty-eight hours before the wedding takes place. Once I confirm that the money is there, Eric and I will see all of you at the wedding reception.

It's good to see that the FBI and local police have been involved. Death to one or all, it matters not to me.

"Well, that's pretty clear, don't you think?" Zack asked, looking at Bevan.

He nodded grimly. "I want to go over this today and tomorrow morning. This bastard has been watching us. He knows some of what we're planning."

Ron agreed. "I need everyone here to make their rounds. Recheck all open areas and entrances. Lane and Zack, I want you two to the roof of the Hilton, and my men to the top of the Wyndham."

Bevan and Ron proceeded to go over everyone's duties for the next two days. Information on the hotel staff, the media, and the bodyguards for the celebrities was checked and cleared. Finally, they reached the point where they felt comfortable with the level of security, and Bevan prepared to depart.

"I'm going to be out of the loop the next two days. Please remember that this isn't just an exchange, but a wedding. We don't want any unhappy memories for E. or Deanna," Bevan said before leaving the room.

Jace walked over to Zack. "You look tired. If you don't rest, you'll be no good to any of us, and your control will be decreased."

"The long sessions with Mr. Joe, the range, the gym, and the worry for Eric: it's all beginning to weigh heavily on me."

"Bring your partner and have dinner with us this evening. You both could use a break."

"I'm not sure Taylor can afford the bill now," Zack said with a hint of a smile.

CHAPTER THIRTY-TWO

Zack stood in the shower, letting the hot water run over her. It had been a long time since she had actually slept. She wasn't sure if it was the company and laughter from the previous night or the third glass of wine, but the peaceful sleep afterward had been welcomed. Zack now felt refreshed, and she knew that Jace had been right. She skipped the gym that morning, knowing it would be filled with guests and agents.

"Partner! Are you awake?" Lane yelled from the connected door, hearing the shower running in her room. "I'm starving. Can you hurry?"

"Ten minutes," Zack yelled back and turned off the shower. She dressed, then knocked on the door.

"I don't think you've ever slept this late since I've known you."

"It was greatly needed, especially with all that's happening tonight," Zack responded.

"Ron, his agents, and the locals are meeting at noon with us for a final run-through before tomorrow."

She nodded. "I hate to miss the wedding, but I think we need to be ready here."

"We can watch the video of the ceremony later," Lane said as they entered the restaurant. "God, I love breakfast bars."

◉

New York, New York
11:30 a.m.

KYLIEGH RETURNED TO the suite after another wonderful breakfast at Junior's. She loved New York, and she had enjoyed this vacation, but now it was time to leave. She packed all the things Aaron had bought for her. For now, she would wear the ring. Kyliegh knew her life with Aaron would be without need or want, but she wondered if the life he talked about would really be enough for him. She rechecked her weapons, now loaded and chambered, and placed them in her bag.

The phone startled her when it rang suddenly. "Yes?"

"Your car is here," a male voice announced.

There was a man waiting at the Lexus SUV for her. He opened the door and took her bags. "Good afternoon, ma'am. I'm here to answer any questions you might have about the car before you leave," he said.

"I just need information on how to work the GPS," Kyliegh said.

Ten minutes later, she was on her way. She couldn't understand why Aaron was having her drive, but it conveniently settled the weapons issue. Aaron always had his reasons, but he was hesitant to ever share them, even with her. Kyliegh looked at the sky and hoped she would not run into bad weather.

Alexandria, Virginia
4:00 p.m.

RON, LANE, AND Zack sat with Taylor as he transferred the money to the five different accounts that Caydon had given him. Jace stood behind her husband with her hands on his shoulders. He waited for confirmation from each bank, then shut his computer.

"It's done; now we'll see if he keeps his word," Taylor said.

"He will," Zack said with certainty.

"What we have to worry about now is his promise to take you," Ron said.

"That will never happen," Lane responded darkly, cracking his knuckles.

"Regardless, everyone should be on their marks tonight and tomorrow. No changes unless they're given to you by me," Ron said.

"Understood," Lane said.

"So everyone have some fun tonight, but be alert. Try to keep the drinking to a minimum, and Lane remember you're the adult here." Ron chuckled and dodged a paper cup that Lane threw at him.

"At least it's a party bus for Deanna and her friends," Zack said.

"One of my men will be the driver. Are you going, Jace?" Ron asked.

"Yes, and Taylor is going with the men," Jace said.

There was somber silence for a moment, then Lane broke the tension with a change of subject. "Has anyone seen the geek?" Lane asked.

"I did about an hour ago. He and Bevan were in the gym," Ron said.

"I don't know whether he's more nervous about getting married or telling Deanna about all of this later," Zack said with a laugh.

"I wouldn't want to have to tell my new wife that I'd been lying to her for the last month," Taylor said.

"Hopefully he won't *have* to," Lane said.

"She probably knows but has faith in what he does and the people he works with," Jace said knowingly.

"Then let's not disappoint either of them," Ron said.

◉

5:00 p.m.

AARON SAT IN front of his computer at the Wyndham, checking the five accounts to make sure that the money had been transferred. He really had no doubt that Taylor would follow through, but there was always that chance. After Friday, he would finalize payment to his men, dispose of Zaveen Keens's body, and disappear with Kyliegh.

"I take it he paid," Dan said, walking in.

"Of course. What other option did he have?"

"Everything is ready. I've lowered the dosage of the drip so that Eric will begin to wake. Once he begins to come around, I'll add something for nausea. He's such a wimp," Dan said, sneering.

Aaron laughed coldly. "I doubt he feels that way, after everything that has happened to him."

Dan shrugged, then told him, "I have a tux ordered, and a stylist and a manicurist are coming early on Friday. They've been paid well to keep quiet."

"I want our men on the roof once the wedding party leaves for the ceremony. I would prefer that you not kill the FBI agents—too messy—but that will be at your discretion. Pick up the package as Eric is released."

"As I said, we're ready," Dan said before leaving to check on Eric.

"If you are a patient man . . ." Aaron said, opening a bottle of champagne.

CHAPTER THIRTY-THREE

Thursday, February 13, 2003
4:00 p.m.

Eric slowly opened his eyes and reached for anything he could throw up in. He was so fucking tired of being drugged by that piece of shit, Dan. The room was so damn dark and it smelled bad. "God what is that stench? Oh, that would be me."

Eric slowly sat up and found a light. "Thank God," he said. He then made the dim room a little brighter with another click of the switch. "I'm in a hotel."

He stood and swayed. Once he finally felt steady, Eric stumbled to the window and opened the curtains. Staring back at him was a huge piece of wood covering the entire viewing area. "Figures."

Eric walked to the door, already knowing that there would be either a guard or some kind of lock so that he couldn't get out, but what the hell, he had to give it a go. He looked out through the peephole and was surprised to find no one in sight. He turned the knob with rising hope and tried to open the door. Nothing. He pulled harder. "Come on, damn it!" He could hear something knocking when he jerked at the door; they had put latches and locks on it. "Fuck it!"

Eric abandoned the attempt and turned back to his room. He began to opened drawers, looking for the phone. Anything that could identify his location had been removed: the television was gone, and even the hotel sundries had been replaced with generic items in the bathroom. The towels were plain with no markings. For all he knew, he was at a Motel 6.

The only things of interest in the room were a new sweat suit, tighty-whities, and flip-flops. Eric resigned himself to the consolation of a shower to wash away the weeks-worth of grime from his body. Eric spent almost thirty minutes washing away the stink and dirt of Niihau down the shower drain. He brushed his teeth, used the deodorant, and finger-combed his hair. He walked out of the bathroom just as the door to his room opened.

"Nice to see that you're up and clean," Dan said.

"Fuck you. Where's the razor?" Eric responded.

"Right, like we'd give you any type of weapon."

"Oh yeah, I'm so proficient with one as a weapon; just call me 'double edge,'" Eric responded sarcastically.

Dan ignored the flippant remark. "No nausea?"

"Just a little. Any chance for a meal?"

"In about an hour, but I want you to drink this first." Dan handed Eric a large Gatorade.

"Grape's my favorite," Eric said with mock thanks. "I can only assume we're at the location where the ransom exchange will take place."

Dan gave no response. He simply took Eric's nasty clothes and left without another word.

Eric walked over to the door and heard two metal latches being locked. "It's a curse to be right all the time."

7:30 p.m.

ZACK STOOD AT the front door of the Hilton, waiting for Deanna, her six attendants, and at least another dozen women. The men had left about an hour previously due to an early dinner reservation. It would be a long night for Bevan and Lane. Her schedule was dinner and barhopping until someone passed out, got arrested, or the bus ran out of gas. She looked up as Jace, Laura Benjamin, and Liz Edwards walked out of the elevator, followed by Deanna.

Deanna hugged her. "Zack, it's so good to see you. I wish Eric was here."

"Me too."

"We've been upstairs looking at Deanna's gown," Jace told Zack. "It's absolutely gorgeous, and it's her own design, of course. I see why you're making the news and increasing celebrity clients," Jace said, turning to Deanna.

"Thanks, but some days, I just want to be on the farm in a pair of jeans and a sweater."

"Maybe we can do that in the spring—all of us," Jace said, looking at Zack with meaning.

"I would love that. Maybe Ron, Liz, and the kids could join us," Laura said.

Ten minutes later, the bus was loaded and they departed. The maid of honor stood up and opened a bottle of champagne. "Let the party begin!" she said, and the bus erupted in cheers with music and dancing in the aisle.

Zack looked at Jace with a playful smile. "It's gonna be a long drunken night."

CHAPTER THIRTY-FOUR

Friday, February 14, 2003
3:00 a.m.

Zack had escorted everyone to their rooms at the Hilton, having obtained a luggage carrier for those who couldn't stand. The other agents and she had made three trips with drunken bridesmaids to their rooms, but everyone was finally tucked away. Once Laura and Liz were safe in their rooms, Zack sat for a few moments with Jace in her and Taylor's suite. It was a good night for reminiscing over happy memories.

"Tonight brings back memories of the night I first met Taylor," Jace said, smiling.

"I was there, remember?" Zack laughed. "Taylor found you, and when he walked up and asked you to dance, it was like you were Cinderella."

"I had such a feeling of meeting someone familiar when I look into his eyes. It was like we had known each other for a long time, and that time was repeating itself," Jace said. She took a deep breath.

"It was something that was meant to be. Sometimes, forces go beyond what we can understand," Zack said, taking her hands.

Jace reached and hugged Zack. "At one time, I would have said you were exaggerating, but not anymore."

"I need to go. The men are coming back, and some of them are going to need some help," Zack said with a knowing laugh.

"I'll see you tomorrow. Promise me that you'll get some rest," Jace said, concerned.

Zack assured her that she would, then left the suite and walked to the elevator. As she made it to the first floor, three limousines pulled up with the men. Zack waited for a moment to see if she would be needed. To her surprise, most of the men were in pretty good shape. The groom, however, was another story; Lane and Bevan had to pull E. out of the car. Lane put him over his shoulder, and Bevan took several pictures, laughing.

"Zack!" Bevan called out when he saw her approaching.

"I see you had a good time. Uh, you do know that he has to be awake and at the church by two, right?" Zack asked jokingly.

"Not a problem. I have an old family remedy for this kind of a night," Bevan said, and they followed Lane inside.

"Go to bed, partner. I'll see you at seven in the breakfast bar," Lane said, adjusting E. on his shoulder for better balance.

Zack caught the next elevator up to her room. She walked to the window and looked out into the night, knowing what was at stake. After a few minutes, she headed to the shower. The water felt good, and she eventually relaxed enough to contemplate sleep. In a few hours, everything they had planned and worked for would come to an end.

After getting out of the shower, she sat on the edge of her bed and looked intently at the raven fetish. "Help me."

8:00 a.m.

ERIC WAS AWAKENED by a knock, then the unlocking of the door to his room at the Wyndham. He looked over at the only thing that had been left by his captors: an alarm clock.

"For God's sake, it's eight in the morning. What the hell do you want?" Eric asked groggily as he turned on the bedside light.

"I want nothing, Mr. Shaw," Caydon said.

Eric sat up quickly when he realized who had entered the room. Anger filled him.

"Breakfast is being brought up as we speak. You have twenty minutes to eat, then Dan will bring a man and woman in to see to your grooming needs. Please do not speak to them or ask any questions. If you should choose to ignore me, I promise you that I will kill both of them and leave their bodies here with you."

"Wow, such an appreciation for human life you have. How can I refuse?" Eric responded.

Caydon ignored the comment, and the door opened behind him. Adam brought in a tray with food and coffee for him, and Dan followed with a tux, shoes, and a coat.

"Twenty minutes," Caydon reminded him.

Eric went to the restroom and splashed water on his face, his hands shaking.

10:30 a.m.

ZACK STOPPED IN to check on Deanna and the hungover attendants in the bridal suite at the Hilton. She was surprised to see that everyone was up, with their hair and makeup being done, and no one was vomiting in the bathroom.

Zack had heard everyone talking about Deanna's dress, and she just had to see it. It was an original design that would certainly be copied once it was seen that day. It was a floor-length, long-sleeved gown made of lace, with a fifties flare. Beads and crystals twinkled along the bust, sleeves, and down the entire length of the dress. There was a white velvet coat with fur on the cuffs and hood. It was beautiful. Deanna would wear the coat with the hood up down the aisle, and then she would remove it at the altar.

"Zack!" Deanna called out as she saw her enter the room.

"I just came by to check on everyone," Zack said.

"I got your family recipe for hangovers. I can't have anyone looking bad today," she said with a wink.

"I wish you the best, and welcome to our family."

"Stay warm and take care. And Zack?" Deanna said, looking intently at her. "Finish this."

"I intend to," Zack said, then left with purpose.

LANE HAD GONE to Zack's room, looking for her. He hoped she had been able to sleep. They had to be sharp that day. He started toward the elevator, thinking she had possibly gone to see the bride.

"There you are," Lane said as she stepped out of the elevator.

"Problem?"

"No. We got E. up, and after the first round of vomiting, he's good. I gave him an old family recipe for hangovers."

Zack laughed. "I guess every family has its secret recipe. How's Bevan?"

"Good, and I checked everyone's weapons."

"I truly hope nothing happens in the church. Oh, and Deanna knows," Zack said.

"Knows what?"

"Everything."

Lane cringed. "Is she mad?"

"Actually, no. She's like the rest of us: ready for this to be over."

He nodded understandingly, then asked, "What time is everyone leaving to go to the church?"

"The men are going at two; the limousine will pick up the rest of the bridal party at three," Zack said.

"It's getting colder outside, but it will be late before the snow begins. We have one more meeting before everyone takes their positions. The church was checked last night and this morning. Two men are there now with the florist. Again, I don't think the church is where the problem will be," Lane said.

"I agree. I think the reception will be the key. For that, we have a list of all the guests who RSVP that will be checked at the door as people arrive."

"Good plan. By the way, did I see your bow?"

"Yes. It makes less noise."

Lane looked at his watch. "Time for the final briefing, and I hear that the hotel made prime rib sandwiches for us."

"Have you got PayDays for tonight?" Zack asked.

"You know it."

CHAPTER THIRTY-FIVE

4:00 p.m.

Dan and Adam moved the unconscious bodies of the two FBI agents who had been assigned to the roof of the Wyndham. Dan had Tasered, secured, and sedated the agents so that Aaron's men could replace them on the roof. He watched as his men now took their places and waved to Zaveen, then checked in on the frequency that had been assigned. Dan could not believe how stupid those FBI agents had been, writing down their codes. He bet Zaveen and Lane had nothing on them that would compromise their assignment if they were captured. As Dan left, he stopped and checked on the FBI agents. He had wanted to kill them, but Aaron had refused to sanction his request.

Dan needed to get back to make sure that Eric was dressed and to finalize all the transportation that would be needed that night. Once they were back at the house in Mathews, his job would be complete. Aaron would transfer a final payment to his account, and he'd assured Dan that Zaveen would be properly disposed of without the need of assistance from Dan.

He knocked on Aaron's door and walked in, saying, "They're all in position."

"Good. Sit down and have some champagne; the wedding is about to take place." Aaron turned the sound up on the television.

"Nice. Adam put the cameras in good positions," Dan said.

"Watch this." Aaron zoomed in on Bevan and Ethaniel.

"I need to check on Eric and make sure he's getting dressed. I'll be back in a minute."

"Bring him over. I'd like for him to see this."

Dan walked across the hall and opened the door. "Aaron wants to see you."

"Should I wear the tux or the sweats?"

"Sweats for now," Dan said.

Eric walked out into the hallway, confused as to why he was being allowed to see his surroundings.

"Eric, come in and sit down, please. I see you took full advantage of the amenities in the bathroom. You look almost like your old self. Dan, would you get some champagne for our guest? This is a celebration," Caydon said.

Eric took a glass of champagne and sat down. He looked at the television and realized where he was. "This is Ethaniel and Deanna's wedding."

Caydon took the remote and zoomed in on Taylor and Jace. Then he focused on Bevan and Ethaniel. A moment later, the camera followed Deanna and her father as they walked down the aisle to the altar. "You see, I can infiltrate any place, any time."

Eric clenched his jaw, fighting to appear calm as he answered. "Taylor paid the ransom, didn't he?"

"Why, of course, and we will be going to the reception shortly," Caydon said.

"I guess I should shower and get dressed, then," Eric said.

"I will expect you to be on your best behavior at the reception. It will be just the two of us."

"No, I won't cause any problem. Just take your money and leave."

"I intend to do just that. It's been a pleasure meeting you," Caydon said mockingly.

"I can't say the same. I intend to piss on your grave," Eric said. He finished his drink in one long swallow. "Now, if you'll excuse me, I need to get ready."

Eric followed Dan back to his room. "You'll be leaving around eight," Dan said before locking the door.

Eric kicked the door in frustration after Dan left. The reception was either in this hotel or within walking distance. That meant that Zack was close. He sat down in the middle of the floor. He had to calm down, to try to focus. Eric felt like a fool, useless and unable to help the woman he loved. "Zaveen, I'm here. Please hear me. I love you."

5:00 p.m.

ZAVEEN CHECKED IN over the radio frequency with the agents on the roof of the Wyndham, then walked toward Lane on the roof of the Hilton. The wind had increased, and snowflakes were beginning to cling to her face. She looked up to the sky as a chill ran deep to her soul. Just as she reached Lane, she heard Eric. *I love you.* At that moment, the dam broke. Visions of Caydon, Dan, and Eric flooded her mind, along with the fact that the two FBI agents at the Wyndham were down.

Lane looked at his partner and knew immediately that something was wrong. "What is it?"

"We have a problem," she said urgently, running to the back of the building. She took her bow and shot both of the men on the roof of the Wyndham without hesitation.

Lane stood in shock for a moment before his mind could catch up with Zack's sudden actions. "I assume those weren't our men."

"No."

"Where are our agents?"

"Sedated. Don't worry, they're alive—for now," Zack answered.

"And Caydon?"

"He's in the Wyndham, preparing to come here to the reception."

"With those two down, there's now less to deal with. Do you have any idea how many more there might be?" Lane asked.

"I can only see Dan and Caydon. I need to get down there and be on the floor."

"No. You need to stay put until the wedding party arrives. We have a duty to protect everyone from here," Lane reminded her.

"You think Caydon will walk through the front door with Eric, don't you?" Zack asked.

"I'm counting on it."

CHAPTER THIRTY-SIX

8:00 p.m.

The hours seemed to drag before the first bus arrived at the Hilton for the reception. It contained several celebrities and their bodyguards. The media circus began, with flashes from cameras and interviews from reporters. The local police had set up an area for the media away from the door, which thankfully kept the constant flow of guests continuing without a bottleneck. Zack and Lane watched as three more buses arrived with more guests and the wedding party. Finally, the limousine with Ethaniel and Deanna arrived. Lane searched the area with his scope. They waited as the sea of guests dwindled to just members of the media.

"Anything?" Zack asked.

"Not yet."

A moment later, time seemed to slow as Zack saw them. She reached urgently for Lane. "There."

Lane watched as two men in long coats walked slowly to the front of the building. "Zack, you have to let Ron know he's here. Be careful."

"Watch your six," Zack said, and she left the roof.

Lane continued to scan the ground for Dan. "Where are you?"

The first shot hit Lane's right thigh, and as he turned, the second shot caught him in the chest. He tried to focus; a blur of white was coming straight at him. Lane was able to get one shot off before everything went black.

AARON WALKED ARM in arm with Eric to the Hilton. He had been informed before he left the suite that both of his men had been killed by Zaveen. Adam now would have the main job of removing

Lane and clearing his path for escape. As they approached the hotel, Aaron stopped and looked up. The flash of light let Aaron know that Adam had been successful.

"You should relax. Enjoy the reception, Eric. Very soon, you will be free to go and live your life," Aaron said.

"You fucking bastard. My greatest joy will be watching you die in the street," Eric hissed.

"Such anger after the wonderful vacation you've had since November," Aaron chided.

Eric tried to shake away from him, but he felt the jab of Aaron's gun in his side. He stopped resisting, but still spat, "Your plan will never work. You're outnumbered now."

"True, Eric, but as always, I have the upper hand. Now smile, and let's have a drink before greeting the bride and groom."

"You're not serious," Eric said in amazement.

"Oh, but I am, and I have a gift that you will give them," Aaron said. He took out an envelope filled with money. "Now, let's get that drink. Rum and Coke, right?"

"With a twist of lime."

THE CROWD WAS immense, and the multiple food stations only added to the chaos. Bevan smiled on the surface and shook hands with friends and family, but he was ever vigilant to the problem at hand. He saw Ron walking toward him in a hurry.

"News?"

"Zack is down here," Ron said urgently.

"She left her position on the roof?"

"She killed two of Caydon's men, who had replaced ours at the Wyndham. Our men are on their way to the hospital. They were heavily drugged and barely alive when we found them," Ron told him.

"And Caydon?"

"He and Eric walked through the front door and straight to the open bar. He even had an invitation."

Bevan looked up as E. waved to him. "I have to go and stand in the receiving line. They decided to keep it to just the bride, groom, best man, and maid of honor. Where's Zack now?"

"Not sure, but she won't be far from Eric and Caydon," Ron said.

"Keep everyone steady. We *cannot* have a firefight in here."

TAYLOR HAD BEEN restless since returning to the hotel from the church. He and Jace had found their table with Laura Benjamin and Liz Edwards. Jace had attempted to calm his fears, but all he could think about was his brother. The money had been paid, and he knew Zack was safe with her partner, but he still had a sense of dread.

"Taylor, would you get me some ginger ale?" Jace asked, touching his arm.

He smiled. "Nausea?"

"A little."

He stood and turned to go. There they were: Eric was standing with Aaron Caydon in line to greet the bride and groom. He started to move toward them, but he felt a small but strong hand grab his arm.

"No, he'll kill Eric if you approach them. I have this," Zack said, and Taylor sat down again. He turned to say something to Zack, but she had disappeared into the sea of people. He looked at Jace.

"Let it go, Taylor. My ginger ale, please."

"Ginger ale, coming up, and a strong bourbon for me," Taylor said, and he walked to the nearest bar.

THERE WERE ONLY two individuals separating Eric and Aaron Caydon from the bride. Eric felt Caydon release his arm. At that very moment, he wanted to turn and attack his captor, to choke the life from him.

"Steady. Control your thoughts of killing me, and be polite. If you do not play your part, I will make Ethaniel a widower where he stands," Caydon said quietly.

"I'll never play a part so well," Eric said under his breath.

BEVAN COULD NOT believe what he was seeing. Eric and Caydon were about to be received by Deanna. All he could do was watch and hope that everyone knew to let this play out. He reached into his pocket and released the safety on his weapon. Bevan looked toward the door, where Zack had positioned herself. He saw that all the exits had been covered; everyone was waiting to see what would happen next.

DEANNA LOOKED UP and smiled at Eric. "Eric!" She hugged him and kissed his cheek. "I didn't think you were going to be able to make it. E., look. Eric's here."

E. looked from Eric to Aaron Caydon, who he knew well. His color faded, and he reached for his pocket, but he was stopped by Bevan.

"I wouldn't let anyone stop me from being here to celebrate your happiness," Eric said, trying to keep the strain out of his voice.

"And who's your friend?" Deanna asked gamely.

"Reginald Baltmorth, at your service," Caydon said in a chipper English accent, bowing. "My thanks to Eric for inviting me to this celebration."

"Welcome," Deanna said graciously.

Eric moved to E. "Congratulations."

"Thanks," E. said stiffly, his hands shaking.

"Mr. Long, my sincerest congratulations, and please accept this small gift," Caydon said, handing E. the envelope.

Eric moved to Bevan. "I'm happy to see you, Bevan."

"And I you," Bevan returned. He looked next to Caydon. "Thank you for joining us this evening."

"Why of course, sir, and it's so good to meet you," Caydon said.

"You'll be staying for the celebration, Mr. . . . ?" Bevan asked.

"Baltmorth, and yes, for at least one more drink."

"I look forward to talking with you, then," Bevan said, never blinking or removing his gaze from Caydon's face.

"My pleasure, as always." With that, he and Eric disappeared into the crowd.

Bevan looked toward Zack, who had already begun to move, when the lights in the room suddenly went out. The bridesmaids screamed with delight as flashing lights and loud dance music began. He turned to check on E., who had grabbed his bride and pulled her to the floor in a protective embrace.

"Bevan, the timing is off. It's too early," E. shouted over the pulsing music.

Bevan looked for Zack, but he couldn't find her in the dark crowd. He gazed back to the place where Caydon and Eric had been standing a moment earlier—they were gone. He pushed his way through the crowd and found Eric hugging his brother and crying. "Where's Caydon?" he asked them urgently.

"I don't know! When the lights went out, he let my arm go, and then he was gone. Where's Zaveen?" Eric asked.

"I'm not sure."

Ron found his way over to Bevan, holding the envelope that Caydon had given E. "You need to see this."

Bevan opened the envelope. There was what looked to be up to $50,000 in cash, along with a note.

So good to see you again, Bevan, but I have places to be and an agent to kill.

"Who else saw this?"

"Just E. We need to go *now*. I just received word that a chopper has landed on the roof."

DAN WAS DELIGHTED with how easy Zaveen had made her capture for him. She had been so focused on Aaron and Eric that his movements had gone totally unchecked. He carried her unconscious body to the roof, where Aaron and the chopper were waiting. Twenty more minutes, and he would be free to live the life he wanted.

BEVAN AND RON headed to the stairwell. Waiting for the elevators with so many guests around would be too slow, and Caydon was about ten minutes ahead of them.

"I hope you're up to this," Ron said.

"Did you forget who the marathon runner is in my house?" Bevan took the steps two at a time.

"I hope Lane has things under control up on the roof," Ron said.

Bevan was worried about the fact that Lane had not contacted them. That could mean only one of two things: he was unconscious, or he was dead.

LANE COULD HEAR talking, mumbling more than actual speech. Why was he so fucking cold? He opened his eyes and saw a chopper with "FBI" printed on the side. He didn't remember anything about a chopper in the plan. Then he saw him: Aaron Caydon. He was taking Zack's body from another man. He tried to sit up and then remembered that someone had shot him. His leg hurt and he was bleeding, but it seemed that the cold temperature had slowed down the progression of his injuries. Lane looked for a weapon; the only thing he saw was Zack's bow. His radio had been taken. They probably had thought he was dead. He was sore, bleeding, and really pissed, but he was not dead.

"We need to leave. The weather in Mathews is still clear, for now," the pilot said.

"Meet me at the house," Caydon told Dan, then shut the door.

Lane hoped that whoever had shot him hadn't searched his boot. He reached into it and found his knife. His vision was blurry, but he had to try. As Dan turned, Lane released the blade as hard as he could. His aim was low: the knife lodged in Dan's inner thigh. Blood began to run quickly from the wound, and he knew that the femoral artery had been hit.

"Shit!" Lane said. He'd only meant to injure the man, not kill him.

The door to the roof slammed opened, and Bevan and Ron ran to where Dan had dropped. They disarmed him, and both quickly realized that he was bleeding to death.

"I need EMTs on the roof *now!*" Ron yelled into the radio.

Both men turned and drew on the door as it opened behind them. Eric came running to where they all had knelt. He dropped and grabbed Dan by the jacket.

"Where'd he take her, you fucking bastard—tell me!" he screamed, shaking Dan.

Dan smiled, coughed, and spat blood in Eric's face. "You'll never find her."

EMTs arrived swiftly, but nothing they could do would save him. He died within minutes.

"Excuse me; I could us a little help here," Lane called from the other side of the roof.

Bevan ran over to Lane's side. "Jesus, Lane, you gave us a scare when you didn't check in. But it looks like you'll pull through." He motioned to the other side of the roof. "Looks like you got Dan. Any idea who the dead man in the white snowsuit is?"

"Must be the bastard who shot me. I thought I had missed him. I'm having a slight problem trying not to bleed or freeze to death here. Get me inside, and bring him," Lane said, pointing to Eric. "Wait, did he just spit on the other dead guy?"

"The EMTs are going to want you to go to the hospital," Bevan said.

"Not going to happen. I know where he took Zack."

11:30 p.m.

THE EMTS CONTINUED to argue with Lane down in the hotel room about his injuries and the need for more medical care.

"Listen, both of you. I've been hurt worse wrestling with my brothers. Give me a piece of bubble gum and an ice pack, and I'm good," Lane said.

"We won't be held responsible for whatever happens to you if you refuse treatment," the male EMT said, shaking his head.

"Then leave."

The EMTs packed their equipment and left the command center. Ron had called up the other agents and local officers from the reception, and he'd obtained a map of the area that Lane had heard the pilot mention. Taylor, Jace, Laura, and Liz also joined the group to listen. Eric stood at the window, looking at the graying sky.

"Yo, Eric. This involves you, so listen up," Lane said. Eric turned to face the group, and Lane continued. "Caydon has taken Zack to a house in Mathews. Eric, tell us what you remember of your prison there."

Eric thought for a moment, sweat beading on his forehead as he concentrated. "There weren't any windows. The floor was concrete, but the walls were made with rock or stone,"

"Rock, stone, which one?" Bevan asked.

Taylor walked over calmly and put his hand on Eric's shoulder. "Brother, close your eyes and remember. If you were taking photographs of it, what would be important to you?"

Eric closed his eyes. "Stone—the walls were made of a natural stone, and it was deep beneath the house."

"An antebellum home," Laura said.

Bevan looked up at his wife with pride. "But which one? There must be at least twenty in that area."

"Yes, but there are only two with deep cellars of stone," Laura said. She looked at the map and, taking a pen, circled two houses. "It has to be one of them."

"How did you know that?" Liz asked in amazement.

"Six months ago, I took a tour of homes in that area. I remember the guide going into detail about the deep cellars and the composition of the walls."

"What are we waiting for? We need to go now," Eric insisted.

"Guess the kid is going with us," Lane said.

"Damn right, I'm going."

"Well, we're going back to the party," Jace said. "But keep us updated."

Taylor hugged his brother. "Bring her home, Eric."

"I've called for transportation and reinforcements to meet us outside of Mathews," Ron said.

Bevan put on a vest and began to check his weapons. He looked over at Laura.

She smiled. "Don't be too late, will you?"

Bevan kissed her. "I'll see you tomorrow."

"Don't wait up," Ron said, and he kissed Liz.

"Meet me at Bevan and Laura's. We're going to take the Shaws home with us to avoid the media in the morning," Liz said.

"Well, ladies, I feel like dancing," Taylor said, and he walked them to the door. He turned and nodded his head at the men, who were armed and about to leave.

The radio acknowledged that their choppers were on the roof. "Saddle up!" Lane said.

CHAPTER THIRTY-SEVEN

Mathews, Virginia
Saturday, February 15, 2003
1:00 a.m.

Kyliegh heard the van arrive, and she knew it was Aaron. She was packed and prepared to leave at his word. She heard multiple footsteps enter the house and head down the cellar stairs. After a few moments, the footsteps came back up and retreated out the back door. She walked over to the window and watched Aaron shake the hand of a tall man before the man drove off in the van. Another of Aaron's privileged secrets that would never include her.

Kyliegh dressed, went downstairs, and put the kettle on for tea. She stood thinking about her arrival to the house earlier that week. If it hadn't been for the GPS, she would never have found it. An older man had greeted her at the door and had taken her luggage, showing her to her room. An envelope had been on the bed, containing information that Aaron would return late Friday night and that she should be ready to leave when he arrived.

The caretaker had given Kyliegh a brief history of the home and a partial tour before he'd departed. The kitchen had been warm and inviting; it had a stocked fridge, water warming on the stove, and her favorite tea next to a cup. The fireplace warming the main room had been cozy, reminding her of a winter evening back home. It seemed the only thing missing to complete the comfortable scene was a cat lounging before the fire.

Over the next two days, she had explored the grounds and the house. She'd found it disturbing that the door to the cellar had been locked. Had that been Aaron's doing, or was it just to keep sightseers out? There were no windows looking into the cellar, so it had been impossible for her to see what was hidden there.

Aaron walked into the kitchen and wrapped his arms around Kyliegh, jolting her out of her thoughts. "Hello, my love," he said, nuzzling her neck.

"Do I have time for tea?"

"Just one cup," Aaron said. He saw that she was wearing the ring he had bought her, and he smiled in approval. He unlocked the cellar door, saying over his shoulder, "I have something I need to finish while you drink your tea, and then we can go."

Kyliegh made her tea and walked into the main room, where Aaron had made a fire. She stood in front of the fireplace, but she couldn't shake the cold she felt. The locked door was Aaron's doing, and whatever he was finishing in the cellar sent a shiver through her body.

AARON STOOD OVER the body of Zaveen Keens and smiled. He was thankful that Dan had left everything prepared for him, and now all he had to do was start the IV drip hanging above her. He knelt down and shook her. "Time to wake up."

Zack opened her eyes and looked around the room. There was duct tape over her mouth and chains around her arms, legs, and chest. She stared at him aggressively.

"No fear in your eyes; interesting. I'll see if I can change that by describing the way you are going to die. First, a history lesson taught by the story of a beautiful, intelligent spy who was killed by one of your relatives, Deelyn Ernest Johns Bowen."

KYLIEGH FINISHED HER tea and walked back into the kitchen. The door to the cellar was open, and she could hear Aaron talking, but no one was answering him. She crept closer to the cellar door and began to listen to his story. The cold she had felt in the main room was nothing compared to the horror building as he continued to speak. Kyliegh knew with certainty that whoever Aaron was talking to was going to die.

ZACK WATCHED AS Caydon stood above her, as still as a prized trophy. She listened as he continued his monologue, trying to keep her anger and heart rate down.

"Bevan Benjamin is a brilliant man, and I am intelligent enough to know that you and your partner were fully briefed on me. You are probably aware that my time in the military over the years placed me in many situations of advantage during the wars," Caydon said, watching her eyes searching around the basement.

"As a child, I was able to come and go on American military bases, deliver food to German strongholds, and take part in French resistance raids. All of this occurred without suspicion being cast upon me. I was a ghost, floating in and out of any situation that would be to *my* advantage, not the governments. I garnered favors and debts that many families have paid and will continue to pay for years to come. What type of favors, you may wonder. I have always been very good at killing without thought or feeling, even at a very young age. But I was also able to save individuals and ensure that they ended up in positions of power before and after the fighting was done. The results of my actions have made me the rich man I am today and who I will be for generations to come."

Zack knew that even Bevan had no idea how far Caydon's power reached or where it would go.

"There is a story, though, that is most interesting. It involves a beautiful French woman turned German spy, Jacqueline Antoinette

Monfaire. She was a master of torture and deceit. Jacqueline infiltrated the Allied forces as a reporter, and she fell in love with an American reporter from Hawaii. His affections were not for her but for an American army nurse, Susan Bowen. Any of this sound familiar?"

Caydon watched, but there was no change in Zack's eyes or body movement.

"Then let me continue. As I said previously, a child is not a threat, and most of the time, he is ignored even when seen. I was present on the American base when Jacqueline injected Susan's friend, Nancy Small, with heparin, then kidnapped and eliminated Susan. The cuts on the small nurse bled as though she had been sliced deep. They were similar cuts to the ones you now have from the boning knife that your relative Deelyn eventually killed Jacqueline with. After that, Deelyn dumped Jacqueline's body on the steps of a Gestapo office in Paris."

He watched Zack's eyes travel along the tubing from her arm to the bag above her. He knelt down to within inches of her face. "Yes, it's heparin. I regret that I cannot stay to watch you die or to observe when the recovery team finally discovers your corpse. I now have the life I want and someone to share it with. Again, I have won."

KYLIEGH LEANED AGAINST the doorframe and closed her eyes. *He's going to murder an agent!* How could this be? The man she had shared a bed with, made love to, accepted an offer of marriage from: he was not a man, but instead was a genetically modified, murderous monster. She could not stay there, would not be a part of this madness. Kyliegh slowly backed away. She had to disappear.

BEVAN WATCHED EVERYONE quickly move from the helicopters to the two vans that were waiting for them in Mathews. The local police had two cars waiting that would lead the way to the locations in question. Time was slipping away, and Bevan knew that if they didn't hurry, Caydon would be gone and his agent would be dead. He watched as Eric climbed into one of the vans.

"Dude, I know you want to go, but . . ." Lane started.

"Shut up. I'm not about to sit on the side and wait for you," Eric said, ignoring Lane's comment.

"You're just going to be in the way," Lane responded.

"Fuck you. I've been boxed and shuffled across the world since November. I will not stand by while he kills Zack. I'm sick of that bastard! I may not be able to shoot a gun, but I didn't just lift weights for my health. Let's go."

"Let it go, Lane," Bevan said.

Ten minutes later, the groups splintered off in the vans to the two houses in question, each to their fate. Bevan made a call over his radio to Ron, who was in the other van. "Ron, keep in touch with updates."

"Will do. Keep safe, or we'll both be in trouble with the wives."

"Can't have that," Bevan said, then signed off.

"How much further?" Lane asked from beside him.

"Not far. We . . ." Bevan started, but he never finished, as the patrol car in front of them exploded.

THE SOUND OF the explosion made Aaron smile. He looked down again at Zaveen, continuing his speech. "Looks like the cavalry will be delayed, and that is my cue to leave. Let me say again, I do wish that I could stay and watch the light in your eyes leave, but the knowledge that you will die is enough. I do have a parting gift, though."

He made a cut across the left side of Zack's face, then buried the boning knife just above her right breast. She screamed in agony through the duct tape. He smiled.

ZACK HAD BEEN listening to Caydon ramble, but her main focus had been on slowing her heart rate. She knew that help was coming, but it might be too late. She watched as the knife struck, and though she tried not to scream, the noise escaped through her teeth and against the duct tape.

Zack watched as Caydon started up the stairs. He was going to get away again, and this time, he would disappear forever. With each step he took, darkness began to close in, and her eyes were difficult to keep open. She watched him turn around.

"Good-bye, Zaveen Keens."

LANE HAD BEEN the first to get to the patrol car, and he had pulled both men out. One officer was dead, and the second was hurt badly. The ambulance that had been following them was now busy. The sudden catastrophe was keeping them away from the house. He knew that this was Caydon's doing and that his partner was in trouble. He had to find a way to get there.

"Bevan, where's that map?"

Eric was at his side, and he was instantly on the same page. "We have to go, to find a way around this mess."

"Caydon is hoping that this will keep us at bay. It looks like, by foot, it's maybe another ten to twenty minutes to the house," Bevan told them.

"OK, he won't be using this road, so there has to been another one leading out," Lane said, looking around.

"There," Eric said, pointing to a dirt road partially obscured by a thin grove of trees.

"Here." Bevan handed Eric his backup revolver. "Point and pull the trigger."

Eric took the gun. "See if you can keep up," he said, taking off running with Lane at his side.

Bevan contacted Ron over the radio. "How far are you from us?"

"Not far."

Bevan gave directions to the house via the back road, then took off to catch up with Lane and Eric.

KYLIEGH HAD TAKEN one bag and was beginning to leave when the unbearable thought of another person, particularly an agent, dying at the hands of Aaron stopped her. She had wavered between opposing loyalties for years, but she could do so no longer. She would have to find a way to save the agent.

She took the Kahr 9mm, chambered a round, and waited for Aaron by the Lexus SUV that she had driven from New York. She took her ring off and put it in her pocket. Kyliegh took a deep breath and smiled as Aaron approached her.

"Time to go," he said.

"I'm ready," Kyliegh replied, and she entered the SUV as if all was normal. She began adjusting the heating controls on the center console, keeping her left hand well within Aaron's eye line.

Aaron immediately noticed her ringless hand. "Where's your ring?"

"Oh no, I took it off when I washed my hands. I'll run back in and get it."

"Quickly," he said.

Kyliegh got out and ran back into the house, heading straight to the cellar, which Aaron had left unlocked. She ran down the stairs and was shocked by the grisly scene below. Blood was dripping from every cut—so much blood! She took the tape off the agent's mouth and pulled the IV out of her arm. Blood began to ooze from it.

"Bandage it. He gave me heparin," Zack said with labored breath as she slowly regained consciousness.

"What?"

"Heparin; it prevents blood from clotting."

"God, what has he done?" Kyliegh asked with distress.

Zack's entire body tensed up. "He's coming—hide," Zack told her urgently.

Kyliegh moved to the only hiding place available: beneath the stairs. She heard him begin to walk down the stairs, his steps purposeful and methodical. She took a breath and waited.

AARON HAD WAITED patiently in the SUV, but soon well more than enough time had passed for Kyliegh to find her ring and return. Something wasn't right, but he couldn't believe that she, the woman he loved and intended to be with for as long as she lived, would ever betray him. They had to leave or risk the chance of being caught.

He'd exited the SUV and had entered through the back door of the house. He'd started to call for her, but then he'd seen the door to the cellar open. Aaron could never control where his mind went when someone betrayed or disappointed him. His thoughts went to a dark place, where reason or thought did not exist, only the need to act. She could not be trusted, and those he could not trust died.

He started down the stairs. "Kyliegh, what are you doing? If you come now, I will forgive this small indiscretion. This has nothing to do with you. It is business, and you have never interfered with my business. My love, come. We must leave," Aaron said in a controlled voice.

There was no answer. He continued to make his way down the stairs when something grabbed his ankle. Aaron lost his balance and fell to the hard rock floor. He tried to get up, but something hit him across the back of his head, and darkness took him.

KYLIEGH THREW THE piece of rusty pipe to the corner. She had to make sure that he was completely out, so she kicked him. When he didn't move, she went back to the injured woman. The chains were making it impossible to bandage her, and time was most important. She took the Kahr and shot the locks off of the chains, then removed them. Kyliegh then took off her shirt and tore it into pieces to bandage as many wounds as she could, then helped the woman to sit up.

"Can you walk? We have to get out of here," Kyliegh said.

Zack winced, but she began to rise. "I'll try."

Kyliegh put an arm around the tiny woman. "I've got you, lass."

Zack looked at the tall redhead as they headed up the stairs together, and she realized that she recognized the accent. She was having trouble focusing, but she began to put the pieces of the puzzle together. "Are you Kyliegh?"

"Yes."

Zack delved into Kyliegh's mind, looking for information to determine whether or not she could be trusted. "You know Cian?"

"I work with him," Kyliegh said.

"Bitch!" Caydon's voice suddenly echoed in the cellar below.

LANE, ERIC, AND Bevan kept an even but hurried pace. The unknown area and darkness made the going rough. Each man had fallen at least once due to the unstable ground and the presence of water-filled ditches, but all had recovered quickly and continued on.

Lane worried that they would be too late and that Caydon would escape. If that happened, he would make it his life's goal to find and deliver the justice that the villain deserved.

"Where are we?" Bevan asked.

"Not far, maybe another five minutes," Lane said.

"Stop!" Eric said suddenly.

"What?" Bevan asked in alarm.

Then they all heard it. "Gunfire!" Lane said, and the three ran toward the sound with dread.

KYLIEGH SAW AARON stand up and head toward them. She turned to Zack quickly. "Go, go, get out of here! Shut the door and find a way to lock me and Aaron down here," Kyliegh said and pushed her up the stairs, then turned her focus back to Aaron. "Aaron, stop! Don't come near me!"

"You were my reason for all this, my reason to stop and finally live," Aaron said in a voice full with agony.

"I never asked you to kill anyone. The only thing I ever needed was you."

"You have ruined everything. I could've given you the world, but now I have no choice. When I am finished with you, I will find that Louisiana bitch and choke the life from her," Aaron raged.

Kyliegh heard the door shut behind her, and she knew that it was time to make her move. She took the gun and fired toward Aaron as she moved further up the steps. He stopped moving and laughed. She wasn't sure if the first shot had hit; she needed to empty the clip into him to be sure. She watched until his body fell backward down the stairs. She ejected the empty clip and loaded a new one. Kyliegh waited, watching for movement, any movement. Slowly, she proceeded down the stairs to where he had landed. Aaron lay faceup with blood running out of the multiple wounds in his chest. This time, he would not get up.

ZACK LAY IN front of the cellar door, praying that Eric would hurry. She looked up as the front door of the house was kicked opened. Bevan and Eric entered, guns drawn. Lane had come around the back, and he entered through the open door. Eric reached her first.

"Zaveen! Answer me, Zaveen!" Eric called to her.

"Bevan, get that ambulance here," Lane said.

Zack opened her eyes. "Heparin . . . he gave me heparin."

"Jesus," Bevan said and called Ron. "We need an ambulance here *now*. Tell them she's been given heparin."

"How intense is the bleeding?"

"I don't know how she's still alive," Bevan responded in shock.

Lane ran to the kitchen and brought back towels to make bandages to replace those already soaked with blood. He looked as Eric reached for the boning knife. "Don't! Leave it until we can get her to the hospital."

Zack reached for Lane weakly. "Downstairs . . . Caydon . . . Kyliegh."

Eric picked Zack up and carried her into the main room, where there was still a fire. He held her in his arms. "I'll never leave you again, do you hear me? Never again."

"You're getting blood all over you . . . I'm tired, Eric . . ." Zack said.

"Stay awake, damn it," Eric said and shook her. "Bevan, where's that ambulance!"

KYLIEGH SAT ON the steps, shaking from anger, not fear. She felt like a fool, but it seemed that Aaron had been the master of deceit. He had many years to perfect his trade. If what he had said was true, the man was in his seventies. How could this be?

The people she now heard upstairs would decide her fate. She looked back at the body lying on the floor below and realized how lucky she had been. At that moment, all she wanted was to go home and stand on the shores at Glenfinnan. The sounds of sirens shook her back to reality.

◉

LANE AND BEVAN watched as the paramedics worked on Zack. An IV was started, and protamine sulfate was administered.

"We need to go. She's lost a lot of blood," the EMT announced.

"I'm going with her," Eric insisted.

"Go. We have unfinished business here," Lane told him, then watched as his partner was taken away.

"She doesn't look good," Bevan said.

"She'll make it," Lane said, trying to convince himself.

Bevan turned and looked at the chair keeping the cellar door closed. "I can't believe she had the strength to do that."

"Time to see who's left alive," Lane said, and both men walked to the door. "This is agent Lane Brigham," he called in a commanding voice. "Stand down, and place your hands on your head."

"Lane, it's Kyliegh MacNiel. My gun is at the door. Aaron is dead. Please call Cian."

Lane and Bevan opened the door, guns drawn. Kyliegh stood on the stairs below, hands on her head, her gun where she had said it would be. Lane motioned to her. "Come up."

"Sorry, but until we work this mess out, you'll have to be cuffed," Bevan said.

"I understand. I couldn't let him kill her. I didn't know he was a monster, ageless and soulless," she said with haunted eyes.

Bevan looked up as Ron and the FBI agents arrived. "Better late than never."

"Where's Caydon?" Ron asked.

"Supposedly dead, according to her." Bevan nodded toward Kyliegh.

"Who is she?" Ron asked.

"Apparently, not who we thought," Bevan said.

Lane looked at Bevan. "Let's go make sure he wasn't wearing a vest."

"He never wore a vest," Kyliegh said.

Lane, Bevan, and Ron headed downstairs. At the bottom of the stairs lay the body of Aaron Reece Caydon. The men were not taking any chances, and Bevan and Ron drew on the motionless body as Lane reached to check for a pulse. He opened Caydon's shirt and counted seven center-mass hits. "I don't believe he'll be coming back to bother anyone."

"Lane, check his pockets and remove everything. Find his suitcase and place it in our van. Ron, I need to talk to you upstairs," Bevan instructed, and he took Ron with him back up the stairs. "I want you and your men to take his body and place it in your van."

"Bevan, are you about to play the national security card?'

"You know me so well. I can't have his body used as a prototype for military purposes. One monster was enough."

"Any ideas on what you want me to do with it?" Ron asked.

Bevan reached in his pocket and wrote down a name and phone number. "Call this number. Ask for the man with the name on the paper. Tell him you have trash to burn."

Ron took the number and called for his agents, and within twenty minutes, Caydon's body was gone. The agents were left to secure the area while he and Lane began to talk with Kyliegh.

KYLIEGH HAD BEEN moved into the main room, where Lane had placed a few more logs on the fire. He had removed her cuffs.

"Any chance for a cup of tea?" she asked.

"I put the kettle on. It shouldn't be long," Lane said.

"Thank you."

"I'll call Cian once Bevan is here. By the way, thank you for saving my partner," Lane said.

"I couldn't let him kill her. You gotta believe me, Lane. I dinna know what he was. What's her name?"

"Zaveen Keens," Bevan said as he walked into the room with a tray and offered Kyliegh a cup of tea. "Lane, make the call, and put the phone on speaker so we can all hear."

Lane opened his phone and dialed Cian's number. "Lána, cad é an ag fuck!" Cian yelled. ("Lane, what the fuck!")

"English, buddy. My boss is sitting here, along with someone who says she's your associate."

"Kyliegh?" Cian asked.

"Yes."

"Cian, what can you tell us?" Bevan said.

"As you know she has been working with us on a number of cases involving illegal shipments of guns into the UK. It was my understanding at our last meeting her brothers had sent her to meet a possible new associate for their gun-running business. It seems she lied to me," Cian said.

Bevan and Lane looked at Kyliegh.

"I assume she is sitting there listening," Cian said.

"I am."

"Has she been involved with Aaron Caydon all this time?" Cian asked.

"Possibly but he's dead, and Kyliegh was the one to take him down," Bevan answered.

"Anyone else?" Cian asked.

"Zack is clinging to life," Lane said.

"Well, if anyone can make it, she can," Cian said.

"Thank you, Cian. We'll be in touch if we have more questions," Bevan said, and Lane ended the call. "Kyliegh, you'll need to be debriefed so that we have the full details of exactly what happened here. In order to not compromise you, I'll have Lane do it here and then keep you out of sight until arrangements can be made to get you home."

Kyliegh sat speechless for a moment before finally replying. "Then, before I leave, I have information on a gun dealer in the New York area."

CHAPTER THIRTY-EIGHT

Gloucester, Virginia
Tuesday, February 18, 2003
7:00 a.m.

It had been three days since Zack had arrived at Riverside Walter Reed Hospital in critical condition. Eric had promised not to leave her side, but he'd had to stand down when the doctors said he couldn't come inside while they were working. She had lost so much blood; he still couldn't believe she had survived. Eric had kept checking, asking for information, making a pest of himself to the point that the clerk had said that Eric would have to sit down or she would call security. Finally, a nurse had told him that Ms. Keens had been taken to surgery. He had been shown to a waiting room and told that someone would update him when they were finished. Two hours later, she had been moved into the intensive care unit to be monitored. Eric had been allowed to wait in the intensive care unit, room number six.

The storm that had been predicted had come like the apocalypse, shutting down roads, schools, and airports. For almost two days, nothing had moved out of the DC area. Bevan and Lane had arrived about three hours after Zack had been sent to the intensive care unit. Bevan had found an all-night store and had bought a set of sweats for Eric, along with a razor, toothbrush, and toothpaste. Lane had brought a large bag of fast food. Before they'd left, Bevan had said that they had company business to finish, but that they would return regularly to check on Zack.

Over the last two days, their friends had come: Bevan, Laura, Ron, and Liz. Lane had kept a watchful eye, day after day, and would sit with Zack so Eric could shower and make his visit to the chapel. Taylor, Jace, E., and Deanna all had come to check on them, too. Eric was pleased when Lane brought Kyliegh by to check on Zack before putting her on a plane back to Scotland. He'd hugged Kyliegh over and over, thanking her for what she had done to save the woman he loved.

The doctor had said that it could be a few days before Zack awoke, and he asked for everyone to give her time. She had gone into cardiac arrest during surgery, but she was recovering. She had been sedated, but the medication would diminish with time. Time was now precious, and time was what Eric would give her.

He closed his eyes. A few minutes later, he heard Zack croak, "Think I could get some water?"

He looked up and smiled, overjoyed. "Bottle or tap?"

"Whatever is cold."

Fort Meade, Maryland
9:00 a.m.

BEVAN SAT COMPLETING his report in his office, which included a full synopsis of Eric's kidnapping and release, Zack's capture, and Kyliegh's takedown of Caydon. The only detail omitted was the location of Aaron Caydon's body. He and Ron would play the pass-the-blame game for the next few months until the inquiries about who had the body of Aaron Caydon would eventually stop.

E. and Deanna were finally able to leave that morning for their honeymoon, and he had extended E.'s leave to make up for the stress at their wedding and the lost days due to the weather. Ron and Liz would stay until the end of the week with Bevan and Laura. Taylor and Jace had obtained a hotel room closer to the hospital, where they planned to stay until Zack's release. Lane was in DC for the time being, wrapping up loose ends, but he was still keeping tabs on Zack with reports from her doctor.

"Line two," Darlene called into his office.

"Thank you."

"Bevan, Zack is awake. She should be moved out of the intensive care unit in a couple of days," Lane told him over the phone.

"Good to know. Was the package delivered?" Bevan asked.

"It will be shortly; I had to make a stop," Lane replied.

"Be here in the morning by seven. There is something that needs to be done, and I'll need your help," Bevan told him.

"Clean up?"

"Yes," Bevan said, and hung up. Bevan had completed his internal investigation shortly before the wedding, and it had led exactly where he had hoped it wouldn't.

CHAPTER THIRTY-NINE

Wednesday, February 19, 2003
7:00 a.m.

Bevan had been at his office since five that morning with the warrants he'd obtained. His office and several others had been compromised by Aaron Caydon. It had taken time, but he had been able to narrow down the list to five main individuals who had assisted and allowed him to obtain classified information and shipments of weapons.

Bevan's door opened, and Lane entered with two sacks of breakfast tacos and a gallon of chocolate milk. Bevan raised his eyebrows.

Lane smirked. "Gotta keep my strength up."

"Fine, bring what you have. We're meeting the other agents in the conference room in ten minutes," Bevan said.

"How many?"

"Eight, with you as lead," Bevan answered.

"How many warrants?"

"Five."

"Anyone I know?" Lane asked.

"Unfortunately, yes. We need to go," Bevan said, and he left his office with Lane.

There were several agents waiting when Bevan arrived. When the rest arrived, Bevan laid out his plan to arrest everyone at the same time so that there would be no ability for them to alert the others. After polishing off the last breakfast taco, Lane jumped in with more details.

"I'll be the lead," he said, swigging the last drop of chocolate milk and opening a PayDay. "I want everyone at their points and ready to go at nine. Be quick, and don't allow anyone to touch their phones. They will be taken to separate interrogation rooms and questioned."

"What about lawyers for them?" one agent asked.

Bevan answered. "I'm sure most will ask for one, but this is a national security issue. These individuals are facing long prison terms for the charges that have been filed. I'm hoping that someone will talk."

"Be professional," Lane interjected. "Serve the warrant, and don't answer any questions or carry on conversation. I want you to take your prisoner and leave their office or cubical quickly."

Bevan pulled Lane away from the others as the meeting wrapped up. "I need you to come to my office when you're done. We'll do the last one together."

A few minutes before nine, Lane and the other agents left the conference room and began to make their arrests. Simultaneously, three men and one woman were taken into custody. Their offices were sealed, and their computers were confiscated. When everyone had been situated, Lane returned to Bevan's office.

"Where's Darlene?" Lane asked.

"We have a problem: she hasn't shown up for work. We need to leave now."

"I'll call the locals and have them meet us at her house."

Darlene had been Bevan's assistant since he had been promoted to the office he now held. She had always been prompt, and he could only remember her calling in sick maybe five times. He was concerned that someone had contacted her when the arrests had started that morning, which meant that there was someone else he had missed.

"Lane, call back and have the agents check to see if any of the secretaries left after the arrests this morning. We've missed someone."

Lane opened his cell phone and checked with the agent he had left in charge. "I need you to check for anyone from those four offices that might have left after the arrests, and I need the answers now," he said before he closed his cell.

The drive to Darlene's house was about forty-five minutes, and the morning traffic was slowing them down. Lane's phone rang. "Local or office?" Bevan asked.

"Office," Lane answered, and he opened his cell. "OK, pick both of them up and bring them back to the office."

"Tell me," Bevan stated.

"Right after the arrests, two secretaries left the office. One said that she had a sick child to go get from the sitter, and the other just left," Lane told him.

"I'm more inclined to it being the second, but they both need to be checked," Bevan said as they pulled up to Darlene's house.

Her car was sitting in the drive, and two local units were waiting for them. Bevan had a feeling of dread that she wasn't sick and that the arrest warrant he had for her would end up just being a piece of paper for the trash. "Lane, have the officers stand down until we get inside. For now, this is a welfare check on my employee."

Lane identified himself to the local officers and followed through with Bevan's request. He returned to Bevan. "What now, boss?"

Bevan picked up a colorful gnome on the front step and turned it over. A house key was taped to the bottom. "She told me about this some time ago. She said it was for emergencies."

"Is she married, and does she have any children?" Lane asked.

"She was married. He died a year ago. They had one son; he's military intelligence, stationed overseas," Bevan said.

"Do you think he's involved?" Lane asked.

"At this point, anything is possible," Bevan said, and he unlocked the door.

Both men entered cautiously. They checked room to room and found her in the sunroom. She had sat down in a rocking chair and had placed a pillow next to her chest to muffle the sound of the gun. One shot was all it had taken.

Bevan shook his head slowly. "Someone called her. Lane, find her cell and have E.'s team check on the house phone, quickly."

Lane made a call to E.'s office and requested the information. Then he asked Bevan, "Do you trust that person covering for the geek?"

"Yes. Tell the officers to secure the outside perimeter and to contact their supervisors. I want to keep them informed, but since she worked for me, I need our people involved."

"Be back in a minute." Lane made his way outside and watched as one of the officers called for detectives to meet them at the address.

There was a note next to Darlene for her son, claiming that she was sick and that she couldn't handle the physical and mental deterioration that was ahead of her. But Bevan knew that Darlene wasn't ill. He had received a report on her annual physical just the previous week, once he had begun to investigate her. At the end of the note, there was a simple message for Bevan's benefit.

I left information in my desk at work.

Bevan looked up as Lane returned. "The sergeant asked that we stay until his investigators arrive. What'd you find?" Lane asked.

"What I needed. I don't believe Darlene brought any sensitive information home," Bevan told him.

"Mr. Benjamin?" a female voice called.

"Yes."

"I'm Detective Cynthia Tines. Could we speak?"

Bevan and Lane walked to the front of the house to join her. "Detective, I became concerned this morning when my assistant didn't come to work and had left no message. She had been a loyal and trusted employee for many years. I was shocked to find that she has committed suicide. We have touched nothing."

They all walked back to where Darlene's body was located. The detective shook her head and looked around at the well-kept home. "Did she leave a note?" she asked.

"She did," Bevan answered and pointed to the note.

"Did you touch it?"

"No, it was in plain sight. I would appreciate you contacting me if you happen to find anything that may be of a classified matter," Bevan said.

"Was she in the habit of bringing such things home?" she asked.

"No, but with the illness that was presenting, that could be a possibility."

"Do you have a card?" Sergeant Tines asked.

Lane jumped in. "Here, take mine. That second number is my home phone," he said and smiled sleekly.

"Thank you. I'll call if we find anything. Does she have family?" she asked.

"One son. He's stationed out of the country at this time. I would appreciate the opportunity to notify him," Bevan said.

"I think that would be fine. I'll keep you informed as the investigation progresses."

"Thank you. We'll go and let you do your job," Bevan said.

Both men left the house, Bevan keeping the house key in case they needed to return. "Lane, don't say anything about this to Zack."

"Then I need to stay away for a few days or she'll know. Bevan, did you know that Darlene had some type of mental ability?" Lane asked.

"No. What do you know?"

"Zack once told me that she was able to read or reach into people's thoughts unless they blocked her," Lane said.

"And?"

"She said that Darlene had the ability to block her."

"I wish I had known that," Bevan said regretfully.

"At the time, it didn't mean much, but now it does," Lane said. His phone rang. "Good, keep them there. We're on our way back."

He turned to Bevan. "Both women were picked up. There was no sick child—no children at all—and the other one was packing when they got to her apartment."

"Seems we need to check bank accounts and phone logs on those two."

"Looks like we're going to be busy for a few days," Lane said, and he opened another PayDay.

Bevan nodded in agreement. "I want you to obtain the information and pass it off to the investigators and the prosecutor. I need to make sure that Darlene's son is not involved in any of this mess."

CHAPTER FORTY

Gloucester, Virginia
Tuesday, February 25, 2003
9:00 a.m.

Zack was up, dressed, and ready to leave the hospital. She knew it was going to take some time for the wounds to heal, physically and mentally. She had finally been able to make Eric leave to shower properly, shave, and get some clothes that fit. Taylor and Jace had stayed close for the last week and had checked in daily. She planned to take some extended time off to recover before returning to the NSA.

"Well, you're looking perky this morning," her doctor said.

"Not having to eat hospital food any longer would make anyone perky," Zack responded, smiling.

"I was going to ask if you wanted a prescription for pain medication, but since you have been refusing them, I figured you didn't want one."

"No, I'm fine."

"I need you to follow up with someone in about a week to make sure your blood counts are good," he told her.

"I have someone in mind. A good friend, actually."

"Good. I believe these belong to you. I understand the knife is a family heirloom," he said, handing her the boning knife and raven fetish.

"Thank you."

She looked up as Eric and a nurse entered her room. "Time to go!"

"I'm ready," Zack said, and she sat compliantly in the wheelchair.

"Taylor has the plane waiting. They've decided to hang out with us for a while," Eric said.

"I guess Daniel and Denise were happy we rented the big house," Zack said.

"Yep, and Bill will be making house calls."

"I need to call my parents," Zack said.

"I already did; I told them where we'd be for a while, and they're planning to see us in a month. Bevan and Lane said that they would come while we're there and for you to chill and forget about work."

"That I can do," she said with a smile.

Fort Meade, Maryland
10:00 a.m.

BEVAN SAT LOOKING at the letter and the file that Darlene had left for him. She must have known that at some point everything would lead back to her. Her ability to block Zack had made it possible to get Caydon what he'd continued to demand, but for some reason, she had never sent files about Zack on to Caydon. That information had been obtained elsewhere and the person was in custody.

Darlene's involvement with Aaron Caydon had begun while he was an agent. Caydon had known that she was up for a possible promotion into a highly classified office. He had played on Darlene's emotions and need for retribution. He had overheard her having a conversation about a family member who had been murdered overseas. He had offered to help the authorities find those responsible for it. She had accepted his offer to help, and all that he had asked was for a possible favor in the future. The file held information on the individual who had been murdered and, later, a newspaper article that recorded the torture and murder of several men. The article indicated that these men had been responsible for a number of killings, including that of Darlene's family member.

As time had progressed, Caydon would visit her and ask for information for his assignments while with the NSA. He had watched her career—and Bevan's—progress. He had helped her son when he had entered the military. Caydon had been good at threats, and Darlene's being a woman had made no difference to him. The threat to kill her son had kept the information he'd needed coming out of the office. Darlene had concluded the file with a final note for Bevan's benefit.

If those of us helping him were ever exposed, I would be contacted. He told me that the manner of my son's death would be mine to choose.

Bevan closed the file as Lane walked in. "Bevan, dude, you gotta hire someone new soon. I'm so not a secretary," Lane said.

"And don't I know it. You can't even get my coffee order right," Bevan said, teasing him.

"This box just arrived. What is it?" Lane asked.

Bevan looked at the return address. "Nothing that concerns you."

CHAPTER FORTY-ONE

Waynesboro, Georgia
Tuesday, April 8, 2003
6:00 a.m.

Zack left the big house at the Long-Bowe B&B and headed for the trees. The sun was beginning to lighten the sky. The air was fresh and clean, and the winter chill was slowly leaving. It had been six weeks since they had arrived, and that morning, she had finally begun to feel like herself again.

She'd had Eric set up targets a few days ago, and now she needed to see how well her body had healed. She spent the next two hours searching and hitting every target dead center, except the last one. Zack reached and rubbed above her right breast. "Damn it!" Caydon's mark was healing slowly, but it would heal.

She put her bow down, stretched, and waited. "You're late."

"I didn't hear you leave," Eric said, walking up to her.

"See if you can keep up today," Zack told him.

"You're gonna eat my dust today," he said and took off.

Zack smiled, and within a minute, she was up with him. They made their regular run, and then Zack turned and headed up a hill. When they reached the top, she stopped.

"Tired already?" Eric asked.

"No, I just wanted to sit. My family is coming today."

"I know, and Bill said that Bevan and Lane will be here this weekend," Eric said, sitting down beside her.

"I'm going to ask for another month off," she said after a few minutes of silence.

"Something wrong?"

"No, I just want to be sure I'm ready to go back. Every time I'm here or at home, it makes me think about working away from the city," Zack said.

"Well, you can do anything you want. I can work out of a tent if needed," Eric said and smiled.

Zack reached and rubbed her right shoulder. "I need to lift some weights this afternoon."

Eric helped rub the sore muscles, then kissed her shoulder.

"I need to go to the clinic. Bill wanted to do another test, just to make sure my counts don't drop," Zack said.

"Well, if I'm right—and I'm always right," he joked, "there will be blueberry muffins waiting for us back at the B&B, so we should go."

"If it's OK with you, let's just walk back."

"Tired so soon?" Eric chided.

"No, I just want to smell the morning and listen to the birds."

"I guess I had better stay down wind of you then."

Tulia, Texas
8:00 a.m.

BEVAN HAD FLOWN into Amarillo the day before and had driven to a small hotel in Tulia, Texas. It had taken some time to search through records, to dig into the past of Colonel Caydon, but he had finally found what he needed. He had called to the cemetery, and the plots were confirmed. Arrangements had been made locally, and now all that was left was to meet the caretaker that morning around ten.

Bevan stopped to check out at the front desk of his hotel. "Can you tell me a good place to have breakfast?"

"Right up the road and on your left. I promise you'll not be leaving hungry," the man told him.

Bevan drove about a block and pulled in where the man had told him to. As he opened the door, the smell of coffee and pancakes assaulted him. The sign said "Seat yourself," so he did. Everyone greeted him as he walked past, talking about the beautiful weather, and the waitress poured his coffee without him even having to ask for some.

"Do you need a minute?" she asked kindly.

Bevan looked at the menu. "I'll have the special."

"Bacon or sausage?"

"Bacon."

After she left, he looked around the room. There were farmers in their overalls, real cowboys in boots and jeans, and in the corner of the diner, old men were telling tall tales to each other. It seemed like only a few minutes had passed when his extremely large breakfast was brought to him.

"Let me know if you need anything else," the waitress said.

Bevan took his time, savoring every bite. When his meal was finished, he asked for a coffee to go and directions to the cemetery. The drive was short, and when he pulled into the small cemetery, the caretaker and a man in a backhoe were waiting for him. He was glad he didn't have to search for the graves. Bevan took a box out of the trunk of his car and walked up to the caretaker.

"Beautiful morning, ain't it, Mr. Smith?" the caretaker greeted him.

"That it is. Yes, I'm John Smith. Pleased to meet you. I have the papers you asked me to bring," Bevan said and handed the man an envelope.

"Don't ya worry, we'll do this right. Uh, about the cost . . ."

"Forgive me." Bevan handed the man another envelope.

The caretaker opened it and smiled. "Good, good, then let's be getting on with it." He whistled and circled his hand at the man on the backhoe, gesturing for him to begin. "It'll take about ten minutes to get to the proper depth."

archidamus

Bevan stood in the bright sunshine of the Texas morning with a feeling of peace. As the backhoe finished he waited until the caretaker motioned for him to approach the grave. Bevan walked slowly to the opening and placed the ashes of Archidamus Karsten Werner into the grave. It was then filled, and the ground was leveled. The case file and all information on Caydon's genetic make had been misfiled in his fireplace. His personal information had already found its way into the shredder.

"Well, nice doin' business with ya, but I'll be leavin' so you can say your final respects in private," the caretaker said.

He crawled up into the backhoe cab. Bevan watched him take money out of the envelope and give it to the driver. There was enough to buy his silence and deny that this had been done.

Bevan stood for a moment and looked at the lonely graves of the family before him. The only identification that they had ever existed was the dates of birth and death for Karsten and Liesel Werner. He would have to let it remain as it stood. He could take no chance of having another Aaron Reece Caydon rise from the dead.

CHAPTER FORTY-TWO

Waynesboro, Georgia
Sunday, April 20, 2003
2:00 p.m.

Bevan sat outside of his parents' house, waiting for Zack and Eric to arrive. In the previous weeks, he and Lane had been delayed due to issues at the office that were related to the arrests and the death of Darlene. He had been able to keep the investigators away from Zack, but it wouldn't be long before she would need to give her statement. He would have them come to her instead of making her come back to the office before she was ready to.

Bevan also wanted to have Mr. Joe come and see Zack before she returned to the office. She would not be able to hide her true feelings from him on what had occurred. The report from his father on Zack's condition had been good. She seemed to be healing; her blood counts were good, and his dad had seen her and Eric running daily. His only concern was that she might be working out too much.

Laura and Sarah had been in Georgia for a week already, and it was always nice to come home, to get away from the city life. Even Lane was different when he was there. Bevan had just missed Taylor and Jace. They had gone to New York to take care of business at the newspaper and to finalize the sale of Sherman's brownstone, but they would return for a final visit before they went back to Hawaii.

Bevan stood up when he saw the Long-Bowe jeep. He smiled when Zack got out. "You're looking good."

Zack cut to the chase. "Darlene killed herself?"

"Can't you just say hello first?" Eric asked her, rolling his eyes.

"Eric, I need to take Zack for a walk. Can you tell Lane to meet us out here? I think he's giving my daughter a pony ride in the family room."

Eric kissed Zack on the head. "Try to be gentle with them, will you."

"How long have you known?" Bevan asked.

"When I first saw Laura. I didn't say anything to her, though."

"Partner!" Lane picked Zack up and hugged her. "You've been working out, and you actually have a tan."

"I'm half Hispanic, remember? And I see you're dating Cynthia Tines," she said, instantly picking up the information from his mind.

Bevan looked at Lane in surprise. Lane grinned back. "What can I say? I like a woman who's in charge."

"Let's walk." Bevan informed Zack on the arrests and the file that Darlene had kept. He told her that he wanted her to meet with Mr. Joe, and that the investigators would be coming after that. "Are you up to this?"

"I think I will be. I do want another thirty days off. If I have to take a leave of absence, I will," Zack said.

"I'll check on your time and see what I can give you."

"I'm going to be gone for a few months on an assignment overseas," Lane informed her.

"Tell Cian hello," she said.

"Will do."

"Lane, I need to speak to Zack alone for a few moments," Bevan said.

Lane started to walk away. "I have more pony rides to give, anyway."

Zack waited a few minutes until Lane was out of hearing range. "So, Mr. Smith, how did you pull that one off?"

"I'd tell you, but you already know. That is one secret that you can never disclose."

"Then I need to be honest and let you know that the extra month off that I'm taking is to decide whether I want to come back or not. I need some time," Zack said.

Bevan had felt that this might be coming, but he had hoped that he would be wrong. Still, he knew it was the right thing for Zack. "Take all the time you need."

CHAPTER FORTY-THREE

Sunday, May 25, 2003
4:00 p.m.

Zack sat on the porch swing at the B&B's big house and thought about the previous three months. Her strength had returned, the wound was no longer a bother, and Dr. Benjamin had given her a clean bill of health. Most of her time had been spent eating blueberry muffins and taking lessons on holistic remedies from Donna and Denise.

Mr. Joe returned to the B&B to spend a few days with her. The sessions with him had been stressful, but she managed to control every thought, even with his constant mental interjections. Mr. Smith's actions remained secret. The investigators who came were pleasant, but they had a job to do. They interrogated all aspects of the incident, policy, procedure and all actions taken. What they didn't know was Zack had always been one step ahead of them with every question.

Taylor and Jace had returned early in May from their trip to New York, and Jace was now beginning to show more of a baby bump. They needed to return to Hawaii before she was much further along; they had a doctor at home who Bill had been sending updated reports to about Jace's progression.

Zack had received calls from Lane. He said that Cian's wife was due before Jace, and that she looked like a pregnant leprechaun. He had been in contact with Kyliegh on the case he was working on. She had made the decision to leave Scotland before the next New Year, her destination yet to be decided.

"There you are," Eric said, joining her on the porch.

She patted the seat next to her. "We need to talk."

"Well, that sounds ominous. First I have something that belongs to you," Eric told her. He took her engagement ring out of his pocket and placed it back on her finger.

"I thought I'd lost it or that Caydon had taken it."

"One of the nurses brought it to me after they took you to surgery. It was covered in blood, and one of the diamonds was gone. I just got it back today," Eric said.

They sat in companionable silence for a few minutes. Then Zack said, "I've been thinking about going back to work."

"Good. One of us should have an income."

She smiled at him. "I've made a decision . . ."

Zack never finished, as Taylor ran out onto the porch. "Jace is bleeding! Bill is on his way."

Zack and Eric ran inside and upstairs. Jace was sitting with a towel between her legs. The door downstairs opened, and Bill called to them. "Bring her down; we need to go *now*."

"I can walk," Jace said, trying to stand up.

"No, you can't," Zack said. Taylor picked her up and headed downstairs.

"Take her to my car," Bill said.

Everyone piled into Bill's car, and a quick trip was made to the hospital. Jace was taken to the maternity unit, where she was quickly triaged. An ultrasound was completed, and she was admitted for overnight observation. When they were allowed into the room, Jace had an IV and was somewhat annoyed by everything that was going on.

"You are such a nurse," Zack said.

"Jace, it appears you may have a small placental abruption, so you will be here for a few days, and your trip home is not possible at this time. I would suggest bed rest for a few weeks at least. I'll have a specialist come see you in a couple of days," Bill told her.

"Then we'll stay, and she can have the baby here," Taylor said.

"Uh, I'd appreciate it if you'd include me in your decisions," Jace told him with irritation.

"Once the specialist sees you, I feel you'll be able to go back to the B&B. But you'll need to rest, and I'll need to check on you more regularly," Bill said.

"As long as I don't have to stay here. I would never get any rest here; no one knows how to let patients rest in a hospital," Jace said moodily.

"Jace, this time you have to be the patient," Zack said sternly but lovingly.

"Please," Taylor pleaded.

"Good, we're agreed then," Bill said. "Now I'll take anyone back to the B&B who wants to go. Taylor, she's in good hands here. Call when you're ready to come home."

"Taylor, please go back with them. You're not going to want to be around me tonight," Jace said.

"I'll be back tomorrow," Taylor promised before leaving with the others.

THE DRIVE BACK was filled with questions from Taylor. Zack watched as Bill tried to reassure Taylor that these things did happen and that they could be resolved with rest and time. When they got back, Taylor shook hands with Bill, then turned to Eric and Zack.

"I need to call home and have Bentwood tend to some business issues that are pending. Sometimes being rich *does* have its advantages."

"Well, how about we get back to that conversation we didn't finish," Eric said to Zack. "How about we sit in the swing at the guest house; that's my favorite spot."

They walked over to it and sat down. The boards made a creaking sound as Eric pushed them in a slow rhythmic sway. Eric pulled Zack to him. "What were you going to tell me?"

"I've made a decision to leave the NSA. It seems I can be of help here until Jace has the baby. I'll need to go back to pack up my apartment and give my notice, but I think I should find something with just a little less stress."

"Any idea what you want to do?"

"Maybe some consulting. There are many areas I can be of help with: missing persons, lost children, and I'm sure Bevan will be able to use me on certain cases."

"Is there money in that type of work?"

Zack laughed. "Yeah, I think I can make a decent living."

"Good, you had me worried there for a moment," Eric said and hugged her. "You know I'm joking. You should do whatever you want to do, or you can do nothing at all. Taylor increased my allowance."

"I guess the only thing left is to plan a wedding. I do have a favor to ask on that."

"What, do you want a million-dollar wedding?" he teased.

"No—an Irish wedding," Zack said happily.

"But . . . we're not Irish."

"That's OK. I think they'll make an exception."

He shrugged. "Sounds good. Pick a date."

"March 17, 2004: St. Patrick's Day. I need a little time to pull this together, and Jace needs to be there."

"Oh, good. I need some time to save up," Eric said jokingly.

Zack stood up. "I'm going to walk up to the main house. Daniel and Denise need to know what's going on and that we're going to be here for a while."

"Bring back some pie," Eric told her.

She waved at him as she left. Eric looked up as Taylor walked toward him with two beers a moment later. He called Taylor over. "Sit, bro. We need to talk."

"Where's Zack going? Wait, pie?" Taylor said longingly.

Eric laughed. "Hopefully she'll bring back enough for you."

"What's on your mind?" Taylor asked.

"Zack's resigning," Eric told him.

"Really? What's she going to do?"

"She said something about a circus and mind reading. Thought we'd travel the circuit for a few years," Eric responded playfully.

"OK, and when are you planning to do this?"

"After we get married next year in Ireland. I'm gonna need a best man."

"I think I can manage that. You know, I really thought I'd lost you," Taylor told him, his voice getting a bit hoarse.

"Not a chance. But did you ever get a refund on me?"

"Actually, Bevan was able to get all but $10 million of it back. I really didn't care about the money. All that mattered was you."

"Ah, stop it; you're gonna make me cry. But thanks," Eric said.

"Anytime," Taylor said and wrapped his arm around Eric's shoulder. "By the way, any job prospects?"

"I've been doing some work for a small magazine in town. Zack threatened to shoot me after the first month of hovering over her, so I decided to check things out and got the job. It will last for as long as I'm here."

"So I can cut your allowance in half?"

"Uh, no. I've got a wedding coming up and a fiancée with no job," Eric responded.

Taylor laughed. "Here's to my child and to your wedding."

"I'll drink to that. Oh, look: pie!" Eric said and nodded toward Zack, who was walking back with a basket.

CHAPTER FORTY-FOUR

Sunday, June 1, 2003
9:00 a.m.

Jace was coming back to the B&B's big house later that day after a week in the hospital. The downstairs bedroom was set up so Jace didn't have to walk upstairs. The previous week Zack had contacted Bevan to inform him she was sending a letter of resignation. He hadn't seemed surprised, and said the NSA would be able to use her as a consultant. She was surprised to learn there was still paid time left that included three weeks of vacation pay. Zack knew with the wedding she would now need more money. She had been taught at an early age by her parents to be frugal and prepared. The savings account that she'd never borrowed from would now be used until she could begin to accept consultant jobs. Zack confirmed the wedding date with Bevan and he assured her everyone would be there.

Zack wanted Jace to be settled at the big house before she and Eric headed to Alexandria to pack up her apartment. The apartment manager had been more than agreeable to allow her to break the lease once informed of all that had occurred. They would then go home to Louisiana. Eric would ask her papa for his permission to marry her. Traditions were still important, and her mama would expect him to make the proper request.

Zack had also called Lane to ask that he make arrangements and contacts for her at St. Teresa's Church in Dublin. She was sure that the church would want the two of them over there at least a month before the wedding for premarital counseling. Zack smiled, thinking about how happy her mother would be—and hopefully excited—about going to Ireland. Lane had said he would have Cian call in more favors to help with the arrangements.

She heard the front door open, breaking her out of her thoughts, and she ran out to greet Jace and Taylor. "For God's sake, Taylor, I can walk!" Jace said as she came in.

Zack laughed. "Everything is set up for you in the downstairs bedroom: the TV has been moved, movies have been bought, and I got you some books to read."

"Great. I hope this issue doesn't last the rest of the pregnancy," Jace said.

"Bill said he'll be over to check on you and the baby this evening," Taylor said.

"OK. Someone get me some pie while I go change and get in bed."

"I hope she didn't want cherry," Eric said mischievously, walking in with a nearly empty pie tin in one hand and a sticky fork in the other.

"I heard that."

CHAPTER FORTY-FIVE

Morgan City, Louisiana
Sunday, August 10, 2003
6:00 p.m.

Zack and Eric had accomplished everything they had planned since leaving Waynesboro. They had sold everything they could in terms of furniture, and she had boxed and shipped what was left to her parents' house. When they had arrived home to Louisiana for the Fourth of July, it had seemed the whole parish was there celebrating. Eric had managed to take her father aside and properly ask for permission to marry her. Her papa had said yes, of course, and then he had made an announcement to the entire parish. It had become more than a celebration of independence; it became a very drunken engagement party.

During their time with her parents, Zack had never spoken of what had happened to her, but her papa had known. Her mama had been hesitant at first about having the wedding in Ireland, but Zack had explained her reasons, and both her parents had agreed to honor Zack's wishes. They would go to Ireland.

She had been happy to be back home, and she had a habit of disappearing into the land for several days at a time. Zack had known that Eric would understand the need she had to be alone on home ground. She would always love him for giving her space when asked. After she returned from her most recent time out in the land, they sat outside, looking at the stars.

"Are you ready to leave?" Eric asked.

"Not really. It's always hard to leave. But . . ."

"Zack, there's a call for you," her papa said.

Zack sat up, saying "Jace," and Eric knew all too well the look on her face. She ran into the house and grabbed the phone. "Taylor?"

"We're at the hospital. It looks like this baby is coming a little early: Jace is in labor!"

"We'll leave first thing tomorrow. Is she OK? No bleeding?" Zack asked.

"No, her water broke, and they aren't going to stop the labor. For now, everything is good," Taylor said.

"Taylor, I expect an expensive cigar," Eric yelled toward the phone, close to Zack.

Taylor laughed. "See you tomorrow."

"Everything good?" her papa asked cautiously.

"Yes," Zack said, beaming.

"Good, then we drink to the birth of family," he said.

CHAPTER FORTY-SIX

Waynesboro, Georgia
Monday, August 11, 2003
4:30 a.m.

Taylor stood inside Burke Medical Center, looking at his son, who had been born just minutes earlier at 4:26 a.m. The neonatal physician had been present at Bill's request due to Jace's early date. Their son may have been early, but his lungs were working well. Jace had done beautifully, and the labor process had progressed quickly.

"Bill, I think he's going to be OK, but I want to watch him in the nursery. Let's weigh him and let Mom hold him for a few minutes before we go," the pediatrician said.

"Any guesses at the weight, Taylor?" Bill asked.

"No. He looks so small," Taylor said as he took some pictures with the disposable camera he had bought on their way to the hospital.

"Five pounds even," the nurse announced.

"I think you were maybe a week further than you thought, Jace. If his sugars are good, I think he'll be able to go home with you in a few days," Bill said.

Jace took her son, and tears ran down her face. She held her son close and kissed him. "I'll come to the nursery and feed him once my legs are working again."

Bill laughed. "Dr. Delbert Ulysses Baxter, anesthesiologist, is a good man, but he may be just a little heavy-handed with the epidurals. We call them a 'Dub's special.' Now, let me take the first family photo.

Bill took several pictures to save this moment. Taylor also insisted on a picture of Bill holding his son.

"I need to take him to the nursery," the nurse said after a few minutes.

Taylor took his son and placed him in the bassinet. "Can I go with you?"

"Of course. You can watch everything we do from the windows. The bands on the baby match yours and Mom's. Don't take the band off until you go home."

Taylor walked over and kissed Jace. He followed the nurse to the nursery and watched them place his son in a warmer. The baby was measured, given eye medication and shots, and then something wonderful happened. The nursery door opened, and the nurse poked her head out. "Mr. Shaw, would you like to give your son his first bath?" she asked.

"Is that permitted?"

"Yes, and when your wife is able to come, he needs to eat," she told Taylor.

Taylor bathed his son with the help of the nurse. The baby seemed to enjoy having his hair washed. "Do all babies have this much hair?"

"Some do. It seems he has taken after his father," she said, smiling.

Father: another title he now had, and another huge responsibility. He was happy to have another person to watch over.

CHAPTER FORTY-SEVEN

Jace and Taylor had been allowed to bring their son home from the hospital after a few days of him being closely monitored in the nursery. He had nursed well, had lost only a few ounces from his birth weight, and had gone through several packages of diapers already. The neonatal doctor had given his blessing for them to leave the hospital, knowing that Bill would be watching over him until they left for Hawaii. The fact that Jace was a nurse had certainly helped, as well.

As they drove home to the Long-Bowe B&B, she knew that everyone would be waiting for them at the big house. "Taylor, everyone is going to want to hold him, and Eric is already bugging me about the name," Jace said.

"That's fine. I bought several bottles of hand sanitizer."

"You didn't," she said, laughing.

"Well, a dad's gotta be careful. You know how Eric is."

ERIC WAS WAITING at the door. He was so excited to be an uncle, and he hoped that one day he would be a father. At least, he hoped that's what Zack wanted, too.

"Of course I want children, but not as soon as Jace," Zack said, reading his thoughts as she walked up behind him.

"Our children will never get away with anything," he said and hugged her.

"They're coming. You go hover, and I'll help Donna and Denise finish with the food in the kitchen."

"They have no idea how lucky they are to have this expert photographer here," Eric said before he ran out the door.

THE BIG HOUSE had been decorated in multiple shades of blue, and a sign that said "Welcome Baby No-Name" hung above the table, which was filled with food. When Taylor and Jace walked in with their son, Jace was surprised to see E. and Deanna. She looked around the room and found Bevan, Laura, and Sarah were there too. She looked in the kitchen and saw Lane standing there, drinking a beer. She realized just how lucky and blessed they were to have such great family and friends. Everyone circled and began to make comments about who he looked like, and about the fact that he was so small.

"Small, but loud," Taylor said.

"I want to know if you two have given that child a name," Denise said.

"We have," Jace said.

"Then we should hear it and have a toast," Bevan said.

"I have the champagne right here," Bill said, and everyone picked up a glass, ready to toast.

Jace looked at Zack and smiled, and Taylor began his speech. "First, we want to thank everyone who is here. You are our family— all of you. This year has made me realize that it is those closest to you that matter, not money or possessions. Though our son is small, his name is not. Please raise your glasses to our son, Samuel Benjamin Brigham Shaw."

"To Samuel!" everyone said, clinking their glasses.

IT SEEMED THAT though the big house had had its sorrows through the years, now it was filled with good news and happiness. That day in particular was filled with love and cheer, not only for Samuel, but for Zack and Eric, too. Zack watched as Taylor held his son as though he had always been a father.

"Jace, can you find Deanna and meet me outside?" Zack asked.

"Wedding plans?"

"Yes. Don't worry, it won't take long."

She walked out and sat down on the steps. "You look good," Deanna told her.

"I feel good. I assume E. told you that I resigned."

"Yes, but whatever makes you happy, you have to do," Deanna said understandingly.

Jace walked out holding a tray containing a pitcher of sweet tea and glasses. She filled them and handed everyone a glass. "Now, what can we do to help you with your Irish wedding?" Jace asked with excitement.

"Deanna, I don't have a lot of money, but I want an Irish lace wedding dress. I would be honored if you would design something for me."

"I would be thrilled, and it will be my gift to you," Deanna said.

"Jace, I need someone to stand with me."

"Of course! Any idea on colors?" Jace asked.

"Actually, I found tartan plaids in our family names. They include a very pale blue, and you can pick anything that you want to wear in that color."

"I'll get started on the dress when we get back, and I'll need you for at least two fittings. Have you and Eric decided where you are going to live yet?" Deanna asked.

"Yes, we bought some land from Bill and Donna. The contractors start in two weeks to clear the land. If the weather remains good, the house will be finished before we leave for Ireland. The priest is insisting that we come to Ireland a month early for classes before he will marry us. I knew that was coming, though. Cian has made arrangements for housing over there for everyone, and he assured us that this will be one wedding to remember," Zack told them.

"We've decided to stay here through Christmas. We'll fly home to Hawaii after the first of the year, and we'll meet you and Eric in Ireland mid-February," Jace said.

"This is wonderful. I'll clear my calendar, and we'll be there by the first of March in case there are any issues with the dress," Deanna said.

"Thank you."

"We're family; it's the least we can do for you," Deanna said.

CHAPTER FORTY-EIGHT

Zack left the hotel, telling Jace that she needed to go for a walk. St. Teresa's Church seemed to be the best place where she could go to think about all the good and bad that had happened in her life in the last year.

Since the birth of Samuel, it seemed that the world had begun to spin quickly. Zack felt blessed to have seen Samuel change almost daily. He had gained weight and learned to smile, and she loved to hold him. It had been difficult to see them go back to Hawaii that first week of the New Year, but the two months after that had gone by quickly.

Eric had continued his job at the magazine in Waynesboro, and he'd also taken jobs around Augusta and Atlanta. He was building a good business, and his work had made the front cover of two society magazines in Atlanta. The house in Waynesboro had progressed, even with some weather issues, and the contractor had assured them that it would be completed when they returned. Bevan had cleared her for consultation jobs with the NSA, and with jobs also coming from local law enforcement, she had kept busy.

Their trip to Ireland in the beginning of February had been long, but having Lane and Cian meet them at the airport had made it worth the flight. Eric had been ushered quickly to the Guinness Storehouse and had been properly introduced to hearty drinking early in the day. Lane had made all the arrangements at the church and with the priest. She and Eric had been rushed through marriage classes that normally took months. Of course, the large donation to the parish hadn't hurt.

Zack looked up when the priest sat down next to her in a pew inside the church. "Are you good, lass?" he asked.

"Yes, Father. I just needed time to be thankful for all that I have been blessed with."

"If you need confession, I'd be happy to hear you," he said.

"Thank you, but not at the moment."

"Then I'll leave you. Peace be to you."

"And to you, Father."

"It'll be a glorious wedding." The priest stood to leave, then hesitated. "If you change your mind, I'll be in the confessional for a while."

Zack smiled and watched him walk to the confessional, where several people were waiting. The wedding would be small, and she had asked that the decorations be kept minimal. They would be surrounded by those closest to them; everyone they had asked had come. Aaron Caydon had attempted to destroy them, but what he had done had actually strengthened their bonds.

She looked up as the door opened, and Eric sat down next to her. "I thought I might find you here."

"I just needed a bit of time."

"Are you having second thoughts? Because I feel really Catholic now."

She laughed. "Well, that will make my parents happy."

Eric put his arm around her and pulled her close. After a few minutes, he said, "Aaron Caydon is gone."

"I know, but he will always be a part of our lives, of our memories," she said.

"Then I'll just have to see what I can do to make more good memories. We should go. Everyone was asking for you, and I think Deanna needs one more fitting."

"You know, she's considering launching a line of clothing for petite women, including wedding dresses," Zack told him.

"That could make her even more popular than she already is," Eric said.

He took Zack's hand, and they walked out of the church, both ignoring the cool breeze that greeted them on the street.

CHAPTER FORTY-NINE

St. Patrick's Day, March 17, 2004
2:00 p.m.

It seemed strange that she had chosen a Wednesday for her wedding, but it would always be special. She thought about St. Patrick and the story of how he had banished the snakes from Ireland. This day, she hoped that their celebration would banish the darkness that had touched so many in attendance.

Zack's wishes had been kept: simple decorations were in the church, and all those who were closest to her and Eric were present. Deanna had created a beautiful cream-colored Irish lace wedding dress that fit her small stature and was appropriate for the day. She looked at her reflection in the mirror, admiring the long sleeves, the fitted waist, and the small train, along with the veil made of the same lace band and netting, which complemented her short hair. Zack had agreed to let Deanna use a photograph of her for her newest release of petite designs for the next fall. She looked at Jace, who was glowing in another Deanna special design, which was light blue and tea length.

"Are you ready?" her papa asked, taking her hand gently.

Zack heard the church bells begin, and the quartet that Lane had arranged began to play. She looked at the shamrocks in her bouquet of white roses and smiled. "Yes, Papa. I'm ready."

The doors opened, and Jace walked to the entrance. Taylor joined her, and they proceeded to the altar. All eyes turned to the back, and everyone stood as they entered the sanctuary. Zack could see that Eric was wearing a sash with Shaw colors across his tux, just for her and their special day. She smiled, thinking about his polite refusal to wear a kilt.

When they reached the altar, Eric stepped down to take her hand. Zack kissed her father and wiped away his tears as he gave her hand to Eric. Their wedding mass proceeded smoothly; even the babies were respectfully quiet that day. She had asked for similar vows that Cian and Cara had repeated. When their promises had been made, ribbons of blue, green, and yellow bound their hands. Once the blessing had been given, they were announced as man and wife. Eric bent down and kissed his bride, then picked her up, hugging her tightly.

"I'll never leave you again," he whispered in her ear.

Eric put her down, and they turned and walked to the back of the church. Taylor walked up to Zack and hugged her. Then he said formally, "Congratulations."

"I see Lane talked to you about Irish wedding traditions," Zack said, smiling.

"Zack!" Cian said. He and Cara walked up, presenting her with a bell.

"Thank you."

"Attention, everyone! My wife and I have one request. We are going to have one wedding photo with everyone here, since you are the most important people in our lives. Then, on to the celebration!" Eric announced.

As everyone proceeded to the altar and were arranged so that no one was missed, Zack happened to look up and saw a tall figure standing in the shadows. She smiled as Kyliegh nodded to her before disappearing. Zack looked at Lane, and he winked.

Family and friends walked to the front doors of the church. The priest threw them open, and they walked out into the sunshine, bagpipes and laughter on the street. The darkness had disappeared, and for once, the voices in her head were silent. The only sound she could hear was the voice of Eric saying that he would never leave.

EPILOGUE

A tall man exited a limousine parked in front of a single-story home. The yard had been recently mowed and the hedges had been trimmed.There was a fresh coat of white paint on the small fence that encased the front yard. He looked at the flowers in multiple pots leading up to the front door that were attracting bees and butterflies.

The man held the carved wooden box that had been left with his employer tightly as he approached the door. He rang the bell and stood back waiting for an answer. As the door opened he could hear children laughing, and looked down at the dogs barking at him. The woman smiled at him.

"Sorry about all the barking."

"Caren?" the man asked.

"Yes."

"I have a delivery from your brother."

"Aaron?"

"Indeed. He has entrusted this box to you, with his blessings," the man said as he handed it to her. He then turned and walked back to the limousine.

Caren took the box into the kitchen and opened it. Inside were two envelopes. The first contained a letter.

My dear sister,

I regret that I cannot be there to share this great joy with you, but I must leave for an unknown amount of time. I have found love and happiness, and I want you to know that you will always be in my heart.

Aaron

Caren opened the second envelope and stood in shock for a moment. There was a cashier's check made out to her for $10 million. She called out, "Stephen! You need to see what my big brother has given us!"